HELL HOUSE

A LOU THORNE THRILLER

KORY M. SHRUM

TIMBERLANE
PRESS

HELL HOUSE

AN EXCLUSIVE OFFER FOR YOU

Connecting with my readers is the best part of my job as a writer. One way that I like to connect is by sending 2–3 newsletters a month with a subscribers-only giveaway, free stories from your favorite series, and personal updates (read: pictures of my dog).

When you first sign up for the mailing list, I send you at least three free stories right away. If free stories and exclusive giveaways sound like something you're interested in, please look for the special offer in the back of this book.

Happy reading,

Kory M. Shrum

For anyone who believes in the unbelievable

1

Hellman House nursing home loomed tall beneath the midnight moon. Spotlights encircling the building illuminated its solemn exterior. Most of the windows were dark, given the hour. But a few shone like open, watchful eyes in the night.

Billy Mays parked his car in the lot at the bottom of a hill. By the time he reached Hellman's back doors, his calves ached. Not that anyone would hear him bitch about it. Sure, the others often complained. Many didn't think it was fair that the visitors' parking lot, conveniently located by the front entrance with no incline at all, sat mostly empty, never more than half filled, even at their busiest times. To those *whiners*, it was unfair that the staff were forced to hike up the steep path to the rear entrance when it would be so much easier to use the front.

Of course this place seemed full of complaints. It wasn't just the old folks themselves carrying on either. The old people he understood.

If someone else was wiping my ass and force-feeding me, I'd be in a pretty sour mood too, he thought as he swiped his card at the door, waiting for the light to turn green and signal his admittance to the building.

The temperature shift was noticeable as he stepped into the empty hallway, the motion lights clicking on. It must've been over eighty degrees outside, at midnight.

That's August in Florida for you.

The nursing home, in contrast, was like walking into a freezer.

The sweat on the back of Billy's neck cooled as the lights above lit his path to the breakroom at the end of the hall.

He clocked in, put his lunch in the fridge, and affixed his badge and keycard to the front of his scrubs.

He expected a quiet night, like most nights at Hellman. The most exciting thing that happened on the third shift was Mr. Greaney waking up screaming, irate that someone—but never himself, of course—had shit his bed. Then there was Dorothy Brown, who sometimes let herself out of her room and wandered around the place at night.

Once, they'd searched top to bottom, turning all of Hellman's eight floors upside down looking for the little old woman, only to find her in the kitchen with a peanut butter and jelly sandwich in one hand and an ice cream sandwich in the other.

I hope it's an easy night, he thought.

As soon as the elevator opened on the fifth floor, Billy knew this would *not* be the case.

Everyone was there. All the nurses. The staff.

Billy took two steps toward the commotion and stopped. A wall of people blocked his path.

"What the hell's going on?" he asked.

He turned toward the nurse on his left. It was one of the new hires. A short Filipino named Manuel, fresh from Florida State's nursing school.

"Somebody died," Manuel said, removing a handkerchief

from the pocket of his scrubs and pressing it against his forehead.

"So what?" Billy said. Half of these residents would be dead and replaced within a year. They didn't have many long-term residents at Hellman. "They're old. They die all the time. So why's everyone out here like this?"

"Because she killed herself," a voice said.

Billy turned to find Rachel beside him. Her red hair was pulled up off her shoulders, revealing her long thin neck. Billy puffed his chest without realizing it. Rachel Frisk was easily the hottest woman at Hellman House, and he couldn't so much as think of her without his mind turning her last name into *frisky*. And oh, how he would love to get *frisky* with her.

She was one of the third-shift RNs, which meant her salary was almost three times what his was as an orderly. But he'd been considering overlooking that and asking her out anyway.

She had a two-year-old son at home. Maybe she'd give him a chance if she was looking for a stable guy to play daddy.

Billy blinked. "What do you mean she killed herself? Who did?"

"Dorothy Brown," she said plainly.

"Dorothy Brown?" he said, immediately thinking of the way the woman had looked when he'd found her in the kitchen with a peanut butter sandwich in her gnarled grip. "She's—she was—a sweetheart."

Rachel arched a brow. "Sweethearts don't kill themselves?"

The news unsettled Billy more than he'd expected. His stomach hardened. He suddenly felt very sick. "How'd she do it?"

"They think she got ahold of some pills," she said. "There'll be an investigation, I'm sure. They'll have to figure out who fucked up."

Manuel puffed out his cheeks and exhaled. "She would

have had to stash them for a while to have enough. Nobody caught it. We won't even know what she had until the tox screen comes back."

"Who's going to tell the family?" Billy asked.

"You see that guy in the suit?" Rachel nodded in the direction of the crowd gathered around the nursing station, blocking the hallway and access to the remainder of the floor.

Billy spotted him. He was tall and looked way too put together with the slick hair and suit. Especially for someone visiting a nursing home at midnight.

"A hundred bucks says he doesn't let any of us tell the family what really happened to her. They'll probably tell them she died in her sleep. Or from a medical complication." Rachel reached up and tugged her ponytail. A few shorter strands fell free, framing her face.

God, she's hot.

When he tore his eyes away, Manuel was frowning at him. At both of them, actually, though Rachel's gaze remained on the man in the suit.

"They're going to make us lie to the family?" Manuel said. "That's illegal."

Rachel laughed. It was a tight, short bark. "It doesn't matter. The administrators don't care about stuff like that. They care about keeping this place open and occupied."

"It's unethical," Manuel countered.

Rachel's voice turned condescending. "Grow up, Manny. Do you think this will be the first time they've told such a lie? Homes like this are made and broken based on their reputations. If patients are offing themselves here, somebody is going to ask *why*. They can't have that, now, can they? What's a little lie if it keeps the money coming in?"

With that, Rachel broke away from them and stepped into the elevator. With the press of the button, the doors closed.

She's heading to the sixth floor to finish her rounds, Billy thought. *And why shouldn't she? Can't ignore our patients just because one died.*

But Dorothy, his mind rebelled. *She'd been such a sweet, kind soul.*

Billy just couldn't imagine Dorothy hurting herself.

"Moira is going to be devasted," Manuel said beside him.

He was right. Moira and Dorothy had been two peas in a pod from the moment Dorothy showed up eleven months ago. And at her age the suicide of her best in-house friend might be what finally finished off her heart. Something the previous four heart attacks hadn't managed.

"Don't tell her until the morning," Billy said. "She struggles with sleep enough as it is."

2

———

Louie Thorne woke to birdsong and the soft orange dawn stretching lazily against the wide bedroom windows. It was such a cheerful contrast to what she had been feeling a moment before. Dark foreboding. Suffocating panic. A cry that still echoed in her mind.

She sat up, listening to the morning stir with its own wakefulness. Even from their bed, Lou could see the Arno River flowing outside. Water sparkled iridescent on its surface.

"What's wrong?" Konstantine asked, his voice thick with sleep. His eyes were a beautiful hazel green in the morning light.

"I don't know," she said. "I felt something. I was too asleep to catch it."

He stretched. "*Sì. Capisco.* It is very difficult to get up now."

He didn't mean this moment in particular. He meant their new arrangement. Ever since they moved into this villa together, their mornings had stretched longer and longer. In the past week alone, they hadn't untangled themselves from each other until well past noon.

"It's the beautiful view," Lou said, watching a small bird with a turquoise throat land on the balcony's iron rail, the marmalade sky serving as its backdrop.

"*Molto bella, amore mio.*" Konstantine's fingers trailed down her bare thigh. "Why is it you frown like that?"

Was she frowning? If so, it was because she could not shake the heavy feeling pressing firmly against her chest.

She threw back the covers and stood. "I need to go."

"It must be very serious, if you will go before coffee," he said, sitting up and placing his back against the headboard.

The sight of him made her second-guess her decision. He was very beautiful, with the deep red comforter laid across his lap and his chest bare.

And she suspected, based solely on the mischievous look on his face, that he knew how he looked to her.

"Are you sure you don't want to come back to bed?" he asked. He fluttered his eyelashes at her.

"If you call that a bed," she said, a jab she'd used quite a few times in the last two months.

When Konstantine said he'd wanted a larger bed, they'd argued. One of the first of several domestic fights that Lou had quite enjoyed.

She had insisted on keeping his original mattress, the one she'd fallen in love with, even though Konstantine had explained he'd only had a queen because it was all that would fit in the loft of his old apartment.

He had insisted that now that they had the villa, and a bedroom bigger than most of the apartments in Florence, a king-sized bed was more appropriate.

She thought she had won the argument—until he'd simply replaced it one day.

The only saving grace was this mattress was even more

comfortable than the one he'd discarded. A possibility Lou had not considered. Not that he needed to know that.

He laughed. "You love this bed. Admit it."

"Never." She pulled on black cargo pants and a soft black t-shirt from her armoire against the wall. She wasn't sure exactly where she was going, but she had sensed the night pressing in along with those crushing feelings of suffocation.

And it was always best to wear black when moving in the night.

"I just want to check on something," she said.

"What?"

"TBD." It was something Piper said all the time.

Konstantine's brow scrunched. Clearly he wasn't familiar with the American expression. "What is TBD?"

Dressed, she bent down and brushed a kiss across his lips. "Don't worry about it."

"Take a gun. At least," he said, grabbing the front of her leather jacket and pulling her into another kiss.

She opened the nightstand beside him and pulled out the Beretta concealed there.

"It's like you don't know me at all," she said, and bit his lower lip.

After grabbing her mirrored shades, she crossed their bedroom to the empty closet. It had been Konstantine who'd removed the shelves and converted the space for her personal use.

As she stepped into the closet, he said, "*Stai attento, amore mio.*"

"I'm always careful." She closed herself up into the dark.

She took a deep breath, relaxing her body, every muscle and tendon, as her mind cast itself across the world, trying to rekindle the connection she'd first made while asleep.

It helped that there was still tension, a general unease

wherever she was headed. Had the danger passed completely, Lou might have had trouble locking in on the location.

The darkness softened, and Lou passed through it. The Florentine villa was replaced with the sharp sting of bleach and antiseptics. Something fell against Lou's shoulder and she reached out to touch it.

A handle. Wood, by the feel of it. Either a mop or a broom.

Her eyes adjusted to the lack of light, focusing on the outline of a door directly in front of her.

Another supply closet then. She found herself in them often enough.

The only mystery was what lay on the other side of the door.

Lou took a moment to slip the Beretta into the waistband of her pants, leaving it snug against her lower back.

Then she slid her mirrored shades over her eyes and opened the door.

Was it a hospital?

The room was dimly lit, with someone sleeping in the elevated hospital bed with its protective rails. Their chest rose and fell gently, though it was hard to see from where she stood if it was a man or a woman. The covers were pulled up past the sleeper's shoulders, with only the thinnest wisp of gray hair exposed.

Lou took a closer look at the room. At the furniture. The television. The plants.

A nursing home? she wondered. Or somewhere that offered long-term care.

Too much effort had been made to make the rooms seem like home.

Voices caught Lou's ear and she crept past the sleeper to the door.

Slowly, she eased it open and peered out into the hallway.

A cluster of nurses stood beside a water fountain. Their faces were drawn. Their body language tense. One held herself. Another clasped the back of her neck with both hands. The third kept rubbing her forehead as if she wanted to be rid of the skin there.

"This is a fucking mess," one of the women said. She was the oldest and had at least twenty years on the other two.

"They just wrapped up the investigation over Mr. Chavez. I can't do another round of interrogations. I always feel like they're trying to get me to confess to murder."

It was the woman clasping the back of her neck who'd spoken, her voice rising to match her growing panic.

"And we can't quit," said another. "If we quit it'll be just as suspicious. We might as well write 'I did it' on our foreheads."

"No one has called it a murder yet," the older woman said. "We don't even know if it is murder. It's *supposed* to be a suicide."

"I told you—" The nurse released her neck.

The older woman spoke over her. "No, I told *you*. That if you want to keep your job you'd best keep that to yourself. You didn't see anything. Or if you did, you didn't understand what you saw."

She spun away, leaving the other two women alone.

After a heartbeat of silence, the one closest to Lou said, "I'm the one who gives—*gave*—Dorothy her medication. She couldn't swallow pills for shit. There was no way she took all those and killed herself. I don't care what they found in her bed."

"I know." The redhead patted the other nurse's arm. "I know. Honestly, I don't even know why it matters. She was eighty-six. It wasn't like she had her whole life ahead of her."

"Because someone *died*."

"Someone *old*."

Lou withdrew into the shadows behind the door, considering the details she'd gathered. An old woman, a resident of this nursing home, was found dead in her bed at eighty-six. Possible suicide. Or she was murdered.

The Beretta resting against her back felt ridiculous given the situation. The whole situation, this place, didn't match the feeling that Lou had woken to. That suffocating darkness. The helplessness. She'd expected to find something more sinister than a nursing home with suicidal patients.

Could she be wrong?

Had she come to the wrong place? Was the distress she registered with her inner compass—that guiding power inside her—the distress of a confused old woman? Or maybe she'd been sensing the panic of the nurses who would soon find themselves interrogated?

What the hell am I doing here?

Lou had destroyed crime families and sex-trafficking rings. She'd saved exploited children.

The last place she'd ever expected to find herself was in a nursing home.

The lumpy form sat up in its bed. An old man with his gray hair sticking up straight on one side squinted and scowled at her.

"Mabel, is that you?"

Lou said nothing. She simply pulled herself deeper into the shadows. With any luck, the old man would forget he'd even seen her.

But he didn't blink and frown like they often did when she merged with the darkness again. He began to shout.

"Hey! Hey! Intruder! Stranger! There's a stranger in my room!"

The door to the room flew open and two nurses barged in. "Mr. McDermott!"

"Henry, why are you yelling?"

"There's an intruder in my room. I saw him! I saw him!" the old man wailed.

"Henry, please. You're going to fall from the bed again."

"Turn on the lights!" Henry screamed, shaking the safety rails on his bed. "Turn on the lights, damn you!"

The redheaded nurse crossed to the wall and flipped the switch. The room flooded with light.

But there was no intruder. They looked under the bed, behind every corner, and in the bathroom and closet. Yet no matter where they checked, there wasn't a soul in sight, save the three of them.

"See, Mr. McDermott. There's no one here but us. You're perfectly safe."

"I know what I saw, damn it!" the old man cried, even as he allowed himself to be tucked back into bed, his pillows adjusted. "It was an intruder."

"A ghost is more like it," one of the nurses whispered under her breath.

"Shut up," said the other, settling the old man back beneath the sheets, taking extra care to fuss over him, knowing it would ease him more than anything else. "Hysteria is the last thing we need right now."

3

____

It was days like this when Robert King wondered if he was in his right mind. He couldn't be. Surely. No one in their *right* mind would have moved to New Orleans just to endure this unrelenting heat.

He'd been standing outside this café, waiting for his coffee, for only *four* minutes, and now he was soaked. Sweat dripped from his temples and hairline. His shirt, which had been a decent, crisp button-down that morning when he'd put it on, was now drenched.

This was typical for an August morning in the city, when it was possible for temperatures to reach the nineties before noon. Yet every summer, somehow he was surprised again by the terribleness of it.

This is why the tourists never come in the summertime, he thought bitterly.

"Robert?" a voice called.

He turned to find a girl with an iced latte in a to-go cup held high in the air.

"Here," he called out. "That's me."

She handed him the coffee, took one look at his clothes, and said, "Let me get you some extra napkins."

"Thanks," he said, embarrassment washing over him. Then again, he was already embarrassed that he'd caved and bought an *iced* latte. He'd come to believe coffee should be black and hot as a rule. *Oh, how the mighty have fallen.*

"Robbie!"

King turned again, looking up the street in the direction of the precinct, and found Detective Dick White walking toward him, his hand up in a friendly wave.

"Robbie, my man. You're a fish."

King could do nothing else but grin and bear it. "I guess I'm not built for these Southern summers."

"Here." The girl offered him the extra napkins, pressing them into his damp hand, before excusing herself to make the next customer's drink.

"Is this your fourth or fifth summer with us?" White asked.

King tried to do the math himself, but it was hard to think with this muggy humidity pressing against his brain.

"Something like that," he finished weakly. "But you're none too dry yourself, White."

White gave a good-natured laugh. "I've got another shirt in the car."

"You ordering something?" King sidestepped, unblocking the entrance. It'd only just occurred to him that maybe White wanted to get a drink, too.

My brain really is useless on days like this.

"No, I called you earlier and you didn't pick up. Then I just saw you here across the street."

King checked his phone. "So you did. I'm sorry, I didn't hear it."

"Not a problem. I was just wondering if you'd heard from Rita Golden."

The name didn't ring any bells. "No. I don't think so."

"Golden is an old friend of mine from school. We both went to Louisiana State. She got married and went north. And I came home and joined the force. I gave her your number."

"She in trouble?" King asked. He didn't think White would take it upon himself to set King up on a date, not since he and Beth had started seeing each other.

"At least a *bit* of trouble, I'd say. Hard to tell how serious just yet. Might be really serious, or it might all blow over. Either way, she could really use somebody in her corner."

King took a long, deep drink of his coffee. The cold wave of relief washing over him was wonderful even if he was irritated by the clink of ice against his teeth.

"I'm intrigued," King said, pressing the paper napkins to his forehead.

White swatted at a mosquito buzzing near his ear. "She inherited one of them old plantation houses up there in Vicksburg a few years back. Got a lot of land too, both from her marriage. When he ran out on her, she had no choice but to take over the runnin' of the place. Now, a local girl, one of the housekeepers I believe, has gone and fallen out a window. She's dead."

King frowned. "That's unfortunate."

"It is. And now Rita's fielding a lot of questions from the police and a lot of pressure from the locals, not to mention the girl's family. They want answers."

"Understandable," King said, taking his turn to swat at the mosquito. "But I don't know what I can do for her."

"Rita could use a legal-savvy person in her corner. Someone who could work as a liaison with the authorities and get this whole mess cleared up."

King arched a brow. "I don't know the first thing about Louisiana outside New Orleans, and both you *and* Mel like to tell me I don't know much about NOLA either. What do you keep saying?"

"The Quarter ain't the city," White said.

"That's right. Wouldn't you be of more help to her? I can't imagine the police force from a small parish would even give me the time of day."

"You'd be surprised. They're pretty laid-back around there." White flashed his best *come on* smile. He'd used it on King before. "Besides, I can't leave town now. We're trying to get the kids ready for school. But you know Louisiana laws well enough and you're good with folks. You've got what my mama called *the charm*."

King laughed into his coffee. "Ms. Golden must be a very good friend if you're buttering me up like this."

"The truth is, Rita had a really hard time at school. People weren't kind to her. Then Johnny Golden showed up, took an interest in her, and it seemed like she was going to get her fairy tale ending."

"But she didn't?" King asked, swirling the ice in his cup.

"No," White said. "Johnny left her and she's been struggling to hold it together since. Just hear her out if she gives you a call. That's all I ask."

And how could King tell him no?

He couldn't. Not when King considered how much help White had offered him since he'd arrived in the city. Plenty of cops could have told him to piss off or at the very least call him an uncle for keeping his nose in police business after retirement.

White hadn't done any of that. He'd been more than happy to take King under his wing, consult him on cases, and vouch for him when things got dicey. He'd gone out of his way to include him and make him feel welcome before anyone else on the force had.

"If she calls, I'll see what I can do." King lifted his coffee in salute. "I promise."

White slapped him on the shoulder. "Good man. Thanks, Robbie."

King waved goodbye as White crossed the street to his unmarked police car and disappeared behind the wheel. He waved once again as the car passed him on the road.

King moved to wipe his damp face again, but the paper napkins he held in his clutched fist were already soaked through.

He swore and tossed them in the metal trashcan outside the café before heading up Royal Street.

God, I hate this heat.

PIPER GENEREUX WAS SURPRISED THAT SHE'D MADE IT INTO the office before King. She'd seen him in the shop talking to Mel that morning, and assumed he was heading straight in even as she finished up her training session with Mel's newest shop girl.

Her heart clenched at that. It wasn't that she was jealous of the three new girls Mel had hired to work at Melandra's Fortunes and Fixes. Every single one of them seemed sweet. Well, Dana wasn't *sweet*, exactly. She was emo and morose, but that was great for the vibe of the occult shop. No one sold *spooky* better than an emo chick.

No, it wasn't the girls. After all, Mel needed the help.

It was simply that Piper was down to only a couple hours at Fortunes. And she missed it.

She missed Mel's calm, steadfast presence. She missed the smell of incense that hung in the air and the chance to practice fortune-telling. She'd even stopped reading fortunes in Jackson Square.

She'd been too busy.

Now her life was full of schoolwork, and working at the Crescent City Detective Agency.

And she loved it—school and working as King's assistant. Absolutely loved it.

She was sure now that she wanted to work in the crime field for the rest of her life, either as a detective or maybe as a federal agent.

But she also wanted the *woo*.

I just need to find the perfect balance, she told herself. *I've got to stop whining. I'm so freaking lucky.*

How many would-be crime fighters would kill to work at an honest-to-God detective agency with someone as knowledgeable and patient as King?

The bell above the agency's door dinged and Piper looked up from her laptop. It wasn't until that moment that she realized she'd been staring at her computer screen without really seeing it.

"Good morning," King said.

"Good morning," she replied. Then she frowned. "Are you okay? You look really red in the face."

"It's the heat."

"You changed," she noted. She'd known he would as soon as she'd seen him that morning. A button-down and khakis? In *August*? There was no way those clothes would stay dry. He'd been smart to trade them out for the breezy collared shirt and shorts he wore now. Even if it was weird to see his super-pale legs.

He came around his desk and pulled out his chair. "Did we get any calls from a Rita Golden?"

Piper lifted the top sheet of the legal pad she used to record all of the messages and calls she fielded for King. But the log was still pretty short, given the hour of the day.

"I don't see any Goldens," she said. "Why? We got a new case?"

Piper's heart flittered in anticipation.

This, she thought. *This is how I know I'm in the right place.*

"Not yet," King said. "Maybe she won't call."

"Vague much," Piper said.

King shrugged. "She's a referral from Detective White. He said he gave her my number, but I forgot to ask if he meant my cell or the office. Just keep an ear out for her, all right?"

"If she calls the office when you're not here do you want me to give her your cell number?" Piper asked.

She flicked her pen against the legal pad.

"Yeah, thanks. Route her to me if she calls in."

"Will do." Piper scratched a note to herself in the top corner of the legal pad, underlining the name Golden so she wouldn't forget. It was possible to go through a lot of names in a day. Mostly it was disgruntled lovers calling to get a quote for how much it would cost to track their significant other for a few days, in an attempt to uncover suspected adultery.

King dabbed at his forehead and neck with a handkerchief that Piper had only ever seen him use in July and August. He couldn't look more like a tourist if he tried, but she didn't tease him about it. She knew both he and Mel were self-conscious of the fact that they hadn't been born and raised in New Orleans like she had.

"By the way, how's it going with the Patel case?" he asked.

Piper straightened in her seat. "Resolved. I just closed it this morning."

King arched a brow. "Did you get the dog back from the ex-husband?"

"Turns out," Piper began, "that the ex didn't steal the dog. Pickles had, in fact, wandered out the back gate, and Moses found him and took him in."

King's brow scrunched. "Pickles? And Moses? A little late for him, isn't it?"

"Pickles is the dog. Moses is a little old man who lived down the road. Though maybe he is two thousand years old. You never can tell in New Orleans. Oh! I also closed the Fuller case."

"And you discovered...?" King prompted, with the air of someone who wanted the latest gossip.

"That, yes, she was cheating on her wife with the sister."

"With the married sister? Or the younger one who'd been teaching abroad in—"

"Korea," Piper finished, keeping to herself that she suspected the younger sister was staying abroad to avoid such family drama. "And no, not her."

King pinched his eyes closed. "There are too many people in this. Use their names."

"There's Clara, who hired us. There's her wife, Bianca. Then there's Mini, who is Clara's sister. Then Samuel, the husband who is married to Mini."

King sat back, clearly trying to absorb the information.

Piper, being a lesbian herself, was less surprised. A woman claiming to be straight just because she was presently with a man had meant little in her personal experience.

"The wife sleeps with her sister-in-law. So Mini must've been—" King began.

"A closeted bisexual or maybe just bi-curious?" Piper offered. "Either way, they're all going to therapy together, which I thought was nice. They want to work it out."

Piper had really liked the husband, Samuel. It was clear he wanted to make it work with Mini despite the infidelity. Clara also wanted to forgive her sister, so it looked like Mini might come out of this relatively unscathed.

Piper was less confident that the wife, Bianca, was going to be forgiven.

But that wasn't Piper's problem. She was doing good just to keep her own relationship with Dani afloat. This was her first time being someone's full-time live-in girlfriend. She liked it.

"How many cases have you wrapped up this week?" King asked.

"Fuller was the fourth."

"And how many of those were solos?"

"Three of them."

He smiled, and Piper couldn't help but match it.

"You're doing great," he said.

Her face burned. "Thanks. I have a good boss."

Ever since King started giving Piper her own cases, she felt different. Trusted, maybe? Respected? Whatever it was, it was damn good. Every time she wrapped up a case on her own, gathered the evidence, ran the interviews, worked with the DA when it was called for—all of it made her feel more and more capable. She was beginning to believe in her abilities as an investigator.

I can do this.

It was a refrain that popped into her head more and more these days.

I can do this.

Piper might miss working at Fortunes and Fixes, and reading fortunes at her little table in the Square. But this—

Nothing compared to *this*.

The office phone rang, and Piper reached across the desk and lifted it from the receiver.

"Crescent City Detective Agency," she said. "How can I help you?"

"Is Robert King available?" a voice asked. There was steel in that tone and something else Piper couldn't quite place. Anger? Irritation?

"I'm happy to check and see if he is," Piper said. "Can I just get your name please, ma'am?"

"Rita Golden," she said. "Tell him a mutual friend gave me his number."

"Sure thing. If I could just put you on a brief hold." Piper pressed the hold button and waited for the light to blink red, signaling their privacy.

To King she said, "Rita Golden is on line one for you."

"Is that so?" King reached across his desk to his matching phone. He lifted the receiver before pressing the blinking red button. "Ms. Golden. I was looking forward to your call. What can I do for you?"

4

———

Lou left the nursing home with a sense of unease. Before returning to Florence, she'd slipped through the dark to the parking lot outside, hoping to get a better view of the building itself.

The air was hot and humid the moment she'd stepped from the supply closet into the open night, even though her GPS watch told her it was after midnight.

From the shadows beneath a row of palm trees, Lou regarded the building. It stood on a hill beneath the moon. Clouds passed over its luminous face, adding to the stoic atmosphere.

The building itself was spotlighted by a row of lanterns. Two of the lights were pointed directly at the large sign which read *Hellman House.*

Nearly all of the license plates in the parking lot were Florida plates.

Hellman House, a nursing home in Florida.

Not her usual haunt, but she couldn't shake the unease she'd felt ever since waking with that sensation of claustrophobia. Suffocation. The pitch black—which she usually loved and felt drawn to—pressing in on her in a way she hadn't experienced since she was a child and afraid of her power.

After one final look at the place, she slipped, letting the darkness overtake her. She abandoned her place beneath the palm trees and returned to the closet nestled in their Italian villa.

She opened the door to find the bed made. The sunlit bedroom bright and empty.

After she washed the Florida humidity from her hair, she found Konstantine in the kitchen.

He looked up from the stove. "*Amore mio*, do you want eggs?"

A pastry box full of croissants sat open on the counter beside a bowl of yogurt and a plate of cut fruit.

"I'd say this is enough," she told him, moving half an orange to her plate.

She added a mound of yogurt with honey and berries as he poured her a cup of coffee.

It was easier for him now that they had a kitchen big enough to accommodate an American coffeemaker. She'd only had to show him once how to use a filter and water to brew the coffee as strong as she liked. Yet his allegiance remained with his moka, so she was not surprised to find that he made himself a cappuccino once she was settled in the window seat with her breakfast.

They ate in silence, his hand resting on her thigh as she tore the pastry apart with her fingers.

Once he was down to only his coffee, his plate cleared, he said, "You returned quickly. There was no trouble?"

"I couldn't find it." Sitting in the sunlight with a delicious mug of coffee in one hand and her belly full still wasn't enough to fully chase away her unease.

"Where did you go?" he asked over the rim of his cup.

"A nursing home in Florida," she said. "Hellman House."

When he blinked but showed no recognition, she tried to explain what a nursing home was and the purpose it served.

"Ah, *sì. Casa di riposo*," he said. "Corruption?"

"A killer," she said. "I think."

"It is a shame." He returned his cup to its matching saucer with a clunk. "They are so vulnerable. *Dobbiamo prenderci cura di loro.*"

Lou only blinked at him, and his smile widened.

"It is bad to hurt the vulnerable, no?" he asked.

"*Sì. È un peccato*," she agreed, and he tilted his head ever so slightly.

"*Brava.*"

He'd been encouraging her to improve upon her Italian since she'd moved here. When they walked around the city together in the evenings, he let her speak to the shopkeepers and the servers. But Lou wasn't a conversationalist even in English.

"*Che piani hai per oggi?*" he asked.

"I'll go to New Orleans. It's been a few days since I've checked on them."

"And then?" he asked. "*E poi?*"

"I want to learn more about Hellman House. The nursing home."

He took her empty mug to the kitchen sink along with their empty plates. The plates went in the dishwasher, but the mug he refilled for her before sliding it across the counter.

"What about you?" she asked. "*Che piani hai?*"

A smile tugged on his lips. "I need to meet with the Neapolitans today. Dante and Carmine."

"I thought you were on good terms with the mafia in Naples."

"Not mafia. Camorra," he said. "And *sì*. I am. For now."

"Are you meeting at the church? Will the kids be around?" she asked.

"*No.* We're meeting in Pelago. I own a hotel there for exactly this purpose. Il Castello di Rico. There's no need for anyone to know where we live."

We live.

"I suppose you'll shout if you need me," she said, and took a drink. "Or cry out in pain."

He frowned at her, unamused. "There will be no problems today."

Famous last words, she thought.

And yet she accepted his kiss on her cheek before fisting his shirt in her hands and pulling him closer.

He laughed, low in his throat. "*Sì, amore mio?*"

She kissed him on the mouth. "Don't forget that you promised me the best Florentine pizza for dinner tonight. And then dessert. Gelato?"

His eyes darkened with hunger. "*Sì*, I remember."

She released him. "Then I'll see you tonight."

King left Piper in charge of the office at one and went home for lunch. Or at least, lunch was part of the reason he'd left. The other part was because he was hoping to catch Mel.

When he entered Melandra's Fortunes and Fixes, the scent of verbena hung in the air above the racks of tarot cards and candles displayed for every occasion and spell arranged on the shelves. The wall of Mardi Gras beads had been switched with the hoodies and t-shirts, for better window placement. The movement had also given her an extra wall's worth of room for new merchandise.

Mel had told King years ago that she'd wanted to do this

rearranging but hadn't had the money or the time. King was glad things had improved for her.

The purple curtain was pulled back, telling King that Mel wasn't giving a reading now.

A moment later, one of the new shop girls confirmed this.

A cheerful Black girl with glitter on her cheeks said, "Hi, Mr. King! Mel's upstairs."

She was a cute girl, bright-eyed and friendly. She couldn't be more than seventeen, or if she was in her twenties—and that was the oldest King was willing to entertain—she had a baby face.

He was a little ashamed that he didn't remember this one's name, and he didn't want to ask. Dana he remembered. With her black hair and thick eyeliner, she stood out. But the other two were like matching pixies. And their names were close too. There was an Amanda and a Miranda.

"Lady with her?" King asked.

"She sure is, Mr. King."

"Thanks." King mounted the stairs, past the six-foot plastic ghoul guarding the steps to the apartments above. Lady barked before he even knocked on the door.

Good dog, he thought. They'd gotten the Belgian Malinois for protection. She *should* bark anytime anyone approached Mel's door.

On the second knock Mel opened it. She wore her fortune teller clothes. That's what she called this ensemble. To King, she looked more like a pirate wench. He supposed an eye patch was really the only difference between the two.

She wore a deep red scarf wrapped around her head with gold beads twined in her hair, to match the gold bangles on her wrist that he'd never seen her without. Her eyeliner was dark around her eyes but she'd forgotten to draw the mole onto her cheek as she sometimes did. Her lips were red too, to match the head wrap and the dress, he supposed.

"Mr. King," she said, as if they weren't best friends. As if he hadn't asked her a *thousand* times to please just call him Robbie. Or hell, even Robert would do. "You wanna come in for a bit of lunch?"

"I already ate," he said. "But I'd like to come in if you've got a minute."

"Of course."

She moved to the side, inviting him into the apartment that was a mirror of his own across the hall. Kitchen first, with its checkerboard floor. A living room just beyond it with a door that led to the wraparound balcony.

Lady stood in the kitchen, tail wagging, her ears up at attention.

King gave her a good scratch and bent to pat her rump affectionately. "Good girl."

He leaned against the counter while Mel resumed making her ham and cheese sandwich. He helped himself to one of the salt and vinegar chips from the open bag.

"I just took a case up in Vicksburg. Aren't you from around there?" he asked.

"That's a little farther north than where Grandmamie had her place. What's gone wrong in Vicksburg?"

"A seventeen-year-old girl died. She fell out of a window. Probably."

"What do you mean, *probably*?" Mel asked with an arched brow.

"The owner, Rita Golden, insists that it was a setup by her rival. Apparently another plantation owner in the area has it out for her. White knows her and asked me to help run interference with the local authorities so she gets a fair shake."

"They won't like that," she said. "Some outsider comin' in and sayin' he knows better than everybody else."

"That's what I told White."

"Then why you here eating all my potato chips, Mr.

King?" She snatched the bag away from him and took her plate to the kitchen table.

"I figured you're from the area. Maybe you'd like to come with me and help me out."

"To a plantation house in Vicksburg?" she said, taking a bite of her sandwich. "Who would run the shop while I'm away?"

"You've got the girls."

"They're *girls*," she said. "How long we talking?"

"Three days? Maybe four?"

"And when would we leave?" she asked.

King wasn't sure what to say. "Later this week. Maybe."

Melandra put her sandwich down. "You didn't actually get the case, did you?"

"She's supposed to call me back tonight to confirm," King said. And that was true.

He'd talked to Rita on the phone for all of five minutes before the woman's voice had changed. He was certain that she was about to offer him the case, but for whatever reason, she'd hesitated. She said she'd needed to check a few things.

But he was sure she was going to call back.

He was *sure* of it.

"*If* you go to Vicksburg to investigate this plantation death, you want me to go but you don't know when," Mel summarized.

"As early as tomorrow, as late as Friday," King agreed, resting his elbows on the kitchen table.

"You going to leave Piper here?" Mel asked. "I'd go if Piper were in charge. But I can't leave the whole show to the new girls."

King didn't have it in him to cut Piper out of the investigation. Not when she'd spent the better part of the afternoon reading articles about the plantation aloud to him.

Mel reached out and patted his hand. "You two go. I'll

stay here and keep an eye on things. Besides, who would take care of Lady?"

"We could bring her?" Though he doubted Rita would agree to having a dog in her manor. "What if the locals give me a hard time?"

And that brought him to the second reason he'd wanted to ask her. "And what if it really was a ghost that killed her?"

Mel sat back in her chair, both brows raised now. "Excuse me?"

"It's just rumors." He was trying to approach this subject as respectfully as possible. "But there are a lot of articles online about how haunted the mansion is."

"And?" Mel arched a brow. "People put a lot of things on the internet, Mr. King."

"Supposedly it's one of the most haunted houses in Louisiana."

Mel rolled her eyes. "Everything down here is supposed to be the most haunted *this* or the most haunted *that*. So what if there is a ghost?"

King's heart skipped a beat. "You see ghosts?"

Mel tipped her head. "Not like Grandmamie. All I can tell you is that they don't kill people. It'd have to be a much darker presence for something like that."

"That's not what the *Vicksburg Inquirer* wrote," King said. "Apparently the locals are convinced that the ghost of Joseph Freeman killed her."

"Dare I ask who Joseph Freeman is?"

"He haunts the top floor of the Margo Manor. Two of the women who used to work there as maids claimed they felt someone pinch their butts and grab their hips, but when they turned around no one was there. The top floor just happens to be where the girl fell from."

Mel couldn't have looked more incredulous if she tried.

"This girl who died was a maid? The one who fell?" she asked.

"That's right," King said. "And maybe if she's still there, you can speak to her for me. Or him. The ghost."

"I'm not a medium and I'm certainly no ghost hunter." Mel threw her napkin down on the table. "You and I both know a ghost didn't kill that girl. Someone read that story and made it look like a ghost did, hoping everyone would be dumb enough to believe in ghost stories."

King shrugged, holding up his hands. "I don't know anything except that the locals will take to you better than me."

Lady placed her head on Mel's leg. Mel rubbed the soft patch of fur between the dog's sweet brown eyes.

"*Ma grande*," she cooed. Without looking up, she said, "*If you go to Vicksburg and find yourself dealing with ghosts, then I'll come up and meet you. That's the best I can offer.*"

King knew better than to push her. "All right. Does that offer stand for troublesome locals too?"

Mel sighed. "Why not?"

KING'S PHONE RANG JUST PAST MIDNIGHT. BEFORE HE could get his eyes open, he worried it might be Piper. Or maybe Mel had gone out and gotten herself into trouble? It wouldn't be White unless they'd found a body somewhere in the city, and even then, he wouldn't be the detective's first call unless it was somehow related to one of King's cases.

But it wasn't any of King's friends.

When he answered the phone, it was a frantic female voice on the other end.

"Mr. King? Mr. King!" she called out. In the background, a horrible screeching was coming through the line. Was their connection bad?

"Yes? Hello? Hello?" King sat up in bed, trying to switch on the lamp as he moved his phone from his right ear to his left. "Can you hear me?"

"It's Rita. Rita Golden," she yelled over the screeching sound.

King pulled his ear away from the phone. "Rita?"

"Yes! Rita Golden!" she spat. "How soon can you come?"

5

———————

Lou finished her coffee on the villa's balcony. It was ten in Florence, but in New Orleans it was still the middle of the night. She'd have to wait until the afternoon if she wanted to catch King and Piper at the office.

A little sparrow landed on the feeder to her right, singing a cheerful song before flying off with a sunflower seed in its beak.

Lou listened to the Arno River lapping at the edge of the canal, the sunlight sparkling on its rushing surface.

Then she closed her eyes. Threw her mind out, casting it like a net, searching for—

Who could use some help? she thought.

The compass inside her whirled and clicked. It built momentum. It spun and spun until it snagged like a hook through her navel, pulling her muscles tight.

The terror trembling through the line made her stomach turn.

Lou stood, placing her empty mug on the table to be dealt with later, and stepped back inside the villa. She paused only long enough to grab her gun, jacket, and shades off the foot of the bed before stepping into the bedroom closet again.

The darkness embraced her, softened for her as if it had been waiting for her to return. Before she drew a second breath, she was through.

Louie's boots settled on the damp earth, the smell of recent rain hanging thick around her.

"Please! Somebody!" a woman screamed, the words choked with sobbing.

Lou turned toward the sound of it in time to see a man draw back a blade, preparing to strike.

Lou moved through the dark without thinking. One moment her body was beneath the thick branches of a soaked maple tree and the next she was between the woman and the knife.

Lou seized the wrist holding it and twisted hard, wrenching the bone from its socket before it could find its mark. The attacker, seeking to escape the newfound pain shooting up his arm, fell into a crouch automatically. Lou took his knife with her free hand.

Light drizzle splattered the snarling face looking up at her.

Without letting go, Lou spoke to the woman. "Are you hurt?"

The man tried to twist free, mistaking Lou's distraction for weakness, and Lou applied more pressure.

He screamed louder, and Lou asked the woman again, "Are you hurt?"

"He cut me." The woman peeled open the shredded sleeve of her jacket to reveal a deep gash beneath. It was bleeding, but Lou had seen worse.

"And he hit me in the face."

Lou could see that, too. A bruise was forming on the woman's cheek.

"I think I need a doctor," the woman said. Her teeth began to chatter.

Lou suspected it wasn't the rain or the state of her clothes that caused the shaking, but a fall in her adrenaline.

"Get your stuff together. I'll be right back," Lou told her, nodding in the direction of the busted purse off to their left.

The purse had either been dropped in the struggle or torn from her grip. It lay in a heap fifteen feet away, its contents strewn across the wet grass. A white plastic card, either a credit card or a license, shone bright with moonlight.

Lou was fairly confident the purse belonged to the woman. It seemed like only the three of them occupied this —what? Park? It was hard to know for sure given that all she could see was wet grass punctuated by tidy trees and a few ill-placed lamps along a concrete walkway.

It was possible that shape in the distance was a park bench.

"You're leaving me?" The woman looked ready to grab hold of Lou and never let go.

"I'll be right back," Lou reassured her. "I just need to put him somewhere he won't cause any more trouble."

It was dark enough for Lou to soften through the darkness where she stood, so she did. There was no point dragging the man out of sight before traveling in that special way of hers. The woman had already seen Lou appear between her and the knife. They were past the point of discretion or secrecy now.

The warm, rainy air was instantly replaced with chilly fog. Nova Scotia was cold even in August.

Tall, straight pines hundreds of years old stretched into the starlit sky. The fog hung over the lake, giving the water an eerie placidity. The sound of insects and frogs swelled even at this hour, and Lou caught the sound of something scampering up the tree to her right.

She released the man onto the muddy embankment.

When he tried to run, she kicked him hard with a well-placed boot. He hit the earth on his hands and knees and Lou plunged his blade into his back, just to the right of the spine.

He let out an ear-splitting shriek.

"Don't go anywhere," she whispered, watching as he frantically tried to pull out the blade he couldn't reach.

Back in the park, the woman stood in the rain, shivering, her poorly packed purse clutched to her chest with her good arm close and the other gingerly resting on top. Blood dripped from her elbow onto her white tennis shoes.

"Come on," Lou said, reaching for her gently. It was a request to touch her.

The woman came forward, and as soon as Lou's fingers brushed her damp jacket, they moved through the dark.

A hospital lurched into view, burning brightly in front of them. The sight of it made Lou think of Hellman House. The way it had beamed on its hilltop.

Lou guided the woman from beneath the dark tree line, across the parking lot and to the emergency entrance cut into the hospital's side.

She released her at the doors. "Go on."

"Wait," the woman called out. "It's not much but I'd like to give you a little something for helping me. You saved my life back there."

She opened her wallet and took out two twenty-dollar bills, all the cash she had.

But she offered them to no one.

Louie Thorne was already gone.

THE MAN SCREAMING ON THE SHORE OF HER NOVA SCOTIAN lake hadn't even heard her return. He was too busy trying to get a good grip on the knife handle jutting out of his back.

Lou grabbed it and twisted it, eliciting another tortured howl from the man's throat.

With her other hand, she grabbed the collar of his jacket and hauled him into the lake after her, floating him across the surface as she waded out into the slate-gray waters.

The fog hung around them as they moved, adding more moisture to her hair and cheeks. It hardly mattered. There was no staying dry where Lou was going.

"Please," the man begged. "Please, for the love of fucking god, I'm sorry. I'm so fucking sorry. I didn't mean to—"

His words were swallowed by the water as Lou pulled them both down beneath its surface.

He twisted in her grip, trying to free himself. Like others before him, he thought he could use his weight to pin her, using the submersion to his advantage.

Of course, he didn't know what Lou knew.

Lou let him thrash, smiling to herself as the waters changed from gray to red, warming as it did.

Still she held him tight. Once she was sure they'd fully crossed over, she grabbed ahold of the handle again and pulled, freeing the blade at last. The moment he was free, he shoved against her.

Lou let him go, surfacing in La Loon with the blade in her hand.

A nightmare landscape met her. The water lapping at her chest was blood red. Ripples washed toward an ink-black shore with foliage as thick as if made with an impressionistic brush rather than given any true definition.

The sky held two moons above the mountains resting in the distance.

The whole place smelled of sulfur. It felt like cotton in Lou's nose. Konstantine had said it was the smell, more than the landscape, that made him wonder if this place was Hell.

Lou liked the smell. She liked all of it.

She pulled herself from the lake and shook water from her coat. A flick of her wrist cleared the droplets from her shades before she slid them into her pocket.

She remained on the shore, blade in hand, watching her captive tread circles.

"You'll want to get out of there before they eat you," Lou called passively.

She didn't think he'd heard her. Not only because he was splashing like a man drowning but because he'd screamed when he caught sight of the six-foot tail slapping the surface of the water forty feet away, before disappearing beneath the surface again.

Screaming was a perfectly acceptable response, Lou thought, to realizing that a monster was in the water.

The man looked back and forth between Lou waiting on the shore with a blade and the shimmering ripples where the beast had disappeared.

Before he could decide who was the bigger threat, he bobbed once beneath the surface.

Only his hands remained above the water.

He surfaced, screaming, only to be pulled under again a second later.

This time there was no sight of him except for the ripples left in his wake.

Lou waited on the shore, watching the waters grow still again. A few bubbles rose to the surface and popped. Then there were no signs that someone had been there at all.

I hope Jabbers won't be too sad to have missed a meal, she thought, and began walking toward the cliff face in the distance, the lake growing smaller at her back.

It wasn't difficult to find the opening to the passageway cut in the side of the cliff. She'd walked this route so many times through the oil-black field that ran alongside the lake that she'd worn down a footpath.

At the entrance, she removed her phone and turned on its flashlight, shining it into the dark.

It had been smart of Konstantine to insist that she get one of the new waterproof phones. If it had been anything less, she would have destroyed it by now.

With one hand on the stone wall and the other holding up the phone, whose light bought her a mere foot or two of visibility, Lou made her way deeper into the mountain.

Not for the first time she thought that water had probably carved this tunnel. It had that uneven look etched into the stone that reminded her of a trip she took as a child with her parents to the Grand Canyon. Water had carved its way through the Arizona desert, giving the canyon its distinctive shape. And Lou suspected that it had done the same to this mountain.

Maybe whatever scientific laws governed this strange, alien world weren't so different from those back home. Even if the creatures that ruled this land seemed like those born from a nightmarish fever dream.

Cerulean light formed in the distance, beating back the dark until she was close enough to see the pool of water clearly. She pocketed her phone and stepped into its glowing blue shimmer.

Lou had expected to find Jabbers there. The enormous beast had taken to sleeping at the foot of her six eggs, feet from the water's edge, instead of her aerie high up the cliff face.

Lou wasn't complaining. It was much easier to reach this new makeshift nest than climb the mountain to her throne of bones.

Yet Jabbers wasn't here.

There were bones. New ones piled on top of those collected in the last few months. Jabbers, being the serpentine beast that she was, had begun gathering them in one corner of the cavern.

The stone floor beneath the eggs was bare. The water was still. The shadowed bone nook empty.

Something else had changed, too.

Lou counted three times to be sure, but no. She wasn't wrong.

There were only five eggs.

She had been certain that there were six. She'd been coming here and inspecting their progress ever since Jabbers had revealed this nest to her months ago.

Her fingers trailed over the warm surface of the eggs.

One. Two. Three. Four. Five—

Her hand found only empty air where the sixth egg had been.

Using her phone's flashlight once more, she bent down to inspect the floor, as if it would offer some clue.

Did Jabbers eat it? Did she push it into the water?

Jabbers was unlike anything from Lou's world, but there were things about her that made Lou think of reptiles and large cats.

Was it normal for reptiles to eat their own unborn young? Had there been a problem with the egg?

Konstantine might know. He seemed to have more of a personal interest in the science and mechanics of this world.

Who knew a mafia boss could have such an interest in science and technology? She suspected he would've been quite the nerd if he hadn't been pulled into a life of crime as a child.

I'll tell him about this when I see him next, she thought.

Her fingers inspected the cool stone floor but found nothing.

6

Piper heard the buzzing of her phone without waking. Instead, her dream morphed to accommodate the sound. In the dream, she'd been walking Lady down by the river. There had been strange multicolored birds floating on the surface, and her mind had been trying to remember the name for them. The Belgian Malinois was walking close beside her at an obedient clip, the leash held loosely in Piper's hand.

Then the dog buzzed, vibrating in place as if this were a perfectly acceptable thing for a dog to do.

Piper stopped walking. "What was that?"

The dog buzzed again.

Piper frowned at her. "Hey, man, are you all right?"

Lady buzzed for a third time and said, "Piper, your phone is going off."

Hearing Dani's voice coming through the dog's mouth finally woke her.

Piper opened her eyes to find she was in her own bed, in the dim bedroom she shared with her girlfriend—her first serious, honest-to-goodness *girlfriend*—Daniella Allendale.

Dani's long brown hair covered half her face, her brown eyes squinting in the dark.

Piper lifted her head from the pillow. "What?"

"Your phone keeps going off," she said again with mild irritation. "I think someone's texting you."

"What time is it?" Piper sat up, rubbing the sleep from her eyes.

Dani checked her own phone. "It's two in the morning."

"It's probably Henry," Piper said. Her friend kept late hours. Piper, too, would just be crawling into bed herself had it been only a few months ago. But since Piper had moved over to the agency full-time and became immersed more and more in her own casework, gradually her hours had shifted.

More than once she'd lamented—if only to herself—that if she wasn't careful, she was going to become old and boring.

"You should check it anyway," Dani said.

Groaning, Piper reached out, fingers fumbling across the surface of the nightstand until she found her phone. She unlocked it despite her several clumsy attempts at entering the passcode.

She opened her messages and found three. "It's King."

She hated the way this man texted. He sent long, single-paragraph messages that were hard on the eyes. Would it kill him to include breaks like a normal person?

"Has something happened? Did someone die?"

"No," Piper said. "Well, yes. Someone died, but no one we, like, *know*."

Apparently Rita Golden had called King back in a panic and insisted on hiring him to investigate the death of the maid who'd fallen—or possibly leapt—to her death. King hadn't been impressed after speaking to Golden on the phone that afternoon.

He'd seemed even less enthused after Piper spent several hours telling him about the ghosts. She must have read a dozen articles about Margo Manor and its hauntings to him as the afternoon had stretched on. She was left with the distinct impression that he wanted nothing to do with this case and only entertained the idea because Detective Dick White had asked him to help.

Piper read the highlights of King's message to Dani. She skimmed over his instructions on what to pack.

Dani snuggled in closer, placing one soft hand on Piper's hip. "You're leaving first thing in the morning? How long will you be gone?"

"He doesn't know. Three days?"

Dani cupped Piper's hand in hers, her gaze still searching Piper's face. "If it's not urgent, why did he text so late?"

"He thought I was at the Wild Cat. Seriously, it's not a big deal. I'm sorry if the phone going off scared you. I'll silence it."

"No, don't." The lines on her face evened out. "You know we can't do that."

She was right. They both knew too many people who might need them regardless of the hour.

"I'll talk to him," Piper said. "I'll just explain that I'm not a cool party girl anymore."

Dani snorted.

Piper sent King a thumbs up and a quick message saying she'd be packed before meeting him downstairs in the morning. Then she clicked off the phone and placed it face down on the nightstand once more.

With the phones off, the bedroom was swallowed by the darkness again. If Piper really tried, she could hear the faint music bleeding through the walls, the chaos from Bourbon Street pulsing in the distance.

She snuggled beneath the comforter, conforming her body to the contour of Dani's back. Dani softened against her.

"What will you do while I'm gone?" Piper asked into her hair.

"Work with impunity," Dani said.

Piper laughed, placing a kiss behind her ear. "I knew you'd say that."

"It'll help with the missing you," she said, and Piper's heart clenched.

"I'll only be a call away if you need me," Piper added.

"A call away and several hours by car. So don't do anything too dangerous."

"I can always ask Lou to bring me," she countered.

"Be careful," Dani said.

Piper kissed her nose. "It's just another murder investigation."

She was going to say, *What's the worst that could happen?* But she didn't want to tempt fate like that. Things went *horribly* wrong during just-another-murder-investigation all the time.

"I'll miss you, too," Piper said, squeezing her tighter.

"I'll probably stay at the office later," Dani said.

"Why?" Piper didn't like the idea of her walking home at night after dark. There were a couple of rough patches between *The Herald*'s office where Dani worked and their apartment in the French Quarter.

"It won't be the same if there's no one to come home to," Dani said.

It was true that Piper was usually home first. It was easy to do given the fact that it was impossible to reach their apartment above the Crescent City Detective Agency without walking through the lobby.

And Piper did her best to be home before dark if Dani wasn't with her. She knew that Dani didn't like to be alone at night. She hadn't had a panic attack in a long time. In fact, she'd been doing great, putting in a lot of work on resolving the trauma left in the wake of the Russian mob boss's torture.

Dmitri Petrov had really done a number on Dani. It didn't help that he'd attacked her when she'd just come home for the night. It made returning home to a dark apartment one of Dani's triggers.

It didn't matter that the attack and hours of torture that followed had been over two years ago. Piper suspected it would take a lot longer than two years to get over getting beaten nearly to death by a bunch of men and having a finger cut off.

"If you want me to stay, say the word," Piper said. "I don't have to go. Or I can get Lou to bring me back and forth."

"No," Dani said. She was smiling but her voice was firm. "This is us. I chase news stories and you chase bad guys. It's a *good* thing that two passionate women spend their lives doing what they love."

"If you need me, I want to be here," Piper said. "That's the most important part of *us*."

Dani turned toward her completely, either because she was breaking her neck looking back like that or because her mind was shifting toward—

The sensuous roll of Dani's body against hers made it perfectly clear what Dani wanted even before she reached up and slid an arm around Piper's neck.

"I thought you had to get up early," Piper said, laughter low in her throat.

"I do, but I won't see you for a few days," Dani breathed across her lips.

Piper hooked a thumb into the waistband of Dani's boxer shorts and pulled, exposing the swell of her hip. She kept pulling until Dani was naked from the waist down.

"Well then," Piper said, tracing a line of kisses up Dani's leg, across her stomach, chest and finally to the curve of her throat. Now she wanted to remove her shirt. "I'd better make this worth it."

· · ·

Lou was sitting at an outdoor Parisian café, her hair freshly washed from La Loon's sulfur stench and her clothes clean, when her watch buzzed. She'd been enjoying the view from her little street-side table, coffee in hand. In August, it was mostly tourists that clotted the narrow alleyways between the centuries-old buildings.

The native Parisians fled to the countryside for summer vacation. That didn't mean that Lou was any less intrigued by the gardens or the yellow taxis running up and down the Champs-Elysées.

The macaron shop across the street had a beautiful display of pretty pastel treats arranged to catch the eyes of passersby. Lou wondered if she should buy some for Dani and Piper, both of whom had a sweet tooth.

Her watch buzzed again, and she turned its face to read the message.

It was King. She did the time zone math in her head. It was almost seven in the morning in New Orleans. The agency didn't open for another two hours, but maybe he had something for her.

It had been three months since he'd offered her a hit list of criminals who thought they'd escaped the justice system unscathed.

She finished her coffee, threw a few euros on the table, and walked toward the narrow alleyway across the street. She'd only just stepped into the gray space between the stone walls when the world shifted, all the color washed away.

She reached out, finding the door handle with her hand.

It opened on the Crescent City Detective Agency.

So she'd been right. King had come into the office early.

Only it wasn't just King who stood there as she entered the room. Piper was also behind her desk, a bag at her feet.

Her eyes were a little puffy from lack of sleep as she packed up her laptop.

King looked up and gave her a nod of acknowledgment. "Hey. Thanks for coming."

"What's going on?" Lou asked.

"We're going to Vicksburg to help with a murder investigation," King said. "Seems like one of Detective White's friends is in a bit of trouble. We'll try to help her out."

"Do you want me to take you?" she asked. It wouldn't be the first time she'd served as chauffeur for her friends.

"No, I want the Buick," he said. "I've got to be able to get around the town and do the interviewing."

"I can take you and the car," Lou said.

"No, I beg you." Piper paused in her packing, her shoulders sagging in defeat. "He promised to let me sleep on the way there and I *need* that nap."

"Then why did you call me?" Lou asked.

"I was hoping you could use your compass to help us figure out whether or not there's actually been a murder or if it's an accident."

"It's not clear?" Lou asked.

"Not at all," King said, tugging the zipper on his pack and sealing his second bag. "And to be honest, I don't have a good feeling about it."

Piper's head shot up. "You didn't tell me that. That might be something you want to tell a person before you take them out to the bayou and ask them to sleep in a haunted mansion, man."

Lou arched a brow. "The murder was at a haunted mansion?"

"Possible haunted mansion," King corrected.

"*Definitely* haunted. It's Margo Manor." Piper's indignation grew as she looked from one face to another. "Come on. I read you *so* many articles yesterday."

"Tell me again," King said, his own irritation showing.

"Why bother? You don't believe in that stuff," Piper said grumpily.

These two are going to have a fun car ride, Lou thought. *He'd better let her sleep.*

King shrugged. "It might help the investigation to know the history of the manor. Or at least to know what people think about it."

"It's supposedly the most haunted mansion in Louisiana. Margo Manor was built in the seventeen hundreds and the family had thousands of slaves to pick their cotton. Then one night there was a fire and almost all of the slaves died. There's a rumor that the owner of Margo Manor started the fire in the slaves' quarters on purpose because his daughter was in love with one of them, but then the fire spread and destroyed most of his estate."

"Why would he set fire to his own property?" King asked.

Both of Piper's eyebrows went up. "Uh, are you talking about the house or the slaves?"

"The house, the land, of course."

Piper's cheeks puffed up. "I don't think it was the owner's intention to burn his own house down. He probably just wanted to scare the slaves and the fire spread farther than he thought it would."

"So it's the most haunted because of all the slaves that died there," he said.

"Not just that." Piper rubbed her forehead. "After they rebuilt the main house and the family moved back in, things started to go wrong in the house. The older daughter had already been married and sent away, but he still had six other kids and a new wife, so, plenty of people for the ghosts to get their revenge on."

"Who?" King asked, pulling a bottle of aspirin out of his bag and tossing it across the room to Piper.

"Oh man, thank you. How did you know my head's killing me?"

"You keep rubbing your head."

She lowered her fist from her forehead. "Oh yeah. Okay."

"Who wanted revenge?" King prompted again.

They waited for her to swallow two pills before she went on.

"Most people think it was the lover. The slave who fell in love with the daughter who was sent away."

"And why do you say it was revenge?"

Piper put the bottle of aspirin into her bag rather than throw it back at King. "One of the kids broke his leg falling down the stairs. Then the wife almost drowned in the bathtub. She claimed that she'd felt a hand holding her under the water. The little kids were also saying that people stood around their bedroom all night and whispered at them, causing them to wake up screaming more than once. One of the little girls even went missing for almost a week, and when they found her she'd been tied to a huge tree in the middle of the woods with bite marks all over her. Spooky shit, man, and you're like, *Oh let's just sleep there.*"

"I didn't realize you were so superstitious," he said.

"I'm not really," she said, puffing her chest. "But I'm also not stupid. There isn't a native New Orleanian I know that doesn't have a ghost story. I've got a friend who to this day won't use any of the bar bathrooms in the whole city because a ghost touched her boob in one."

King looked incredulous. Lou, however, thought this conversation was great.

Lucy would love this, she thought. A heartsick twinge shimmered through her chest. Sometimes she could go for months and months without thinking of her dead aunt. Other times she missed her so fiercely and suddenly that it physically hurt.

"I've always wanted to see a ghost," Lou said. "Aunt Lucy

believed in them. She used to say that if people like us existed, then anything was possible."

King's face softened, either at the memory of his late wife and great love or because he was coming around to the idea of ghosts. Lou suspected it was the former.

"Fine. Maybe there will be ghosts, but more likely, this was an accident. Or maybe there's a real flesh-and-blood murderer on the loose. And if someone *is* responsible for this girl's death—whether it be Rita or someone trying to make it look like Rita—we will find them and hopefully hold them accountable in a court of law."

Piper slid her packed bags off the desk. "Murderers held accountable in the court of law? Now who's talking crazy?"

7

———————

On hot summer days like this, Konstantine was grateful that the thick stone walls of his church kept its interior cool. Its high caverns and domed rooms protected them from the heat collecting in Florence's cobblestone streets. Even the stained-glass window of the Blessed Virgin seemed to repel the harsh, direct light.

He'd passed the day fielding phone calls from his people across the globe, agreeing to treaties, brokering new deals. He'd just had lunch with Stefano when his accountant called with the good news. Their accounts were up, better than they'd ever been even in all the years under Padre Leo's guidance.

Konstantine had much to celebrate.

Are you proud, Padre? Konstantine wondered as he cleared his desk that evening, ready to head home.

Assolutamente.

Konstantine crossed the courtyard, purple with twilight, and disappeared beneath the arch leading toward the nave. He traced the halls, following the growing sound of children's voices.

When the last corridor broke open, he found them—the dozen children in his care—seated around the long table in the dining room, loudly talking over one another.

He cleared his throat.

Nothing. They took no notice of him.

He tried again, and when this still earned him no response, he began singing loudly, throwing his voice over the din.

They turned in their seats, surprised by the intrusion. But as soon as they realized who it was, and that he was *singing* of all things, the children burst into laughter.

"*Tranquilli, bambini,*" he begged them. "Quiet down."

He gave them a moment to settle before he said, "Has everyone done their homework?"

"*Sì!*" they called back.

"And have you done the chores that Matilda has asked of you?"

"*Sì,*" they called again.

"And after dinner, will you take your showers and brush your teeth and go to sleep when you are *told* so that no one is late to school tomorrow?"

He gave Nario, who'd overslept that very morning, a pointed look. The boy returned a shy smile and averted his gaze.

"*Sì, signore!*" the children said.

"*Molto bene.*" Konstantine reached forward and put one hand on Matteo's head and another on Nario's shoulder. "Then I will go home now and see you tomorrow."

Several of the smaller children, Franco, Brando, and Andrea, scrambled from their seats, hurrying to him and throwing their arms around his legs.

He assured each in turn, patting their backs, ruffling their hair, saying all the tender kindnesses that his mother had said to him when he was a child.

"Bene, bene."

Matteo needed no invitation to get up from his seat and claim his hug. Konstantine was careful not to squeeze him any tighter or praise him any harder than the others.

He loved all of the children and was fiercely protective of them. But Matteo was different because Konstantine loved him the way Padre Leo must have loved Konstantine as a boy.

He was a favorite. A beloved son.

And Konstantine did not want to create a rivalry. It had been because Padre Leo had favored Konstantine over his own son, Nico, that Nico had sworn revenge. In that quest for revenge, he'd destroyed Padre Leo's church, where they'd grown up together, and killed half of the Ravengers—their friends—and nearly Konstantine himself.

No, he thought somberly. *I must be careful.*

He wanted the children to love each other. To look out for each other. There could be no rift between them. He must be careful. Always careful, no matter how he truly felt.

No sooner had Matteo released him than another dark head appeared under Konstantine's hand.

Gabriella.

If he hadn't already been schooling his face and emotions carefully, Konstantine's shock might have shown. This was the first time the girl—the only girl in his charge—had openly sought affection like the others.

He gave her the same pat on the back, the same ruffle of her hair, the same calm assurances.

Though he did notice the way Matteo had smiled at her when she retook her seat beside him, and the way Gabriella had nudged him with her elbow and mumbled something under her breath, too low for Konstantine to hear.

Don't tease her about it, he wanted to say, but couldn't.

Once the children were at the table again, their attention returning to their dinners and their conversations louder than ever, he slipped from the dining hall without a sound.

He'd almost made it all the way home before he realized something.

He was happy.

He was honestly, truly happy. For the first time in his life, at least as far as he could remember, he was completely satisfied with the state of his affairs.

All of the children were well. Business was good. There were no wars brimming on the horizon, no rival gangs threatening to destroy him or the people he cared about. He had his health, his wealth, and his power.

Above all, he had his greatest obsession, Louie Thorne, waiting for him at home.

After opening the villa's high gate and mounting the stairs to the living room, he found her in the armory. He saw her before she saw him.

He knew this was an illusion, of course.

Yes, he was looking at her back as she stood in the lit antechamber, examining the guns lining the walls—but this was Louie.

No doubt she'd sensed him coming before he'd even made it through the villa's gate.

Yet she permitted him to look at her back, at her sleek and beautiful form, as she inspected her arsenal.

She reached forward and pulled out the new Benelli he'd hidden there. It was a beautiful creation. Automatic and powerful. It wasn't even on the market yet, but that hadn't stopped Konstantine from acquiring it.

"I can't tell if I'm getting better at finding them or if you're getting worse at hiding them," Lou said, finally turning to look at him. With the Benelli still in her grip, she measured its weight in her hand.

"I think it's you who is getting better," he said.

It had become a little game of his, to hide gifts around the house for her, a game born out of necessity.

If he could simply hand her a gift, he would, but so often she looked pained in those moments. What else could he do but treat her when she was not looking?

It had begun with the American coffeemaker. Though in no world would he call what that machine made *coffee*. Since that first offering, there had been many others.

The guns she always found quickly.

He supposed he shouldn't be surprised, considering how often she assessed her weapons.

The clothes took longer. He was half convinced that she never really looked at what she put on. That was the only explanation for how a pair of Versace boots could go unnoticed in a closet for almost two months.

He went to her and wrapped his arms around her waist. "Are you ready for dinner, *amore mio?*"

"Almost."

He checked his watch. "We will leave in thirty minutes then? After I shower."

Her tone was darker than he'd expected. Usually, when she identified a new target, her mood was bright. Give her a serial killer or fiend and she was delighted. Perhaps the darkness in such souls called to her own darkness.

Without a good target, there was usually a current of displeasure. It wasn't that she brooded exactly, though that's what he'd thought at first. It had taken him a long time to realize that simply when she was bored, she was unhappy.

"What troubles you?" he asked, his chin still on her shoulder. "*Cosa hai fatto oggi, amore mio?*"

"I visited La Loon," she said. "One of the eggs is gone. There were six. Now there are five."

"Maybe something ate it. Or your beast herself."

"That's what I thought. But why would she eat it? Should

I bring her more bodies? Do you think food is a problem?" Her mood was darkening more. That was not the direction he'd wanted this to go. "Maybe she can't hunt because she's always watching them."

"I wouldn't worry about it, *amore mio*. These things happen. Why did you go to La Loon? Just to check on your beast and the eggs?" he asked.

"I killed a man. He tried to stab a woman in the park. She's fine."

"Thanks to you, no doubt," he said. "And your friends?"

"King and Piper are going to investigate a haunted house somewhere in Louisiana. Piper kept calling it 'the bayou,' but I don't really know what that means. Do you believe in ghosts?"

"A ghost committed a crime?" he asked, struggling to follow her thoughts.

"*Sì,*" she said simply. "Or maybe someone was pretending to be a ghost. They haven't figured that out yet."

He shrugged out of his shirt, his thoughts turning toward the shower. "You can explain this to me at dinner."

She took one look at his naked chest, a long, lingering look, before turning back to the rack of guns in front of her. "You'd better hurry."

He did.

It wasn't until they were sitting at the table outside the pizza bistro four blocks from their villa, his hair slicked back from the shower and clothes fresh, that he was able to ask about the nursing home in Florida.

"I haven't figured that out yet," she said.

"It is so sad," he said, taking a drink of his red wine.

"Why?" she asked.

How to explain it to her. Perhaps because she'd had so little connection to the elderly. Her parents had been murdered when they were young, and even her aunt had not yet reached fifty when she'd passed on. There was the detective in New Orleans, who Konstantine knew to be sixty-three, but he wasn't old, not really.

"You had no grandparents?" he asked her.

"Not really," she said. "My dad's and Lucy's parents were gone before I was born. And my mother's family didn't like my father, so we didn't see them much. I only have a few memories of them. None of them particularly pleasant."

"The elderly are like children," Konstantine explained. "They need care like children. We must protect them."

She lifted her wine glass and drank deeply.

"I had a ninety-year-old try to shoot me with his shotgun," she said at last. "He didn't seem especially *vulnerable* to me."

He didn't dare ask why the old man had wanted to shoot her.

After the waiter placed their meal on the table and Lou had taken the bite of her first slice, she asked, "Will you help me research Hellman House? Maybe you can find something about the patients there, or the staff. Maybe even look into their financials in case it's insurance fraud or something. I'm not sure what I'm looking for, to be honest. A motive for killing an old woman, I guess?"

"Of course, *amore mio*." He sat his own wine glass back down on the table, enjoying the light sparkling in her eyes from the nearby candle. How could he express how much he loved this—their life together? How afraid he was of losing it. "And the haunted house? Do you want me to look into its history as well? Do you remember its name?"

"Margo Manor," she replied. Lou looked out over the square, at a fire dancer performing for a small crowd that had gathered around her.

"Why not?" she said. "I like to be prepared."

8

———

King had only been on I-10 for five minutes before Piper was asleep. When he turned to her, ready to offer her the coveted honor of playing DJ for their journey, he found her eyes closed and mouth slightly ajar.

Her head lolled against the seatbelt, cradled like a hammock.

I guess she really was tired.

That was fine. He could make the journey in silence, letting his mind unwind like a dropped spool of thread.

It turned first to his work, to the unresolved aspects of outstanding cases. He considered what his next moves should be in order to bring his objectives to fruition.

Once this work was done, his mind turned to Rita Golden.

He rehearsed what he would say to her when he saw her, how he imagined—*hoped*—the interview would go.

Then there were the employees he needed to speak to. The witness, a fellow maid. The police and investigators.

Only after he spoke to everyone would he be able to reconstruct a clear picture of what really happened.

The phone in his pocket buzzed.

It was Beth, letting him know she'd be back at the end of the week.

Beth Miller, his current squeeze, had been out of town for almost a month. She'd gone to Florida three weeks ago for her son's wedding, a week-long celebration of dinners and potlucks and gatherings meant to include their scattered family members and friends. Then she'd agreed to stay and housesit for two weeks while they traveled Europe. Apparently someone had to keep the house plants and their two rescued pit bulls alive.

Beth had texted him every other day at first, and they'd chatted on the phone. Then three or four days would pass without him hearing from her.

King missed her. He missed their easy way of being together. He missed the sex.

But if he was honest with himself, he knew that he'd be fine if she never came back from Florida.

That's normal, he thought. *Lucy was the great love of my life. Nothing will feel the way it did with Lucy.*

And Lucy had only been dead for a couple of years. If he *ever* got over Lucy, it certainly wouldn't be so soon.

By the time he turned off the exit into Vicksburg, his mental wanderings had stopped. He needed all of his attention to navigate the winding roads and follow the signs directing him to Margo Manor.

The streets twisted beneath the canopy of old trees, and thick honeysuckle bushes and kudzu grew right up to the edge of the road. It had been a while since he'd driven on streets so narrow that they couldn't even accommodate a dotted line dividing them into two lanes.

Around the latest bend, a stoplight hung above the middle

of the intersection. He hooked a right, past a small white chapel. A waterline cut across the chapel's dingy side, telling King that this area had seen high floods not so long ago. Or perhaps no one had gotten around to power-washing the stain off the white boards.

In fact, several buildings on the outskirts of town were still empty and boarded up. He'd heard that many of these towns had struggled to get the financial support they were owed after the storm blew through, and yet it was painful to see.

But even with these markers of decay, the town was beautiful with its enormous trees sagging under the weight of Spanish moss. The branches twisted toward the sky like worshippers in a fervid dance.

It was very green, very lush, and borderline wild.

King was still admiring it, wondering if he should get out of the city more, when he discovered the entrance to the manor.

The driveway was well manicured. The trees had been left quite close to the edge of the concrete and had been allowed to grow in such a way as to form a canopy over the cars as they passed beneath.

Between their thick trunks, bright blood-red bursts of flowers and purple blooms fought for space. Then the canopy ended, breaking open on a blue-gray sky above the manor house.

The house itself was a soft orange, like the skin of a mango. Its shutters were black to match the stately front door. The driveway changed from pavement to cobblestone, and as the tires of his Buick bumped and bounced over the burnt-red stones, he had a sense of traveling back in time.

If it wasn't the look of the place, then it was certainly the footman in full livery standing by at the base of the stairs leading up to the entrance.

When King threw the car into park, Piper woke with a jolt. A red line was embedded in her cheek from the seatbelt.

"We're here," he told her. "Take your time getting out. I'm just gonna talk to that guy for a minute."

"What? Oh." She rubbed sleep from her eyes, unbuckling her belt. "That was fast."

King threw his weight against the Buick's heavy door and stepped out. He pulled at the belt on his pants, hiking them a little higher, before shutting the door behind him. He took a moment to stretch and ease the tension out of his back and shoulders before crossing to the footman.

"Hello, sir," he called out.

The footman's gaze remained forward, though what he was looking at, King had no idea.

The only thing across from the house was the fountain burbling in the center of the circular driveaway. Beyond that, the forest that had been allowed to grow unchecked. It was impossible to see very far into the shadows collected beneath those entwined branches.

He extended his hand toward the footman, but the man did not move. King had no choice but to let his hand fall. "My name is Robert King. Ms. Golden is expecting me. Any chance you could tell us where I can find her?"

"She's in the house, sir," the footman said, his dark eyes remaining fixed on something in the distance, over King's right shoulder.

King resisted the urge to look around again.

"It's a big house," King said. "Where should I look first?"

The car door slammed and Piper stretched in his peripheral view.

"Try the office on the first floor, sir," the footman replied. "There are signs."

His thick Louisiana drawl reminded him of Mel. Half the time when King ran into someone in New Orleans, they might not have an accent at all. In the city, there were transplants from all over the country—and the world—just like him. He suspected that was also why Piper's accent was a mix. Southern, surely, but softer.

But Mel's accent wasn't much different than the footman's, even though hers had softened a bit during her time in the Big Easy. Either as a natural result of living in the city or because she hadn't wanted others to know where she came from.

Mel should be here with us.

King pushed these thoughts away.

"All right. I'll do that. Thank you. Can I leave my car where it is?" King asked.

"Yes, sir, though the parking spots for overnight guests are located on the other side of the building."

"Thanks. I'll move after I speak to Ms. Golden."

Piper was at his elbow now, her bag hoisted up onto a shoulder, looking to King for instruction. He nodded in the direction of the manor's double doors, and they opened as if on their own.

It took King a moment to realize the footman had pressed the disability-assist button.

Sure, the footman was still facing the formidable wall of trees, seemingly unchanged, but his gloved hand was clearly on the large silver button now.

Don't let all this ghost stuff go to your head, King scolded himself. *You haven't even been in the house yet.*

The first thing he noticed once he stepped into the great hall was that it wasn't air-conditioned. Heat hung in the air thickly. He felt like he could reach up and swipe at it like a cobweb.

"If the bedrooms are this warm, we might have to rethink sleeping here," King said, turning to Piper.

Piper snorted. "Sometimes I forget that you're from up

north until you say things like that. Honestly, this ain't that bad."

King spotted the sign pointing to the office and hooked a right at the end of the hallway. The carpets pulled at the soles of his boots until he stopped just short of the door and rapped on its frame.

"Hello?" he called out. "Ms. Golden?"

He heard her before he saw her, her heels catching on the carpet in short, strident steps. Her hair was black.

Her eyes were dark brown and her eyebrows drawn so thickly that they gave her face a stretched look. He couldn't tell if her expression was stern or surprised.

It wasn't that King cared about things like makeup. He had just never seen it so poorly applied to someone's face before.

"Is that marker on her face?" Piper muttered under her breath.

"You're a professional," King reminded her, even though her remark wasn't far off from his own thoughts.

Piper straightened and King felt a little sorry to have chastised her.

"I'm Robert King," he said to Rita, extending his hand. "We spoke last night."

"Detective King," Rita said, and shook his offered hand.

"Robert is fine."

Technically, he couldn't address himself as a detective since it was a formal job title. He didn't belong to a police force or investigative organization in any official capacity.

True, he was a private investigator. Licensed, certainly, but still freelance.

She turned those stern eyes on Piper.

"You didn't tell me you were bringing anyone," she said. Her cold tone matched the clamminess of her palm.

"This is my apprentice, Piper Genereux. She helps me with all of my cases."

He saw Piper's spine straighten ever so slightly.

"Nice to meet you both," Rita said, but she did not offer to shake Piper's hand.

Piper let her hand fall, returning it to the strap of her bag.

To her credit, she didn't turn and give King a pointed look.

Way to be professional, kid.

"Please have a seat." Rita gestured at two high-back chairs in front of the large desk.

Piper took the innermost seat, closest to a large window overlooking a manicured garden. King took the one closest to the door.

Rita situated herself behind the desk, looking smaller than ever. She couldn't be more than five feet tall.

"How would you like to begin?" she asked.

At least she's calmed down, King thought. There was no trace of the desperation he'd heard on the phone the night before.

"We need to ask you some questions," he said. "It will help a lot to clarify your situation and let us know how best to proceed."

"I assumed as much," Rita said. "Richard told me you were very thorough."

Richard. It took King a minute to realize she meant Dick White. No one on the force ever called him *Richard*.

"Yes, he'd know. We've worked together on several cases," King said politely. "Then once I finish speaking with you, I'll head over to the station and see what they have to say before coming back to interview your staff."

Rita turned her wrist, her blood-red nails tapping the face of her gold watch. "Depending on how many questions you have, those yahoos at the station might already have left by then. They cut out by lunchtime on days like this. No sense of urgency with Herb, I'll tell you that. It might be tomorrow before you catch him."

"That's fine," King amended. "If that's the case, then I'll speak to your staff first."

"We'll all be here until six," Rita assured him. "You should have no problem. Though Aubree isn't in today and she's the one you'll want to talk to. She was the other maid working with Nova when she fell."

"Can I get her full name?" King asked. "Nova..."

"Nova Perry. And Aubree Owens is the other one."

Piper was already writing the names down. Rita Golden eyed her, unimpressed, but King wasn't worried. Piper was a wonderful notetaker. This was far from the first interview she'd transcribed. He'd taken her to crime scenes, interrogation rooms, and prisons.

A hot office with a bitchy boss was hardly the most difficult of situations. Her notes would be good.

"How old was Nova when she passed?" King asked.

"Seventeen," she said. "Just. Her birthday was in July."

"And how long had she been working for you?"

"Almost eight months, though I wasn't sure how much longer she was going to last."

King shifted his weight in his seat. "Why's that?"

"She was always turning up late to her shift. Sometimes I would catch her lingering in the garden with Michael Reed. Truth be told, I was ready to fire both of them. But competent workers are hard to come by. There's also the house's reputation to consider."

"I would think the house's reputation would keep traffic up," Piper said, her pen hesitating. "Tourists love haunted places."

Golden looked at her as if she were nothing more than a cockroach to be squashed beneath her boot.

Before Rita could say anything cruel, or even insinuate

that Piper had no right to speak to her, King said, "It's a valid question. Answer it, please, Ms. Golden."

Golden regarded him for a minute, but whatever caustic thing she wanted to say she kept to herself. After several beats of silence she said, "If you *must* know, no. *Traffic* isn't up and hasn't been for quite a while. Before Katrina we would get hundreds of thousands of visitors a year. Now we're lucky if we get a quarter of that. New Orleans isn't the only city in this state that gets devastated by floods, you know."

King remembered the water stain on the side of the chapel.

"The majority of our returns come from weddings, events, but last fall we were washed out completely because of the flood. Weddings are usually booked a year in advance. It's hard to convince people their wedding *next* October will be fine when all they can think about is how *last* October half the town was under water and we have a non-refundable-deposit policy."

You could try canceling the non-refundable-deposit policy, he thought. But he said nothing. Rita definitely looked like the sort of woman who would not take kindly to any advice on how to run her business.

Piper was scribbling something, but King couldn't see from the corner of his eye.

"You said that Nova fell from the fourth-floor window?"

"It wasn't a window," Rita said.

"Oh, I'm sorry," he amended. "I thought Dick—*Richard*—told me she'd fallen from a window."

Rita shook her head. "At the end of the hallway, there are two glass doors that open up onto a balcony. The balcony isn't up to code. It needs to be rebuilt, so I keep those doors locked. On the day she died, the doors were open and she was found on the patio below the balcony."

"If the doors stay locked, do you have any idea how they were opened?" King asked.

"I have a key that opens them. I'm the *only* one who has a key. The day before she fell, my key went missing. I'd say she took it herself and leapt off the balcony, but I found the key in my desk that night after the police and everyone had cleared out. A dead person can't put keys back, so someone must've taken them."

"Are you sure?" King asked. "Maybe you overlooked it and it was in the desk the whole time?"

"No," Rita said firmly. "I didn't. It was gone. Someone took it."

Piper's hand remained frozen, poised above the paper.

"That's why the police are investigating me," Rita said. "I keep telling them that someone must have taken the key out of my desk and put it back, but they don't believe me. No one in this town ever believes me because I'm not from here. They don't like outsiders. Hell, they didn't like me from the moment I arrived, and it's only gotten worse since my husband left."

"How long ago was that?"

"Fifteen years," Rita said, and her mouth twitched.

King noted the tic, but wasn't sure if it was simply a strong emotion that Rita was holding back or if it was a lie. Considering how easy it would be to verify her story, he felt he'd have his answer soon enough.

"What was your husband's name?" King asked.

"John Harrison Golden," she said, with the same mouth twitch.

Piper's hand had resumed scribbling across the page.

Rita didn't seem to notice.

"Fifteen years ago he ran off on me. Left with another woman and never came back. It took me *seven years* of fighting. Seven years of scraping and pinching to make ends meet until I could get him declared legally dead and have the manor and land turned over to me. I had to fight Herb and everyone else in this godforsaken place, and spent a fortune on lawyers and court fees just to get what was mine."

"So fifteen years ago, that's the last time you saw him alive."

"Yes."

"Why do you think he ran off? Why not assume he was kidnapped or murdered or—?"

Rita sneered. "He was seeing someone at the time. I found, shall we say, *evidence*. When I asked him about it, he said he was in love and wanted to be with her. I was supposed to get divorce papers, but they never came."

Tears formed in the corner of Rita's eyes. They were at odds with the furious curl of her lip.

"He made his choice. And I've been here, cleaning up *his* mess, ever since."

There was no denying the hatred in her voice. The cold fury.

"Is it possible your husband is still alive?" King asked. "Perhaps we could repair your relationship with the towns-people if he turned up."

"He won't be back."

Here her tears fell, wetting the thick eyeliner she wore.

"He took nothing with him? No money? No car? No one ever came forward? No one admitted to helping him out? There was never so much as a call to let you know he was okay?"

She shook her head. "I never heard from him again. I suppose he thought he was doing me a favor, by letting the years pass with no contact so that I could declare him dead."

She looked suddenly very tired. King thought this was a good place to stop.

"Is there anything else you want me to know about Nova or your husband, Ms. Golden?"

She shook her head and then checked her gold watch again. "If you hurry you might catch them down at the station before they leave for lunch."

"Have you been formally charged with murder?" he asked.

She scoffed. "Not formally. Though I remain a *person of interest* and I'm not to leave town. As if I have anywhere else to go."

Such bitterness infused her words.

King let Piper finish her notes before he stood and extended his hand to Golden again.

"We'll head over to the station and see what they'll tell us. Any recommendations as to where we can grab some lunch?"

"Freddie's," she said. "It's on the main strip not far down from the station. You won't miss it. This town isn't big enough to get lost in."

"All right. We'll try to make it back before six. Did you still want us to stay the night here in the manor?"

"Yes," she said, rising to meet him. "At least for tonight. Just in case."

"In case of what?" King asked.

"In case it really was a ghost that pushed her."

King had half turned toward the door when these words stopped him. "Is that an actual consideration?"

He'd expected her to deny it. Or, even as stern as she was, make some joke.

But she didn't smile or laugh. The bags beneath her eyes were pronounced and her eyes round with...fear? Sadness? Exhaustion?

"It's better safe than sorry," she said.

. . .

Neither Piper nor King spoke until they turned off
the manor's long driveway, back onto the road that would
take them into town. Piper didn't know why King had felt
compelled to be silent, but she had her own reasons. In fact,
she had *so many* reasons from the minute they'd walked into
Margo Manor.

Finally King asked, "What follow-up questions do you
have?"

"I want to check on the flood dates for the area and also
the financials for the manor," Piper said. "I'd also like to ask
the staff what kind of boss Rita is, and whether or not they
think she could push a girl off a balcony."

"I thought we were trying to prove Rita's innocence,"
King said. "Is this because of the missing key? One of the
staff members could have stolen it."

Piper shrugged, trying to hide her nervousness. "We've
got to keep all possibilities open. Sometimes the bad guy
hires the detectives to help make them *look* innocent."

"She didn't hire us," King said. "White did."

"Yeah, but she called him for help, right? It's the same
thing."

"Just because someone doesn't know how to put on their
makeup doesn't mean they're a villain," King said with a
smirk.

"It's those eyebrows, right? They *scream* villain eyebrows."

"We have to assume she's innocent *until* proven guilty,
Genereux."

"Yes sir," Piper said, and immediately she felt terrible for
making fun of the woman's eyebrows. It wasn't like Piper had
great ones herself or anything.

King shrugged as if it were no big deal. "Besides, Nova
was too young to be a romantic rival. She'd have been a
toddler at the time of John's disappearance. I doubt Rita
killed her for revenge."

"Maybe she has a new boyfriend, and Nova made the mistake of talking to him and Rita just snapped. Like she was triggered or something after what her husband did."

"We'll ask about a potential boyfriend when we do the staff interviews," King said.

"And before that? What do we do next, boss?"

"White thinks the cops will be pretty laid-back and will give us all the help we need. Mel thinks that they'll be cold and give us a hard time for being outsiders poking our noses in other people's business. I say we go find out who's right. Then we can grab lunch at Freddie's."

I better figure out where he stands on this before I say anything, she thought.

Piper said, "What about the ghost?"

King laughed, straightening out the wheel. "It was strange that she tacked that on there at the end, wasn't it? It surprised me."

You don't know the half of it.

"There was a lot *strange* about that interview," she said, her gaze fixed beyond the window. She was afraid that if she looked at him, she'd give it away. She could already tell by the way he kept looking at her that he was trying to figure out what she was thinking.

"If I'm being honest, she was a hard read. I sensed guilt, but not really about Nova Perry's death. And that part about the ghost, what do you think of that?" he asked.

I think I saw a dead guy standing behind her.

After a beat of strained silence, Piper said, "Maybe she didn't kill the girl but she thinks she could have prevented it somehow? But yeah, she totally thinks the ghost is real."

Because it is, she thought.

It's not enough, her mind countered. *He's a cop more than anything. He needs evidence. What can I give him?*

"I'd know that look from anywhere," she added, her eyes

tracing the foliage pressing against the side of the road, but she barely saw any of it. Not the trees, nor the vines. None of the flowers. "We see lots of tourists in the Quarter like that. In Mel's shop too. They have some weird, unexplainable encounter and then they're like, 'Oh shit. Maybe there's something to all this stuff.' That's what Rita looked like to me when she mentioned the ghost."

King said nothing, his forehead wrinkled in thought.

Piper pressed him.

"Maybe she knows something about the mansion or the ghosts but she didn't want to tell us. Heck, maybe she even knows her husband is dead because she's seen *his* ghost."

Piper waited with bated breath.

Come on, she thought. *Be open to this, man.*

"As professionals, it's our responsibility to reserve any judgments about Golden's guilt—or belief in ghosts—until we have more facts."

"Yeah, okay." Piper rolled down the window and stuck her hand out into the humid wind.

I'll have to wait, she thought. *Maybe later I can tell him what I saw.*

9

Lou sat up in bed, an unsettled feeling chaffing against her bones. Beside her Konstantine dozed. They'd had their nice dinner, had come home for a couple of glasses of wine and had fallen into each other's arms soon after.

The soft, contented expression on his face was at such odds with the agitation now coursing through her veins. She slipped from the bed naked and crossed to the balcony window. The high moon struck the Arno's black waters. The ripples made the moonlight spark like stars.

What is it? she asked the darkness. *What's wrong?*

Had she had another dream? Some half-formed fear scurrying around the back of her mind.

It had been so quick, over before she could get a clear sense of the danger lying on the other side of—what exactly?

She crossed to the bedside table and checked her watch. It was four in the morning. The night was almost over. It would be ten p.m. in Florida.

I'll go anyway, she thought. *I'll go and see for myself.*

Lou dressed. She pulled on her loose black pants and a tank top. Then she added her shoulder holster.

What to cover you with?

She reached out and touched one of her father's flannels. It was too soft now, having been worn thin throughout the years since her father's death. It could never hide a gun properly. It was best to stick with the leather jacket.

Lou slid the Beretta she'd been favoring into the holster and pulled her leather jacket off the back of the chair. She gave Konstantine one last, lingering look.

He didn't wake.

Lou entered the closet and closed it quietly behind her.

Is there a killer in Hellman House? she asked the dark.

The darkness softened and the soft slapping of the Arno's waters against the wall of the canal fell away. In its place bloomed a different darkness. Much colder, with the antiseptic stench Lou associated with hospitals, and there was something else.

Wilting flowers?

Something perfumed yet permeating decay.

She stepped forward into the room.

The man in the bed was unconscious or asleep. The tube across his face whistled and hissed with each breath. The heart monitor beside his head beeped a slow, even rhythm.

The blankets wrapping his legs had been tucked in tightly and his bald head shone from the lights thrown by the equipment surrounding his bed.

They're like children, Konstantine had said.

The man lying there certainly looked small in his bed, with its safety rails and neatly tucked blankets.

But how could he be the one Lou was looking for? She didn't think her killer was a comatose patient in a nursing home. She came to the side of the man's bed and looked down on him.

His exposed skin was mottled with—what had Lucy called them? Liver spots?

They were everywhere. On his bald, wrinkled head. Along his cheekbones, in the folds of his crinkled neck, and on the backs of his hands.

Lou lifted his hand and let it fall.

Nothing.

It was as she thought.

Did this guy kill someone ten or twenty years ago? Possibly. But look at him. He certainly wasn't killing Hellman's patients now.

"Who is doing this?" Lou whispered to the dark.

"You can't be in here," a woman said.

Lou looked up and found a nurse in the doorway. Her red hair was pulled up in a high ponytail that fell past her shoulders, and she was scowling at Lou as if she were a thief.

"How did you get in here?" she demanded.

"I came during visiting hours," Lou lied.

"They ended hours ago," she said, her expression not softening. "And this is the critical care ward. It's unsanitary for you to be in here."

The nurse reached for the switch, flicking it with an impatient hand, flooding the room with light. The sleeping patient didn't stir. His heart monitor didn't even register the brash intrusion. The monitor continued to *blip blip blip* as if nothing had changed.

Lou's heart, however, had skipped a beat.

When the nurse turned on the light, she took away Lou's exits.

"I'll be going then," Lou said.

She had no choice but to walk straight past the nurse into the bright hallway.

She felt completely, hideously exposed. And very aware of the gun she carried. Her fingers itched to pull it.

"I'll escort you out," the nurse said. "This way."

"All right." There was no point in arguing with her.

Lou let her take the lead. But they only made it halfway down the hall before Lou sidestepped into another patient's unlit room.

Then she was gone before the nurse turned around.

LOU LIKED LIBRARIES AT NIGHT. TRULY, SHE LIKED libraries any hour of the day. But when they were closed and not a soul stirred in the whole building, there was a quiet that filled her soul, easing her restlessness unlike anything else. Apart from murder, that was.

This one had mice. Or Lou *hoped* they were mice.

The relentless nibbling came from somewhere behind the stacks off to the right where she sat in front of the microfiche machines. The soft, repetitive grinding noise went on and on, pausing ever so often, abruptly, as if the mouse was listening for intruders.

Lou understood why twenty minutes later when an orange tabby leapt onto the table without warning.

Lou had pulled her gun and pointed it at the creature without thinking. Green eyes regarded her with indifference. They slid to her gun, unimpressed.

Meow.

"A library cat." Lou lowered the gun. "Sorry about that."

Meow.

"They must've hired you for the mice." Lou reached out and scratched the beast between its eyes and then down around its ears. It purred, pressing its head into her hand.

A tag hung from its red collar with the name Bartleby inscribed into the gold plating. On the back, *Please return me to the Clermont Public Library if found.*

"Do they know about the mice?" Lou asked him. He pressed his head into her hand without comment.

As Lou searched the old news stories for anything on Hellman House, the orange tabby spread himself wide beside her, his large soft belly easily covering what little space was left on the table by the microfiche machine.

Lou periodically scratched Bartleby's ears while she read.

But the hours stretched on and she didn't find anything about Hellman House. No reports of suspected abuse or mysterious deaths. No reported crimes of any kind. Then again, the news she found on the microfiche stopped in the nineties, before the birth of the internet. If Hellman had its demons they were recently acquired. That meant it was in Konstantine's research domain, lord of the modern computer that he was.

At least she could give him the patient's name, Jesse Elmer. It had been conveniently written on the slate outside his room. She'd spotted it when the nurse had marched her into the hallway.

Maybe learning more about Elmer would uncover the reason why when she'd asked for a killer, her compass had brought her to his room. The library hadn't had any information on Elmer either.

If he had a record, Konstantine would have to find that as well.

"I wish I could find an *awake* Hellman resident," Lou told the cat. "Then maybe they could tell me what's going on."

Meow.

A rattle of keys caught Lou's ear. Then the sound of doors swinging open and shut. The scrape of a mop bucket across the floor.

Guess the Clermont Public Library has a night janitor.

"That's my cue," she whispered to the orange tabby, and scratched his ears one last time.

Lou rose from her seat and walked toward the stacks. She followed the rows of books to the end of the room, where thick shadows waited for her.

Bartleby sat down at the edge of the darkness, as if he knew he couldn't follow Lou where she was going.

Meow.

Lou gave him a final salute. "Good luck with the mice."

Bartleby was still sitting in the same spot, peering into the dark, when Kenny the night janitor found him twenty minutes later.

Cats are weird, Kenny thought, not for the first time. He hated it when they seemed to see something he couldn't. When they stared like that, it was enough to make a man believe in ghosts.

10

The Vicksburg Police Department was a small brick building at the end of the main strip, if King could call it a strip. The options included Freddie's diner, a small fire station, the equally small police station, a grocery store, a two-pump gas station, and a post office. Across from Freddie's was Barbara's, which King largely suspected was a bar given the metal signs featuring recognizable beer brands advertised above its door.

"Do you want to bet that Barbara and Freddie are brother and sister, mother and son, or husband and wife?" Piper asked. "I'd put my money on mother and son."

"I'll take that wager," King said. "My money is on husband and wife."

"How much money we talking about?" Piper asked, wagging her brows at him.

King threw the car into park on the gravel lot outside the police department.

"Twenty bucks."

"Shake on it."

She undid her seatbelt and stretched her hand toward him. They shook.

"Your loss, Genereux."

"Eat it, old man." She flashed a nervous smile. "Too much? Was that too much? I'm trying to work on my cop talk."

"Doesn't even register." He laughed and pushed open his door. "If you stay in law enforcement long enough, you'll hear much worse."

King cracked his neck from one side to the other and checked his pocket for his PI identification and license. He had a larger, framed version back in New Orleans, hanging on the wall behind his desk. These cards were no larger than a driver's license and meant for moments exactly like this, when he needed to prove who he was to someone who would ask.

Please let them have air-conditioning, he begged.

The sweat was already collecting on the back of his neck. As if that wasn't terrible enough, the mosquitos were awful.

King had thought they were bad in New Orleans. But here, at the bayou's back door, they moved in swarms.

"Let's get inside," King said, swatting his neck.

Piper didn't hear him. She was standing outside the Buick with a huge can of bug spray. The can hissed as she sprayed herself in large, generous strokes from head to toe.

Then she sputtered, trying to wipe it off her lips.

"Give me that," he said, spraying himself as vigorously as she had. The cloud of mosquitos dissipated.

It was a welcome relief, even if it had done nothing for the sweat collecting at his hairline and the base of his neck. And a sheen of bug spray over sweat was a terrible feeling on his skin.

The inside of the police station was too dim and too warm. A haze hung in the air with only thin beams of light escaping around the drawn curtains meant to block out the sun. A single bulb burned and a fan turned in lazy circles overhead.

"Whew, somebody smells like the deet," a voice drawled.

"Yeah they do," agreed another, and laughed like a horse.

"What? Y'all don't wear bug spray?" Piper asked.

"Nah, we're bred to repel them skeeters."

All three of the men laughed from where they sat, reclined behind their desks. The one blessed with a horse's whinny was loudest of all.

"Is your police chief in today?" King asked.

"I'm back 'ere," a man called.

The oldest man present, older even than King, sat in front of a computer at the back of the long room, squinting at the screen. He looked up, his gaze going from King to Piper.

"The interstate is east," he said, already dismissing them. "Just hook you a left back past the diner and then you'll—"

"We aren't lost, sir," King said, extending his hand across the man's desk. "I'm Robert King and this is my assistant, Piper Genereux. We've been hired to serve as a liaison with your department for the duration of the investigation into Nova Perry's death."

The men who'd been laughing and cutting up by the door fell silent.

The shift in mood was palpable.

That's never good, King thought.

The slight lift in Piper's brow told King she'd felt it too.

"Is that so?" The old man gave King a polite shake, but it was a bit firmer than it needed to be. "A *liaison*."

"Yes, sir," King said, sticking steadfast to his manners. He pulled his license and identification from his wallet and slid them across the man's desk.

"A private investigator," the chief read aloud. "Licensed by the great state of Louisiana."

Someone snickered by the door.

The chief looked up.

"Don't mind Mark," he said, seemingly satisfied with what he saw. He slid the cards back toward King. "That boy don't know his ass from his elbow. I only took him on because his momma is best friends with my wife."

Mark wasn't laughing now, but something like speech was trying to escape the young man's throat.

"You got something to say to me, boy?" Herb asked.

"No."

"I can't hear you. Speak up," Herb said.

"No, sir." Mark's face was stone.

Herb motioned toward the front door. "Then why don't the three of y'all head out for the day?"

The young men stood, tugging at their brown uniforms before disappearing through the precinct's front door. It closed with a slam behind them.

"Children, every one of them," Herb lamented. Then to King, "Most PIs come from the field. Where were you before you retired, Mr. King?"

"I went through the Minneapolis Police Academy when I was twenty-one and worked on the force until they made me detective. After a few years working mostly murder cases, I applied to the DEA and was transferred to St. Louis. I stayed with them until I retired."

"Drugs," Herb said, scratching his nose. "You should do something about these meth labs in Louisiana then. I swear, I hear about a new one just about every other day. The last one had a baby in the house. A damn baby, if you'd believe it."

"Are you also a career man?" King asked, trying to ride this wave. If he could build a measure of rapport with the police chief, this would be a lot easier for all of them.

He smoothed his gray mustache with his thumbs. "Yep. I've been here in this very building nearly all my damn life, it feels like. And them *boys* you just saw leave out of here, they're all right. They don't have nearly enough respect for the force, and they view themselves more like Wild West gunslingers than public servants, if you don't mind me saying."

"I don't," King said instinctively. He nodded toward the chair beside him, and Piper pulled it up. She was already unpacking her notes and pen before King took a seat himself.

This conversation had the slow feel of small talk to it. King didn't mind. He could use a talker right about now. Someone to give him a clearer picture of Rita's situation in this town and the state of the investigation.

"If you don't mind *me* saying so, sir, Ms. Golden's given me the impression you don't care for her much."

Herb harrumphed. "Is that right? I can't say I'm surprised. If I'm being honest, most of the people in this town ain't been none too nice to her since she arrived here. Some people —good people like my wife—view Rita with pity."

"Why's that?"

"Oh, because of Johnny." Herb laughed, as if he was about to share a dirty secret. "Johnny Golden was one of us. Grew up right here in Vicksburg. You won't find a beautiful woman in town who ain't been on Johnny's arm or in his bed, excuse me for saying it—" He cut his eyes to Piper and dipped his head respectfully. "But I think you get what I'm trying to say."

"He was a lady's man."

"That he was. And fellas liked him too because he was friendly. Like his daddy before him, he had money, but they weren't stingy with it. He'd help you out if you were in a tight spot, if you know what I'm saying."

"I think I do."

"So imagine our *surprise* when Johnny goes on a vacation" —here he put air quotes around the word—"and comes back with a second wife, Miss Rita."

"I thought they met in college?" King said, trying to remember what Dick had said about it.

"She *was* in college," Herb said. "Johnny was in his thirties."

"Had he divorced the first wife long before that?"

"Not at all." Herb laughed, a lazy rumble in his chest. "I think Tricia wasn't gone but two months before Johnny found himself another Mrs. Golden. The only problem was, unlike Tricia, we didn't *know* Rita. And she wasn't like us. Tricia grew up here. She was Johnny's high school sweetheart. Prettiest girl in town right after my Birdie. But she didn't like Johnny sneaking around like the tomcat he was, so she went home to her momma, fair enough. Then Johnny turned up with this new girl."

"Rita," King said.

Herb nodded. "And Rita, well, she was nothing like Tricia. Rita couldn't spare you two minutes if you caught her outside the post office. I get that city folk are in a hurry, but that's no excuse for bad manners."

"So people thought she was rude, and so they were rude back?" King asked.

"Yes and no. Like I said, there were a few women, like my wife, Birdie, who pitied her. Then there were the others who wanted to *be* her."

"Which is probably how Johnny found himself another woman. Any idea who it could've been?" King asked.

Herb leaned forward over his desk and pitched his voice low, conspiratorially. "That was the funny thing about it. This is a small town, right?"

"Right," King said, though he knew Herb would keep talking whether he answered or not.

"And all the ladies here know *all about* the other ladies' business. It can't be helped. We try to mind our own around here, but we're on top of each other, you see."

Sure you are, he thought. "All right."

"So when Rita comes and tells us that Johnny ran off with someone, we'd have liked to believe her. We all knew how he was. Except we got to doin' a headcount and nobody's missing."

"Maybe he met someone from out of town, like Rita?" King figured if a man can find one wife outside of his small town, no reason to think he couldn't find another. "Did he go on any business trips? Conferences? A family reunion?"

"Nope. I spoke to everybody and nobody had seen him. It was like he vanished into thin air. And then the rumors started. Half the people in town thought Rita had killed him. People were taking bets about whether we'd find him walled up in the house or in the ground. The other half of town thought maybe Johnny found himself a pretty girl in Slaughter."

"Slaughter?"

"It's two towns over. Bigger than ours. We all go over there for furniture, and the big grocery store, you know, if we need to hit up the hardware store or somethin'. If there's a car problem that Jackie can't fix, that sort of stuff. And it just so happens that there's some pretty girls in Slaughter."

Herb frowned at Piper.

"Honey, what are you writing in that notepad of yours? Your pen is practically smoking."

Piper looked up sheepishly then turned to King for help.

"I ask Ms. Genereux to transcribe all of my conversations, should I want to review the details later."

Herb spared her a smile. "I don't talk that fast, honey."

Piper forced her own smile. "Mr. King says it's important to be thorough."

King doubted that Herb saw through the façade.

"Well if one of those boys you seen earlier took half an

interest in any real police work like you, I'd get a lot more done around here plenty faster."

King placed his hand on Herb's desk, hoping to draw the man back into conversation. "Herb, tell me. When Johnny disappeared, did you arrest Rita? Did you formally accuse her of anything?"

"No, we didn't have enough evidence for all that. We got warrants. We turned that house upside down and had the property combed. We even brought in those sniffer dogs, but they didn't find anything. There wasn't a drop of poison or a single bullet in that house. We took down everything but the walls. I don't know if you know this, but the thing about historical houses is you can't tear down a wall unless you get a permit—the state of Louisiana is more worried about the condition of that old manor than whether or not a good man like Johnny is walled up inside it. Not that she's gonna have to worry about keeping up on that place much longer."

King frowned. "What do you mean?"

"Rita Golden owes about twenty thousand in back taxes on that place. If she don't turn things around soon, the state is gonna own that house outright."

11

————————

Konstantine wasn't in bed when Lou stepped out of the closet and back into their shared villa. The last of the moonlight had dissolved in her absence and now only the soft glow of early morning stretched across the room. It amused her how Konstantine made the bed each day, and so neatly at that. Not a crease in the comforter could be seen.

Lou wasn't sure if she'd ever made the bed once in her adult life. As a child she'd done it only to avoid a lecture from her parents—and then from Lucy.

The sound of dripping water caught her ear. A thin cloud of steam billowed through the crack in the bathroom door, escaping into the bedroom.

Lou had already showered, but it took her only a moment to decide it was certainly worth it to get into the shower again. She stripped down, throwing her clothes across the foot of the bed, letting her boots drop where they were.

Once she pushed open the bathroom door, the first thing she saw was the large plane of Konstantine's back through the shower's glass. She took a moment to admire the way the water trailed rivulets between his shoulder blades, down the slope of his skin, the smaller streams twining just above his buttocks.

She opened the shower door and stepped in without a sound.

When she slid her arms around his waist, his body tightened.

"Just me," she said.

"*Amore mio*," he said, and his body relaxed against her.

"Yes." She placed a kiss on the back of his neck. "Unless you and Stefano are closer than you've let on."

He laughed, the rumble of it vibrating against the forearms still firmly clasped around him.

"Lucky for you he loves women even more than I do."

"Is that so?" she asked.

He turned toward her and wiped the water from his face. "He is less choosy. He will bed anyone as long as she is beautiful."

"And you?"

"And for me, there is only you."

She shivered, the goosebumps rising on her arms. Slowly her body relaxed in response to the heat and the water splashing her skin. She reveled in it while Konstantine trailed kisses along her shoulders and neck.

"You don't smell like sulfur," he remarked.

"No, I didn't hunt. I went to Hellman," she said. "And the library. I met a cute cat."

Konstantine arched a brow, then nodded presumably in the direction of Octavia, the British Blue, lurking somewhere out of sight. "She will hear you."

She wanted to feel his body against hers.

In Konstantine's old apartment, it had been difficult to shower together *and* enjoy it. The stall itself had been too small, the pressure too weak, and the diameter of the stream too narrow.

None of those defects had followed them to the villa, and Lou was grateful for it. If only so that she could stand comfortably beside him, her skin sliding against his.

While she washed, she told him all about her visit to Hellman, her encounter with Jesse Elmer, and the irritated nurse who'd chased her from the room.

Lou couldn't blame her.

If people were dying on my watch, I'd be suspicious of strangers too.

"Whatever scandal the nurses are worried about at Hellman, they're recent." She told him of her fruitless search for information in the local library's archives as she ran her hands over his body.

"You and your ancient machines," he said, amused. "Why do you love them so much?"

She didn't answer. How to explain to him why libraries gave her so much comfort after her parents died. Other kids had friends and hobbies. Sports. The closest thing Lou had to a sport had been her martial arts training. When she wasn't in a dojo, she was in a library. The smell. The silence. The click, click, click of those "ancient machines."

It was on those ancient machines that she'd read everything she could about her father and his murder. About his work and the crime family who had shattered her world.

Konstantine's family.

"You want to find out if this Jesse Elmer is a killer?" Konstantine asked, seeming to sense the shift in her mood.

Lou ran her fingers through his hair, fisting it. "I don't know if it matters. He can't really be sleepwalking and killing people."

"If they do an autopsy on the woman who died, we will know if it's murder. In a nursing home they might not. They might not warrant the investigation for an elderly patient with known medical conditions. Hellman specializes in those types of patients."

How do you know?

The question was on the tip of her tongue, but it was silly to ask. Konstantine would have looked into Hellman House as soon as she'd mentioned it. And it secretly pleased her that he was as interested in her *work* as she was.

"Everyone there has a medical condition?" she asked.

"Yes. Some more serious than others, but all of them require long-term care. *But*—" He kissed her. "You mentioned that last night was different."

Lou tried to cast her mind back to their previous conversation despite the pleasure of his body pressed up against hers.

"When you arrived, everyone was upset," he added. Water trailed rivulets over his body.

"Yes, they were worried about a scandal and an investigation. That probably means something went wrong," she said.

"Exactly," he said, running his hand down her back, tracing her shoulder blades.

"In cases like that, they will usually perform an autopsy," he said. "So we wait."

"Can you access it if they do?" she asked. "The autopsy?"

He kissed her shoulder again. "I will keep my eyes open for it, *sì*. But sometimes it takes a while for the autopsy to process. What will you do in the meantime?"

What could she do? Keep her compass tuned to Hellman. Should anything happen, she would be ready.

What else?

"I want to talk to the patients," she said. "But I have a feeling they won't talk to me."

"You? No. Not with the leather jacket and sunglasses. You are too *intimidatoria*."

"I can dress differently."

"No, *amore mio*." He slid his hand under her thigh, hiking her leg up so she could wrap it around his waist, her back pressed against the tiles. "It's not just your clothes. It is how you move. The look in your eyes."

He was hardening against her. She could feel it. She reached for him, pulling him to her.

He knew what she wanted.

"Are you free later today?" she asked, the last shred of her concentration unraveling. How quickly her mind resigned itself to oblivion. "You could play the part of concerned son. And I'll be your cold, indifferent wife."

"*Sì*," he said, his eyes mischievous and cheeks red from the steam. He allowed himself to be guided into her, burying himself to the hilt. Taking responsibility for her weight and the rhythm.

"*Sì*," he said into her ear. "You will be my wife."

FREDDIE'S DINER REMINDED PIPER OF ONE OF THOSE airstream RVs from the movies. She hadn't seen wheels on it when they'd mounted the wooden steps and entered through the narrow single door, but if this thing suddenly started rolling, Piper wouldn't have been surprised.

The counter was white with cherry-red seats and the whole place smelled of fried potatoes and coffee. Piper's stomach turned with anticipation.

"Isn't this nice? A couple of new faces," the waitress said with a bright smile.

Piper noted that one of her upper molars was gold.

"Take a seat wherever you like," she continued, plucking a couple of menus off the stand beside the register.

King selected a booth halfway down the aisle, putting his back toward the end of the restaurant rather than the door.

The waitress put the menus on the table.

"Thank you very much," King said, flashing her one of his smiles.

"Thank you," Piper said. "I'd *love* a coffee."

"Of course, honey. And you?" She turned to King.

"I'd also like a coffee, please."

"Sure thing," she said, leaving them alone with the plastic menus.

Piper read her choices and found nothing unusual. It was the typical diner fare. Eggs, bacon, toast, potatoes. Coffee, juices, milkshakes. There were also sandwiches, a BLT in particular that Piper thought looked tempting beneath the photos of pancakes, waffles, and grits.

She'd decided to go with the waffles and hash browns by the time the waitress came back with their coffees, and they ordered before she could escape.

King got the BLT.

"Well?" he asked her.

"Well what?" Piper was already emptying creamer and sugar into her coffee.

"What do you think of it? Of everything we just heard?"

He nodded in the direction of the police station.

Piper pressed her fingers against her temples with one hand and drank half her coffee in one go. Man, she hoped the caffeine would kick in with a quickness. She never waited until this late in the day to have her coffee, and her brain was in full revolt.

"I *think* you're about to make me sleep in a mansion full of ghosts where a woman probably murdered her husband."

King snorted. "Those are just rumors. And the ghosts are made up."

You don't know what I saw, old man.

"It's interesting that they haven't formally charged Rita with anything. Seriously, not even negligence? Or something that might stick? They're only calling her a person of interest."

"Didn't Beth say they only push to charge you if they think you're going to run off? Where the heck is she going to go? It sounds like she would've left ages ago if she could have."

"What about the affair?" King asked. "And having him declared dead?"

"I'd be curious to know how much money he had before he took off. It's possible he kept his real money somewhere else. Otherwise, why would you walk away from a whole-ass mansion if you had one? It's not like twenty bucks in the joint savings or something like that."

"I don't think we'll be able to *legally* obtain information about Rita's financials," King said. "But I'm trying not to get distracted here. We aren't trying to solve the case of what happened to her husband. We're trying to prove Rita didn't kill the girl."

Piper thought again of what she was *certain* she'd seen.

Of *who* she'd seen.

He'd been transparent. Paper thin. That was true. Maybe people like Mel could see ghosts as solid as people. Or perhaps it had to do with the power of the ghost and not the ability—or lack thereof—of the people who saw them.

If someone had asked Piper the day before if she could see ghosts, she would have said no. She got feelings sometimes. When she was standing in some of the old bars around the Quarter, or walking unlit streets at night, sometimes a sensation like someone breathing on the back of her neck would wash over her. But if she stopped and turned, looked around, she would never see anyone. Or anything.

A shadow might seem ill placed, maybe, falling across a building in a weird way.

But she'd always attributed these odd moments to a bit too much rum and her impressionable mind.

She had never seen a whole *person*, or at least, the shade of a person, standing in full view before.

And it had been the middle of the day no less.

True, Piper was more than a little sleep deprived, thanks to Dani's very insistent sex drive, but she wasn't seeing things. She was sure of it.

That's why she'd filled a whole page with her furious descriptions of the dead husband, Johnny Golden.

Or at least, she *thought* it had been Johnny Golden.

The blood on the side of his face. The scar just above his lip. The large ring on his left finger that wasn't a wedding ring. A class ring, maybe?

The polo shirt he wore had a symbol sewn into its breast pocket. Piper had tried to describe it as well as she could so she could look it up online later. She had every intention of internet-searching the heck out of Johnny Golden the first chance she got.

Piper used her phone to do just that. Her heart sputtered when she saw a ring on his hand. It had been a fraternity ring. "This him?"

She showed King the photo.

"That's the one." He looked up from her notes. He was still on the first page. There was no need for her to freak out yet. The ghost encounter wasn't until page three. Then again, if he actually read what she wrote about Johnny, maybe they would be able to expedite their much-needed conversation.

Piper finished off the coffee, wishing the waitress would come back and just inject some of it straight into her veins.

"The balcony was supposed to be locked for safety reasons. It wasn't. The girl fell and Rita was the only one with a key. Though it seems odd that Rita would unlock a balcony and say, 'Oh, hey, maid. Look at this,' and then shove her off. Lock up and put the key back?"

King was scowling in that way he did when he didn't like the evidence. He pushed her notes aside before even finishing the second page.

"We're missing something," he said finally. "I want to see this balcony and the fourth floor."

Piper snorted. "Oh, we're going to see it all right."

The real question will be whether or not it's got a ghost too.

Piper wasn't sure she had it in her to see two ghosts in one day. The first was proving to be shock enough.

The waitress reappeared.

"The BLT and home fries for you." She placed a plate in front of King. "And waffles, bacon, and hash browns for you, sugar. Here's your syrup."

Piper thanked her and slid her empty coffee cup toward her hopefully. The waitress chuckled.

"Sure thing, honey. I got you."

With anticipation, Piper watched her refill the ceramic cup.

King asked, "You wouldn't happen to be Birdie, would you? Herb's wife?"

She smiled, pulling napkins out of her apron pocket and placing them on the table. "I sure am. How'd you know that?"

"We just spoke to your husband," King said.

"Did you now?" the waitress said. Her face lit up. "Oh, are y'all here on police business?"

"We are," King said, not touching his BLT. "We're helping with Nova Perry's case."

Piper resisted the urge to reach across the table and take a bite of it. Instead she cut up her waffle, drenched it in warm syrup and butter, and shoved a thick bite into her mouth.

It was good. Really good.

It was almost enough to make her forget about ghosts.

Almost.

"It's a real shame, isn't it?" Birdie sighed. "She was such a sweet kid. Quiet. Well mannered."

"What do you think happened?" King asked pointedly. "Do you think that Rita hurt the girl?"

"No," Birdie said with an exaggerated purse of her lips. "No, not at all. Rita might be a bit hard, a little cold, but that don't make somebody a *killer*."

Shows what you know, Piper thought.

Except that Piper didn't *know* that Rita was a killer. She was pretty sure she'd seen Johnny Golden's ghost standing behind his wife, but it wasn't like he'd held a sign that said *This bitch killed me.*

It had been more about the look in his eyes that had made Piper think Rita was guilty.

But I don't know, she reminded herself. *I don't know anything.*

Yet.

She would have to treat this like any other case if she wanted to find out the truth. The only problem was that her boss was clearly against the idea of a ghost victim. That meant Piper was on her own with this one. Unless, of course, she could get Lou and Mel involved somehow.

And maybe Dani too. Piper had a feeling her girlfriend's excellent research skills would be put to good use in helping Piper learn more about Johnny and his marriage to Rita.

"Like I said, it's not her fault. We weren't real good to her back then," Birdie said. "Part of it was because Johnny was one of us and we all owed him or his daddy one thing or another. But the other half of it was we knew better than to get attached to her."

"Because of his affairs," King said, finally taking a bite of his BLT.

"That and because of the ghosts. We thought if Johnny didn't chase her off, the ghosts would."

Piper dabbed her damp forehead with a paper napkin.

Birdie frowned at her. "You might want to slow down on the sugar, sweetie. Diabetes is no picnic. I've got two brothers who struggle with it."

"You're right," Piper agreed, feeling a tremor in her hands. "Could I get a glass of water?"

When she returned, King asked, "What do you think happened to Nova?"

"That depends on who you ask," Birdie said, refilling Piper's emptied coffee cup for a second time. "A few people around town is saying that Nova resembled the daughter. The foreman's long-lost lover."

King frowned. "The lover?"

"You've heard the story, I'm sure. About the fire that killed all them slaves. How the oldest daughter was in love with the foreman who watched over the fields, kept the other slaves in line."

"And that has to do with Nova?" King prompted.

"She's about the right age, build, same color hair. Or so we've heard. Who really knows, it's been so long."

Piper could tell King was struggling to keep his face and voice neutral. "You think the ghost pushed her off the balcony?"

Birdie put a hand on her hip and gave King a good-natured smile, showing her gold tooth. "Now, I didn't say I believed anything. I *said* it depends on who you ask."

"Then what do *you* believe?" he pressed.

"Why do you care what an old woman thinks?" she asked, a wicked gleam in her eye.

King flashed his most charming smile. "Oh come on now. Don't sell yourself short. You've lived in this town your whole life. You know the manor, you know the people. I can't think of a better person to ask."

Piper was glad at least one of them could carry the conversation. It was taking every ounce of her concentration just to keep her waffles in her stomach. All this talk about ghosts—and the very clear understanding that she was going to have to sleep in that place tonight—was making her stomach twist and turn something awful.

Maybe some potatoes will help, she thought.

She closed her eyes and forked some hash browns into her mouth.

When Piper opened her eyes again, she noted the silence. Then the way Birdie's gaze was fixed on something beyond the window. Piper followed that gaze but saw only the trees crowding the other side of the road. They swayed slightly with the breeze.

Piper stopped looking for fear she might see a face—or God help her, something worse—hunched there in the dark.

"Some places are just built for tragedy," Birdie said, her voice as distant as her gaze. "You'd think we'd have enough sense to stay away, but we don't. We can't help ourselves."

"Why is that?" King asked.

"Because despite Rita's quirks, despite the manor's history, its reputation, it's still a good job."

"Is it?" King asked, showing surprise for a second time.

"Oh yes," Birdie said, seemingly present with them again. Whatever had held her attention before was gone. "People might not like Rita, but she pays well and she pays on time. That's not always the case around here, when everyone is likely to treat everybody else like a cousin or an uncle twice removed."

"So she's never run into financial trouble?" King asked. He was pulling his wallet out of his pocket, signaling to Piper that their meal was near its end.

"If she has, she's never come to us with it," Birdie said. "Which is a shame. Maybe we would've had a reason to get to know her better."

Piper's stomach tightened again. Two distinct parts of herself were warring with each other. There was the part of her that wanted to be taken seriously, that wanted to prove she was a sensible professional capable of doing a difficult job. Then there was the other part of her, the one who said she had to be an *idiot* if she was going to sleep under the same roof as a murderer and at least one ghost.

When she looked up, the waitress was smiling down at her. "You want a slice of peach pie, sweetie? On the house?"

"Oh no, thank you. I'm stuffed." Piper forced a smile.

"Can I ask you one more thing, Birdie?" King asked. "I'm curious about this Freddie and Barbara."

He gestured toward the windows and presumably the signs outside.

"Freddie and Barbara were my grandparents. Married almost sixty years and lived in Vicksburg their whole life."

"A husband-and-wife team," King said, giving Piper his best *gotchu* smile. "Imagine that."

12

———

Lou found a pimp in East Texas. The gun he held in his left hand was pressed against the side of another man's head while he swore in Spanish. Lou didn't need to know Spanish to know the man pinned against the wall was begging. For what—his life? More time? Only that part was unclear.

No matter what he'd wished for, he got it when Lou wrenched the pimp's gun away, broke the offending wrist, and pulled the pimp backward through the dark. Downtown Dallas disappeared in a final flash of streaked lights.

Lou dropped him on the shores of her Nova Scotian lake, noting the fresh bruises and swollen knuckles across his right hand as he tried to cradle the wrist she'd just broken.

He smelled like sweat and booze.

The verbal abuse he hurled at her lasted only until she slit his throat with a blade. His eyes went wide and stayed that way as she watched him bleed out on the shore.

The pimp was still gurgling his last as Lou tossed the knife into the lake and washed her hands. Then she dragged his body out into the water and dunked them both beneath its iridescent surface while the moon watched silently, without judgment. She'd seen it all.

One world disappeared.

Another rose up to replace it.

This time Jabbers waited for Lou on the shore, her black tail curled around her haunches as if she were a cat.

Lou hauled the waterlogged body of the pimp onto the shore and dropped him at the feet of the beast like an offering.

In turn, the creature cooed affectionately, driving her large serpentine head into Lou's stomach, knocking her back a step with the force of it.

"Hey," Lou said, stroking the cool muscle under her hand. "How're the kids?"

Jabbers replied with a soft chuffing sound before sliding past Lou to inspect the dead body. The pimp's head lolled to the right as the beast pressed her snout to his cut throat, inhaling deeply.

Lou left her to it, retracing her steps across the lakeside field to the base of the cliff. Once again she had to rely on her phone's flashlight to navigate the pitch-black passageway until the glowing bright waters began to share their light.

Her night vision really must be incredible, Lou thought, not for the first time.

Then she'd seen her dive down to the bottom of Blood Lake and haul creatures out of its depths. So maybe her ability to see in the dark so well was a byproduct of her water adaptations.

Lou stopped, her heart sinking.

Two more eggs were gone.

There were shell fragments on the ground, glinting in the shimmering light thrown by the water that lapped gently at the cave floor.

Lou wished she knew what was going on. Was Jabbers

eating the eggs? Was there something wrong with the babies? Could she sense their development through the stone-like shells, maybe? And she'd made an executive decision about which ones should or shouldn't be born?

She'd heard of crocodiles who ate their young because there wasn't enough food around.

Considering how often Lou dropped a body on the shores of La Loon, she didn't think food scarcity was an issue.

Or perhaps the breed—whatever Jabbers was—had a non-compete clause. And it was the mother's duty to keep and nurture only one offspring from one batch. May the strongest survive.

She ran her hands over the remaining eggs, using her phone light to check for cracks, blemishes. Serpentine bodies moved under her hand as if seeking her warmth, even though it felt as if the shells were too hard for them to detect anything at all.

They *seemed* okay. If they were sick or malformed some-how, they wouldn't be able to respond to her, right?

Jabbers slid into view, her long body quickly filling up the cavern. Lou still held a piece of the eggshell in her hand. She held it forward to Jabbers.

Her thick white tongue licked the inside of the curved shell, pulling it off of Lou's hand easily.

It crunched between her massive teeth as she chewed and swallowed it, licking Lou's hand again for any remnants.

Why? Lou wondered as she regarded those yellow eyes in the dark. *Why are you eating them?*

"You look like you're going to be sick," King said. "Did that diner food get to you? The BLT was pretty salty, but I thought it was good."

"It wasn't the food," Piper said as they turned off the main road, back onto the long drive leading to Margo Manor's door.

King frowned, his concern evident. "Then what is it? What's going on?"

Piper hesitated. She couldn't bring up the ghost. Not if she wanted him to keep treating her like a real investigator.

What will he believe? she wondered.

"I just don't feel comfortable here," she told him. There. It was a vague declaration, but King wasn't the kind of guy to dismiss someone else's feelings.

"Because you think Rita is a murderer."

"Yes," Piper said.

King turned toward the soft orange building coming into view.

"We can get rooms side by side," he said. "If we stay together, then I'll hear you scream."

Piper groaned. "Hear me *scream*? Man. It's too late if you hear me screaming."

And what can you do anyway, even if you come?

Guns don't work on ghosts.

Has this guy never seen a movie?

Body snatchers. Psycho killers who will brick them up in the wall and then claim that they've never seen them.

"You look really pale," he said.

"Maybe it is the diner food," she said weakly.

"Or all that coffee. I've never seen you drink so much of it in one go. Do you need the bathroom?"

"No." She reached up and wiped the sweat off her brow. "Yes."

Instead of parking in the circle driveway beside the front door this time, King hooked a right, following the sign into the back lot that said *Overnight Parking*.

He put the Buick in park and turned off the car. For a minute he just looked at her.

"Look," he said. "If you're worried about sleeping here, you don't have to."

"But then you'll be alone," she told him. Surely King wasn't so dumb to think he couldn't be snuffed out in the night.

"Who is going to hurt me?" he asked with a little laugh. "And I'd rather you be comfortable."

How could she convince him that she didn't want him alone in this house either? Johnny Golden was every bit as big as King, if the size of his ghost was of any relevance. If it was, then if Rita could take down her husband, she could definitely take out King.

More than that, she also didn't want him to think she was a quitter.

"If you're staying, then I'm staying," Piper said. *God help me.*

"Then I think we should get ahold of Lou. She can stay in your room with you. I'd feel better if she did, actually, because you're right. We've got a dead girl and possibly someone who thinks murder is the solution to their problems."

Piper wasn't sure what Lou could do about a ghost. Until she saw otherwise, Piper planned to stick to her conviction that guns were useless against people who were already dead. But what if the person she really needed to worry about was Rita Golden?

Then Lou would be great to have around. Not to mention, Lou had other talents. She'd know if Rita was a killer. And she'd know if Johnny was buried somewhere on the manor's property—or anywhere, for that matter. Then if they had to sneak around and find evidence without getting caught, that was one more thing Lou would excel at.

Rita had to have buried him somewhere, Piper thought. *Unless she fed him to gators. That's what I would do.*

If she had decided to throw his body in the bayou and call it a night, it would be long gone by now.

"If Lou stays with you, will you be all right?" King asked, his eyes still searching Piper's face.

She gave him her best grin and hoped it didn't look nearly as tight as if felt. "That should do it."

King went inside to ask Rita about their rooms, and Piper lingered in the parking lot. She walked to the edge of the lot, as far from the big house as the vines and high grass would allow, as if the building itself was listening to her.

She called Dani first.

It rang twice before Dani picked up. "Hey, baby. How are the boonies?"

"*Well*, it turns out—"

"Hello?" Dani asked. "Piper, can you hear me?"

Piper pulled the phone away from her ears and checked the reception bars. Only one.

"Are you kidding me? Could you be any more horror movie right now?"

With a groan, Piper ended the call and composed a text.

Guess there's no reception here at Murder Mansion. Are you getting my texts at least?

Loud and clear, she wrote back.

"Thank the gods for that," Piper muttered.

Can you do a search for Johnny Golden? Married to Rita, an LSU student. Had a couple of previous wives, one named Tricia something. Family-owned murder mansion. Margo Manor. Went missing fifteen years ago. Anything on Rita Golden too.

Thought a girl died? Dani wrote back.

Her too. Nova Perry. Anything about the Goldens, Perry, the mansion. Hell, anything about Vicksburg while you're at it.

Dani replied with a thumbs up, a kiss emoji, and a wink.

Also, if I disappear or die, please know that I love you.

Piper's phone rang in her hand immediately. She tried to

answer but this time it was Dani's voice that cut in and out, unrecognizable.

Piper ended the call with another resigned sigh.

The text came a second later.

Don't joke about that.

"If only I was joking," she muttered.

Sorry.

Piper's phone buzzed again. It was one last text from Dani.

Lou?

On it.

The wind kicked up, circling the lot. The long grasses twisted and swayed. The branches lifted. If Piper listened too closely, it began to sound like voices.

Goosebumps rose on her arms. Reflexively, she looked up, her eyes inexplicably drawn to a window on the fourth floor.

A shadow passed over the glass.

"You ready?"

Piper pried her eyes away from the window and found King standing beside the Buick, his hand on the open trunk's lid. Piper hadn't even heard him come back.

Had she spaced out?

She looked to the glass again. Nothing. The shadow—if that's what it had been—was gone.

"Piper?" King said, pulling her bag out of the trunk.

"I'm coming." She took her bag from his hands. "Let's check out these rooms."

Before crossing the threshold back into the mansion, Piper sent one last text, this time to Lou.

I could use a hand, if you're free.

13

Lou had just changed into clean clothes for the third time that day when her phone went off. She opened the text message from Piper and frowned. She threw her compass out across the ocean, searching for her friend.

She found her easily.

There was concern, certainly. An underlying anxiety that Lou could feel skittering along her own skin. No panic. No immediate fear and danger.

She reread the text.

I could use a hand, if you're free.

There wasn't any urgency in those words. Piper sure as hell wouldn't have written *if you're free* if her life had been on the line.

So what was Lou worried about?

She checked the time on her phone.

She was supposed to go to Hellman with Konstantine in thirty minutes.

"*Amore mio?*" Konstantine called out. "I brought pasta."

Lou listened to him mounting the stairs, wondering if she should disappear before he saw her.

She waited too long in making her decision. Besides, what if she left and it took longer than expected?

Konstantine appeared in the entryway between the bedroom and the stairs that led down to the main living area, his brow pinched in concern.

"What is it?" he asked.

"I need to take care of something before we go to Hellman."

He checked his watch. "You have time. Will you eat when you get back?"

"Yes, when I get back," she said.

"Do you want red sauce or white sauce?" he asked.

"Red." She brushed a kiss across his lips before stepping into the closet.

When the closet fell away, Lou was in an opulent room.

Or it must have been opulent someday in the not-so-distant past. The four-poster bed had lush curtains hanging from its thick wooden posts but was coated in an inch of dust. The windows were high, generously large, though the panes were obscured by more dust. Sunlight cut into the room at odd angles where it could.

The furniture was covered by sheets. The fireplace empty and ash-coated.

Lou heard voices. She moved to the door and creaked it open ever so slightly to widen her view of the hallway.

King walked just behind a dark-haired woman whose heels kept catching on the carpet. Just behind him trailed Piper.

"You will be in this room on the left, Mr. King, and on the right here we'll—"

Piper screamed bloody murder. The sound was so high-pitched and shrill that Lou felt it ring through her bones from where she stood.

Lou widened the door a little more, ready to leap out and defend her friend from what must be certain danger, only to realize that Piper was looking at *her*.

Piper covered her mouth, her face reddening.

King looked stuck somewhere between concern and amusement. "You all right, Genereux?"

Lou eased away from the door, back into the room.

In a strained voice, Piper said, "Yes, sorry. I saw—I saw a spider. A really big spider."

"Is that right?" King asked, his brow arched.

"We are in an old house, surrounded by many trees," Rita said, her annoyance laid bare. "There's going to be spiders here."

"Yes, you're right. So sorry. Did you say this one was mine?" She placed a hand on the door beside her.

"Yes, there's a private bath in each of your rooms and—"

"Great," Piper said, her smile forced. "If you'll just excuse me for a few minutes. I need to use that bathroom."

She disappeared into the room and shut the door behind her.

Lou kept an eye on King for a moment longer, watching him through the crack.

He gave Rita a good-ol'-boy smile. "It's been a long day for both of us."

"I'm sure," Rita said, without returning his charm. "Unless you'd also like to complain about the spiders, let me take you up to the fourth floor."

Lou bled through the dark before they passed her door for a second time.

Then she was in Piper's room. It was similar in style to the one Lou had just vacated, but someone had made the effort to clean it. Clearly this room had been used more recently. The bed looked freshly made. The curtains around the bed and the drapes on the window were free of dust. The sunlight had no problem pouring through the window on this side of the manor. Outside there was a beautiful English garden, also well kept with uniform hedges and blood bursts of red. At this distance, Lou couldn't tell if the flowers were roses or something else.

Piper grabbed hold of her as soon as she turned away from the polished furniture.

"Christ in *heaven*, Lou-blue. You gave me a heart attack."

Lou couldn't contain her smile. She kept her voice low, matching Piper's whisper. "Why did you scream like that?"

"I thought you were another ghost. And you were *terrifying*. Lurking in the dark like that. You scared the shit out of me." Her hand was covering her heart as if she were trying to keep it in her chest.

Lou tilted her head. "*Another* ghost?"

Piper ran her fingers through her hair. "Listen. This is going to sound crazy but just hear me out."

Lou was beginning to wonder if she should've brought a gun for this. "Okay."

She listened carefully as Piper caught her up on the case, filling her in on the details of the dead girl, the missing husband, and the ghost that Piper saw in the woman's office. Lou accepted all of this for what it was.

Fact. Probably.

Piper had never, in all their years together, ever lied to Lou. Lou didn't think she'd start lying now.

Besides, she was more than a little jealous that Piper had seen a ghost and she hadn't.

At the end of her story, Piper ran a hand down her face. "Just tell me you're going to sleep here in this freaky place with me, because if I'm left alone all night I think I might *die*. God, I was so worried about Dani having panic attacks while I'm away and look at me. Look at me!"

Lou placed a hand on her shoulder and squeezed. "I'll stay with you."

"You sure? You don't need to check with your Italian stallion first? Does he care if you sleep with a lesbian for a few nights?"

Lou smiled. "He doesn't care."

Lou wasn't sure that was exactly true. But it wasn't his call.

The relief on Piper's face was visible. "Okay. Fine. Just be here as soon as it gets dark. It's after dark that scares me. I think I can hold myself together as long as the sun's up."

"You sure?" Lou asked. "That was a very loud scream."

"Shut up."

"How many hours until dark?" Lou rotated her watch, illuminating its face.

Piper checked her phone. "A few, why?"

"I've got an appointment."

Piper's brows rose. "You working a case?"

"I am."

"Tell me about it tonight. Maybe we can help each other," she said hopefully. "It'll give my mind something to think about that isn't ghosts or a super-creepy house."

"Stay out of trouble until I get back," Lou said.

"*Ha.*" Piper forced a tight laugh. There was still a lot of tension in her shoulders, but Lou could tell she was relieved that she had promised to stay. "You're one to talk."

KONSTANTINE WAS BARE-CHESTED, HIS TATTOOS SNAKING UP one arm and trailing over his collarbone, when Lou reentered the villa. He lifted a button-down shirt off the end of the bed and slid it on, tucking its ends into the top of his pants. He took one look at her and grinned. "Don't look at me like that, *amore mio.*"

"Like what?" She closed the closet door behind her.

"I will remind you that visiting hours close soon and you have not yet eaten your dinner."

"Forget the pasta," she said.

"*Amore mio*, I *beg* you."

"I like it when you beg."

He chuckled.

"What if I told you I won't be sleeping here tonight? Would that get you into the bed now?"

His pout was immediate. "Why won't you be here tonight?"

She told him about Piper's situation at the mansion. While she spoke, he finished buttoning his shirt and fastening his belt.

"How many nights?" he asked.

"I don't know. Three? Maybe more. However long it takes them to finish this case."

"And what *exactly* will you be using to protect yourself from a ghost?"

"Don't tell me you believe in ghosts," she said.

"With you, I am forced to believe in many things, *amore mio*." He checked his watch again. "But truly, we must go. You have less than thirty minutes before the hours end."

Lou carried them both to the visitors' parking lot outside of Hellman's main entrance.

Konstantine swore in Italian. "This heat."

Lou had to admit it was nearly unbearable. It felt as if someone had thrown a heavy blanket over her head. The contrast to the icy blast of air-conditioning that awaited them in Hellman's lobby was shocking to her skin.

"Can I help you?" a woman asked at reception.

She sat behind a circular desk. Her name tag read *Hazel*.

"We came for visiting hours," Konstantine said beside her.

The receptionist had been indifferent, borderline suspicious of Lou. But now that she'd seen Konstantine, her tone changed. Her cheeks filled with color, her eyes bright.

"This way, sir. They'll be in the family room here on the first floor."

"Thank you."

"What a lovely accent you have," the receptionist said, glancing over her shoulder to Konstantine again.

It was as if Lou no longer existed. That was fine. In fact, that was what Lou had been hoping for.

"I'm Italian," Konstantine said.

"Oh, how nice. I have a little bit of Italian on my mother's side of the tree."

Lou suppressed a smile.

The receptionist led them down the hallway to the door at the end. "Okie dokie. Here we are. You have a good time visiting your..."

"Nana," Konstantine said.

The woman put a hand over her heart. "Your nana."

Once the door closed behind them, Lou whispered, "Nana?"

"I have heard it is a normal name for an American grandmother," he insisted.

They scanned the room. Most of the residents were sitting at one of the long tables in the center. At first glance, Lou estimated fifty or sixty people were present.

"How many people live here?" she asked him.

"Close to four hundred, but not everyone will be well enough to visit, don't you think?"

Lou had no idea where to begin. Was she simply supposed to wander around the room and ask her compass, *Does this one know anything? What about this one?*

"Use your compass, *amore mio*," Konstantine said.

She followed his lead as he approached the nearest table

and sat himself down beside an old woman with crooked fingers and a humped shoulder.

"Good evening, signora," he said.

She looked up from the puzzle she was trying to make with her shaky hands. "Elliot? Is that you?"

Lou scanned the room, searching, hoping. But her compass didn't pull her toward anyone present. Its aim sought someone out of sight. Someone on one of Hellman's upper floors.

Because these are the ones they're comfortable displaying, Lou thought. If they really thought someone was going to complain, or alert their families, they'd keep them hidden away, wouldn't they? They could just say the person was too sick to visit that day.

Lou allowed her compass to widen, extending its focus beyond the room.

Someone who knows something, Lou thought. *Someone who can let me know what's going on.*

A sharp tug pulled through her navel.

She placed a hand on Konstantine's shoulder, then bent and whispered, "Learn what you can. I'll be back."

He didn't protest. He gave her only the barest of nods as she traced the edge of the room, looking for an exit. She found it in the single-stall bathroom, complete with safety rails.

Lou stepped through the dark and into another room.

A woman sat in her bed, the back inclined to support her frail form. As soon as she saw Lou, she clutched her chest, her mouth opening wide.

"Don't scream," Lou said.

Her impending wail evaporated. Her face pinched in fury. "Don't you tell me what to do, young lady. I'll holler my head off if I want to."

"But then who will tell me what's going on here?" Lou pressed.

The old woman's fury softened. "Going on where?"

Lou didn't doubt her compass. This woman knew something. Maybe she'd seen something or heard something. Lou couldn't say. But it was clear that Lou wasn't asking the right questions.

"A few patients have died here," Lou said patiently. "Do you know why?"

"We're old," the woman said, her cheeks flapping. "We do that."

Lou smiled. "Yes. But I think you know what I mean."

The woman reached across her torso, and Lou thought she was going to press the call button to summon a nurse.

Instead, she grabbed a breathing mask and fit it over her mouth for several heartbeats, taking slow, deep breaths.

That more than anything reminded Lou that Hellman was —above all things—a hospital.

And Lou *hated* hospitals.

"Is it hard to speak?" Lou asked, trying to distract herself.

"Everything is hard at my age," she said. "I'm almost ninety."

Ninety.

Was this what it would have been like, had her parents lived into old age? Instead of losing her parents in the flash-bang of Angelo's gunshots, would she have had to watch them die slowly, watch them waste away like this?

Was it a blessing that she'd been spared?

She wouldn't go that far.

"What's your name?" Lou asked.

"Moira."

"The truth is, Moira, I'm a reporter," Lou said. It was an easy lie to tell, and it wasn't her first time using it. "There have been some mysterious deaths here at Hellman. I came during visiting hours so I could talk to somebody and get the truth. But everyone downstairs in the visitors' room seems to be drugged out of their mind. And I have a feeling that's not a coincidence."

Moira snorted. "I wouldn't know. I haven't been well enough to go down to visiting hours myself."

"How do you see your family?" Lou asked.

"What family?" she hissed. "I've outlived them all."

You and me both, Lou thought.

"Moira, have you heard anything? Seen anything strange?"

"I can't get out of this bed. I don't see much. And I hear even less." She tapped the hearing aid nestled in the curve of her ear.

No. I can't be wrong.

The old woman's gaze grew distant. After another hit off her oxygen mask she said, "Well. There was that one night."

Lou leaned toward her expectantly.

"I thought it was a dream. It was after the night rounds, so the drugs were good and strong at that hour, too. I'm sure that didn't help."

"I don't care if it's strange," Lou said. "Tell me what you saw."

She rested her hand and mask on the fold of her covers. "It's just that I would have sworn I saw someone."

"Someone in your room?"

"Yes, standing right beside my bed. There was this shadow. And it was...it was *looming*."

"Someone was looming over you?"

"That was scary but not even the worst part. The *worst* part was that I just had this feeling, this *terrible* feeling."

The monitor reading her pulse began to rise with the memory.

"What happened next?" Lou asked. Because if her pulse didn't come back down, half the nurses on the floor were going to end up in this room before Lou concluded this interview.

"I pressed the call button and the lights came on. The nurses were shaking me, asking me if I was okay. One of them told me I was just having a bad dream."

"But you don't think it was a dream?" Lou pressed.

"No," the woman admitted. "No, I don't. It was that feeling, you know? That terrible presence. Like having the devil stand beside you."

The woman opened her mouth to say more but a cough tore through her throat. One hacking sound after another until her face was as red as an apple.

The monitor beside the woman began to screech.

Lou rose, frozen. She wasn't sure what she was supposed to do.

"Go," Moira wheezed, before fixing the oxygen over her mouth again.

She waved Lou away.

And now Lou could hear the footsteps rushing down the hallway toward her. She had no choice but to step back into the dark.

14

____

The heat was the worst on the fourth floor. King was sure of that. All the heat that had collected in the mansion throughout the day had risen to the top of the house. What little air-conditioning the manor did have didn't make it up this far.

He was sweating before they even reached the end of the hallway.

"All these closed doors here are bedrooms," Rita said, gesturing to each side of the hall in turn. "We keep them shut off. As you can see, this isn't the most comfortable part of the house. So unless we have a large party—which we haven't in a while—we don't bother to do more than a light cleaning once or twice a month up here. Vacuum, dust, turn on the pipes, that sort of thing."

"Is that why Nova and Aubree were up here the day of the accident?" King asked.

"Yes," Rita said. "They'd been instructed to clean the two easternmost units that day. They had completed the first when Nova said she needed a break and stepped out. Aubree began on the second room without her. She said she was almost done when she heard Nova's scream."

They'd reached the end of the hallway. King bent down and ran his hand over the carpet. No glass.

"Has someone cleaned up here since she fell?"

"Not that I'm aware of," Rita said. "Like I said, we don't prioritize this floor, and Herb and his idiots taped this part of the hallway off for over a week. Though what evidence they could have possibly collected I've no idea."

"If she jumped, I wonder why she screamed," King said. Did she have second thoughts? King stood and his knees popped in protest. "You're sure she screamed?"

"I heard it as well as several of the maids. It's quiet out here. Noise travels."

King looked toward the balcony, tracing the wrought iron with his eyes. "Did she say anything to Aubree before she left the room they were cleaning?"

Rita shrugged. "You'll have to ask Aubree about that. Personally, I think Aubree was covering for the girl."

"Covering for what purpose?" King went to the glass doors, inspecting their hinges and handles.

"I told you. Nova had something going on with Michael, the gardener. Everyone knew about it. And Aubree is the kind of woman who likes to be liked."

King didn't miss the way Rita sneered when she said that, as if it was the absolute worst kind of person to be. Someone who *likes* to be liked.

"If Nova said she needed twenty minutes, Aubree would just give it to her. Like the rest of us, I'm sure she thought that she'd just gone off to see Michael."

"But she hadn't," King said.

"No. Michael had just pulled up right after we found Nova's body," she replied. "He was with his brother, I believe."

King twisted the handle on the balcony door. It was locked.

"Then there was the scream?"

"Yes."

King rattled the handle again. "This is locked."

"I told you it was." Rita looked at him unkindly.

"Do you have the key with you?"

With a sigh, she pulled it out of her pocket and fit it into the ornate keyhole beneath the handle.

"You are *not* to step out onto the balcony without signing a waiver," Rita said. "As I *said*, it is in desperate need of repair."

"It held Nova long enough for her to go over the rail," King said.

"With all due respect, you are much bigger than Nova," Rita said. "That girl weighed a hundred pounds wet."

Rita opened the doors and King looked out. He kept his feet firmly on the hallway carpet, craning his neck only as far as his balance would allow.

He suppressed the urge to jump out onto the balcony with both feet and a yelp of triumph.

King inched his toes over the line and put a bit of pressure on the balcony.

Nothing.

"How long does it usually take the girls to clean this floor?" King asked.

"Several hours. I cut down on the housekeeping staff, so it can take one girl as long as four hours to clean one of the suites and bathroom."

King noticed a crack along the balcony's floor.

"Mr. King," Rita said. "I must ask you to please come back inside now."

The fact remained that this was a terrible place to commit suicide *or* murder.

It simply wasn't high enough to guarantee death. A broken leg or back, sure. But if these ceilings were nine feet high, it couldn't be more than thirty or forty feet to the paving stones below.

A death was *possible*.

But King thought that if someone wanted to kill the girl, they would've chosen other means. Could she have thrown herself off the balcony to make a statement? A dramatic message, perhaps?

There would have been a letter or declaration if that was the case.

Was it a crime of passion? Did someone push Nova on impulse? Hard to do when the door stayed locked.

No, it would have to have been planned to some extent, if only to make sure the door was unlocked. But acknowledging that it must have been premeditated only begged more questions.

Was it possible that Nova was killed somewhere else and moved to the patio below?

Maybe the balcony being unlocked was a mere coincidence.

"Who is the coroner for this parish?" King asked. If the body did show any perimortem signs of trauma, the coroner should have noted them in their report.

"Herb's brother Hank is the coroner," Rita said. "But he's already sent the body up to the Baton Rouge medical examiner's office. He said it was necessary given the situation."

Her skepticism was apparent.

King made a mental note to get the case number from Herb and check in with the medical examiner first thing tomorrow.

Somewhere in the house a clock began to chime. It rang seven times.

"If you're about done here, Mr. King, I'd like to return to my rooms. My dinner isn't going to cook itself."

"Of course. Thanks for letting me take a look." King stepped back from the balcony.

She spun away and was halfway down the hallway before she turned and faced him again.

"One more piece of advice, Mr. King, if I may," she began. And just as she had looked that morning in her office, her features had grown tight again.

She's really afraid of something, he thought.

"I'm listening," he said.

"*Don't* wander around the house at night," she said. "The house is old. It creaks. It moans. You might think you hear someone moving around or people talking, but it'll just be us, I assure you."

He arched a brow. "You want me to stay in my room, no matter what I hear?"

"Yes. I think that would be the safest, for all of us," she said. "And please tell your arachnophobic assistant to do the same."

LOU LAY DOWN BESIDE KONSTANTINE, LIFTING THE COVERS so she could slide in close. She placed one hand on his bare chest. With a finger, she traced the grooves between his muscles, the outlines of his tattoos.

"What is it?" Konstantine asked her.

She looked up, meeting his gaze. "What?"

He smiled, his eyes drooping closed. "You do that only when you are thinking."

"Do what?"

He imitated her tracing his chest.

"I was thinking about the 'looming' shadow the old

woman saw. And I was wondering what connection it had to Jesse Elmer."

"They sleep on the same floor," Konstantine said. "There are six rooms between them."

"How do you know that?"

"I may have done some hacking this evening, while you ate your fettuccine."

"Is that so?" Lou came up onto one elbow and looked down on him.

"*Sì*," he said. He looked up at her through his long lashes. "Moira Bradley is on the same floor as Jesse Elmer."

"Do you think he's sleep-killing?" It was a strange idea. "What's his condition?"

"Brain-dead," he said. "Or at least, that is what someone wrote in his medical record."

"If he's brain-dead then he's not wandering the halls killing people," Lou said.

"It's possible someone lied and he isn't brain-dead." Konstantine shrugged. "Or he could have an accomplice?"

Is it Jesse Elmer? Lou wondered. *Is he killing them?*

She waited but her compass did not stir.

"Maybe it's not Elmer," Lou said.

She hadn't had much time before the nurse arrived. What if there was someone behind the privacy curtain who'd hid when she appeared? Or someone in the bathroom?

"Either Elmer is not brain-dead, he has an accomplice, or someone else was in the room," Konstantine said, gesturing as he spoke. "We can work to eliminate the choices."

"Not tonight," Lou reminded him.

"*Sì*. You will be with Piper."

She loved the way he said *Piper*. It was much closer to the way she pronounced *pepper*. Once she'd made the mistake of telling him it was cute, the way he said it, and now it seemed like his accent was stronger.

"What else did you learn about Hellman?" Because Lou didn't believe for a second that all he learned was where Moira's room was and the status of Jesse Elmer's health.

"There *were* a few scandals recently. The first was a nursing strike for pay. Then there was a death two years ago. The family sued for negligence and the nurse responsible was fired. And then there was an affair."

Lou arched a brow. "Please tell me that they weren't abusing the patients."

"No," Konstantine said. "It was a consensual relationship between the director and one of the staff. But he was forced to resign from his position and now they have a new director."

"How long ago was that?"

"Months."

"No suspicious deaths?"

"Hundreds of patients are housed at Hellman at any given time and there is a death every other week. None of them have been flagged for investigation until last night."

Octavia, their British Blue, leapt onto the bed with a little meow.

Konstantine cooed to her, "*Buonasera, bellissima. Vieni qui. Vieni qui, per favore.*"

The cat was all too comfortable walking across Konstantine's chest and flopping down on top of him, blocking Lou's access.

"What was different about last night?" Lou asked once they'd settled.

"The hospital reported a suicide. The family of the woman, Dorothy Brown, say that is impossible. Given the previous case of negligence, the police have opened an investigation."

"Because they don't think she killed herself? Where is Jesse Elmer's room in relation to Dorothy's?"

"It is also on the same floor," he said.

"But they haven't completed her autopsy yet?" she asked.

"No," he said. "But I will keep an eye for it."

Lou checked her watch. It was just past one in the morning in Florence. She threw back the covers and slipped from the bed.

Octavia began to purr triumphantly.

"Are you leaving?" Konstantine asked with a little pout.

"It's almost sunset in Louisiana. I promised Piper I'd be back before it got dark."

"But I will miss you, *amore mio*. We haven't slept apart since you moved in."

She suppressed a smile. "The day had to come eventually."

He stuck his bottom lip out farther. Lou nodded at the cat. "She'll keep you company."

Once her boots were laced, her leather jacket loose around her shoulders, and mirrored shades in place, Lou leaned across the bed and kissed him.

"Come back as soon as it's dawn," he begged.

"That'll be afternoon for you," she said, and stepped into the closet.

What she didn't tell him was that she too didn't want to sleep apart.

15

Piper was beginning to feel like an interloper. As she scurried from floor to floor, room to room, knowing full well that she wasn't allowed to be snooping around, her paranoia grew. If she was being honest with herself, she wasn't sure if she was more afraid of running into the living or the dead.

She held her phone up for the hundredth time. The reception bars remained absent.

"Come on," she hissed. "Seriously? No reception in this *whole* house?"

Even Piper's texts weren't getting through to Dani now. She'd been able to send a few outside, at the edge of the parking lot, but within the manor's walls, she kept getting error messages and red exclamation marks with each attempt.

"What about guests who need to work, huh?" she asked the Civil War portrait beside her. But the longer she looked at its creepy black eyes, the more she felt certain it was watching her.

At the end of the hallway, she threw one last nervous look over her shoulder before bolting for the stairwell.

And she slammed into someone as soon as she turned the corner.

Rita Golden swore, hellfire in her eyes.

"I'm so sorry!" Piper blurted, straightening.

"There is no running in Margo Manor," Rita said, her irritation creasing her face.

"Yes, of course. I'm very sorry," Piper said.

"Did you see another spider?" Rita asked with an arched brow. Or at least Piper thought the woman was arching her brow.

Someone really needed to tell her not to draw them so thickly.

Piper did *not* want to be that someone.

"I need to make a phone call. I was trying to get a signal," Piper said.

"The reception isn't great here. But we do have Wi-Fi," Rita said. "You can get the passcode information from the brochure carousel by the front entrance. You might find that it doesn't work far beyond the lobby. Your rooms are the most air-conditioned, but they are also the farthest from the office where the router is."

If you call that air conditioning, Piper thought. Of course, she knew better than to sign her death warrant by saying this aloud.

When Rita didn't say anything more, Piper forced a smile and inched around the woman.

"Thank you. I'll go get that passcode now."

"I just left your *boss* on the fourth floor," Rita said. "If you'd like to check in with him."

Why was she saying "boss" like that? Did she think King was lying about Piper being his assistant? She couldn't tell what upset her more. The idea that she didn't look like an investigator, or the possibility that this woman thought Piper

—the most lesbian of all the lesbians—was sleeping with King.

"Ew," Piper said, shaking her head as if to clear the thought away.

Rita frowned harder. If that was possible.

"I'm sure he's fine," Piper said, and ran for the stairs.

"No running!" Rita yelled after her.

"Right, sorry."

It was easier to find the Wi-Fi information than Piper had expected. She managed to get her phone to connect and wrote the info down for her laptop too. But Rita proved—irritatingly—to be right.

Once Piper was in her room, neither her phone nor her laptop could make a good connection. The pinwheel of death just spun and spun rather than actually loading any of the pages.

Piper threw herself back on the bed with a beleaguered moan.

That leaves Dani then. Though how she's going to tell me what I need to know, I've got no idea.

"Hope Lou doesn't mind playing errand girl," Piper said.

"I don't," Lou replied.

Piper came up onto her elbows to find Lou leaning against one of the bed's four posts. Her leather jacket and mirrored shades looked at odds with the ornate wood carving.

"Oh my god. You look like a vampire right now," Piper said. She made a box with her index fingers and thumbs and framed Lou as if for a shot. "You've been sleeping in a tomb for thirty years and now you're lonely and here to offer me immortality. *Action.*"

Lou opened her mouth and grinned. "No fangs."

"Bummer." Piper slid off the bed. "Where's your stuff?"

Lou opened her jacket. "This is it."

Piper noted the silk pajama bottoms and the soft t-shirt. But also the holster holding twin pistols.

"You sleep with your guns? How *you*." She snorted. "Where's your toothbrush, man?"

"Already brushed."

"I haven't, and the bathroom is over there, but you better believe I was waiting for you to show up. I'm not going into any bathrooms in a haunted house without a bodyguard. No one who has seen a *single* ghost movie would be so stupid."

Lou didn't complain. After Piper had gathered up her toiletries, Lou followed her to the bathroom. There she waited against the creepy wallpaper, arms folded, the picture of indifference as Piper ran through her nighttime routine.

They were already back in the bedroom when a soft knock came at Piper's door.

Piper jerked the covers up to her chest and hissed, "You better be a human!"

The door eased open, creaking dramatically. A full second passed before King stuck his head around the door. "Everything all right in here? Hey, Lou."

Lou threw a wave from where she sat at the foot of the bed, her back against the post, her arm resting on a bent knee.

"Geez, I'm glad it's you. If that door had opened on its own I'd be screaming bloody murder right now. Did Rita go home?" Piper rubbed her nose.

"This is home," King said, closing the door behind him.

"What?" Piper sat up straighter. "She *lives* here."

"Afraid so. Guess residential commercial property designations are a little lax here. And she wanted me to tell you not to wander around the mansion at night, no matter what you hear."

"Are you kidding me?" Piper's eyes couldn't have gotten any bigger if she'd tried. "Like if I hear someone being hacked up, I'm supposed to just—what? Lay back and think of England?"

King frowned, obviously confused.

"Sorry, this bed is just giving me serious English mistress vibes. Anyway, what did you find out?"

"That there's reception at the end of the road. I was able to place a couple of calls."

Piper placed a hand over her heart. "You drove away from this house *without* me."

"Just to the end of the driveway," he said. "I was gone fifteen minutes tops."

"It's a long driveway! And we both know it takes about fifteen *seconds* to get murdered," she hissed. She pressed her fingers into her forehead. "Forget it. Who did you call?"

"The medical examiner in Baton Rouge. And then, because she wouldn't speak to me, Dick White, who called her, got the report, and then called me back."

"And?" Lou asked.

King lowered his voice. "And Rita might be arrested for murder sooner than we think."

"Oh shit, why? Did she kill the girl too?" Piper clutched her pillow against her.

"We don't know she killed *anyone*. But we do know that Nova Perry was killed and *then* thrown off the balcony. Her autopsy showed blunt-force trauma to the back of the head as cause of death. And someone might believe that happened when her head hit the patio below *except* that the injuries consistent with falling from that height—her broken wrist, elbow, and hip—all happened *after* she died."

"Someone killed her and threw her off the balcony. Damn. But we think it's Rita, right?" Piper pressed. She was still whispering for fear that Rita might hear her somehow. She didn't want to be that idiot who accused a killer of being a killer while sleeping under the same roof.

"There's no reason for Rita to have done this," King asserted. "We have no motive."

"*Yet*," Piper said, squeezing the pillow tighter. How in the world was she going to make King see that Rita was a killer?

"If Rita didn't murder her, what are the other possibilities?" Lou asked. She was also keeping her voice low.

"I want to rule out the other maid, Aubree Owens, and the rest of the staff," King said. "Aubree and Nova were on the same floor together for several hours. Maybe there was a fight and Aubree hit her in the back of the head with something, realized she'd accidentally killed her, and threw the body off the balcony."

"But Rita has the key to the balcony. There's no way Aubree could've acted impulsively."

King gave her a look. "Again, keys can be stolen."

"Do you know she was killed here at all?" Lou asked. "Maybe she wasn't killed here but was brought to the mansion to make it look like a work accident."

"Seems like a lot of effort. It's more likely that she was killed here, and on the fourth floor, even, and then thrown. Too many people could have seen her body being carried up there otherwise. You forget how hard it is for the rest of us to dispose of a body," King said.

Lou snorted.

"So someone killed her on the fourth floor. Rita or Aubree. Those are our lead suspects," Piper said. "I'm telling you, I think it's Rita."

"I could just go and find the killer," Lou said.

"No," King said, his voice sharp. "If we can't find the evidence to build a proper case that will stand in court, there's no point in investigating at all."

Lou crossed her arms and King's gaze softened.

"All I'm saying is that I won't be able to explain in court

how you used your magic compass and powers to find a killer."

Piper sighed. "Oh, if only."

"Since we are *building a case*, we need to rule out Aubree or anyone else who was in the mansion that day before we can go that route. There's also the possibility that Rita's claim that her rival has it in for her might also be legitimate. There's not much money out here. Maybe the rival paid someone a lot to set this whole thing up, knowing that one more scandal would finally run the pariah out of town."

If Piper didn't know better, she would have said that King felt sorry for Rita. And she guessed she could understand. But it was hard to feel sorry for someone after seeing a ghost in their office with their own murderous glare in their glowy ghost eyes.

Piper shivered.

"How can you possibly be cold?" King said, pulling at his collar. "It's so warm in here."

Lou said nothing, but Piper noticed the way her eyes began to slowly scan the room.

Oh geez, she thinks I'm seeing ghosts again when really I'm just freaking myself out.

"All I ask is that you keep an open mind and remember that we were hired to clear Rita's name, not throw her to the wolves. Innocent until *proven* guilty. We need to make sure we've got Nova's killer. We owe the poor kid that much."

And just like that, King succeeded in making Piper feel bad again.

"Okay," she said. "I'll give Rita a break."

Until I see her carted off in handcuffs.

"That's all I ask. Now. I'm going to head back to my room. Yell if you need me." King patted the mattress. "What happened earlier, by the way, when you screamed like the gates of hell had been opened?"

"I saw Lou. She was lurking."

"Ah," he said, and nodded knowingly. "I thought so."

As soon as the door shut, Piper said, "I told you she was a freaking murderer."

Lou grinned.

"Wait. Whoa. Why are you looking at me like that?" Piper's nerves began to vibrate. "You do believe me about Johnny and Rita, right?"

"I believe you," Lou said. Her smile was no less mischievous. "Let's go find his body."

Piper bit her lip. "But King said I can't cheat."

"It's not cheating if you find human remains. That's evidence, right?"

Piper snapped her fingers. "So it is."

LOU WASN'T COMPLETELY CONVINCED RITA HAD KILLED THE maid or her husband, but she wasn't yet ready to burst that bubble for Piper. As King spoke, outlining what he'd learned from the autopsy, Lou had thrown her compass out, searching, seeking Nova's killer.

And she'd found something, a firm tug on the other end of the line—but it was too far away to be Rita Golden. The only thing that Lou's compass had told her with certainty was that Rita's husband was dead.

Once Piper was ready, Lou pulled them from the canopied bed in Margo Manor out into the night.

Blessedly, the breeze slid across her skin, the back of her neck and her arms, but the heat was still ever present.

"Oh my god," Piper whined. "Why is it so loud? It's louder than Bourbon Street out here. What is all of that?"

"Cicadas, I think," Lou said, though she thought she heard some crickets and frogs mixed in.

And Piper was right. The cacophony was extreme, louder

even than her private lakes, which were in some of the most remote places Lou had ever seen. Was it the warmer clime?

Something splashed off to Lou's right. It was too dark to see what it was. Or even to understand what she was looking at, given the thick canopy of trees.

"If there's water, there's gators," Piper said. "I think we need flashlights. I don't feel comfortable standing out here in the pitch black like this. If a gator grabs me and drags me into the water, you better freaking save me."

"I'd try."

"You'd *try*?" Piper scoffed. "There is no try!"

Lou pulled her phone out of her pocket and shone it into the dark. The outline of trees sprang into view, most of them partially submerged by black waters, their bark wet from the water line.

The light caught and reflected several pairs of eyes, but Lou didn't see an alligator. She was fairly certain what had leapt off the log into the water was a frog or a toad.

There was only three or four feet from where they stood to where the earth dropped away and the water began.

"Are we thinking she threw him into this bog?" Piper asked. "If so, he can't possibly still be down there. Something would have eaten him by now."

Lou focused her concentration on her compass.

"Something's here," she insisted.

"I'm gonna be straight with you, Lou-blue, or as straight as a girl like me can be. I don't think I can watch you walk into that. Just the thought is making me feel panicky. I'm a city girl, you know? I've heard horror stories—*so many* horror stories—about people who go into the bayou and are never seen again. I do *not* want to be one of those people."

"Are you worried about ghosts or alligators?"

"All of it," Piper said with a shake of her head. "All of it."

"I'll come back alone," Lou told her. "During the day."

"Aren't you scared of getting in that water?" Piper asked, her mouth hanging open.

How could Lou explain to her that this *bayou*, even if it was full of snakes, gators, leeches, or whatever Piper's terrified mind could conjure, would never compare to that other world?

To La Loon.

To Blood Lake. How could she explain that she'd already swum in monster-filled waters, often with her arms carrying corpses from its depths up to its black shore.

"I've waded through worse," Lou told her, and turned off her phone's light. "Let's go back."

"That's the *sweetest* thing you've said to me all night," Piper said, and threw herself into Lou's arms. "Get me out of here."

16

––––––

King woke to a beam of sunlight striking his face. He pulled back, trying to escape it. Blinking morning tears from his eyes, he tried to remember where he was. Red-and-gold tapestries. The vaulted ceiling. The four-poster bed. Then it came to him.

He was still at Margo Manor. He sat up, shoving the blankets away. In the bathroom, he splashed cold water on his face, brushed his teeth, shaved, and dressed.

He didn't know if it would help, but on impulse, he pulled back the heavy drapes covering the large window. He wanted to let the room get some light in his absence.

He didn't believe in the ghosts that Piper kept alluding to, but he couldn't ignore the fact that the manor did have a presence, a *gloom* about it, that not even this extra sunlight could fully diminish.

When King poked his head into Piper's room, Piper was snoring, her arms sprawled over her head. She was taking up most of the bed. Lou was sitting against the headboard, her eyes closed.

Those eyes opened the moment King's gaze fell on her.

She arched a brow in question, but he waved her away.

They'd made it through the night just fine. That was all he'd wanted to know.

Rita was in front of Margo Manor, giving stern instructions to a footman. It wasn't the same man King had seen yesterday. This one was at least ten years older, with dark circles under his eyes. If King had to guess, he'd have said the man was hungover. King had spent many years that way himself. He could spot a drunk at a distance.

King waited, pretending to look over the brochures filling the rack, until Rita was done. Only then did he approach her.

"Good morning," King said.

"Morning," she said with zero enthusiasm.

King had the distinct impression that she didn't want to talk.

Then he'd better keep it brief. "Do you know what time Aubree will be in today?"

Rita checked her watch. "Four hours. I've already told her that you need to see her."

King wished she wouldn't have done that. If Aubree was guilty of anything, the advance notice would give her time to get her story straight.

"I suppose you want breakfast," Rita said. It sounded like a challenge. "I'm sorry to say that because we've no events this week, the kitchen isn't stocked. I do serve a light tea with sandwiches and salad around four o'clock for myself and the staff. Otherwise, you'll have to fend for yourself."

"It's fine," King said. "I liked what I had at Freddie's yesterday. Maybe I'll pop back in for something else."

"You'll have to," Rita said. She'd fixed her hair and reapplied her makeup since King had seen her last, but she looked as underslept as the footman swaying on his feet by the door. "There's not much else to choose from unless you want to run to the market and get supplies. But I ask that you not keep food in your room. It attracts rodents. The last thing I need right now is a rodent problem."

Did she sleep at all? King wondered. Or was there something keeping her up at night?

She'd warned him of noises, but if there were any, he'd heard none. King himself had slept hard as soon as his head had hit the pillow. He blamed the heat.

"What about you?" King asked.

"What about me?"

"What do you usually eat?" he asked.

"With what time?" She turned to walk away.

"Wait." King wasn't so foolish as to touch her or force her to stay, but he held his hand out. Fortunately, that was enough.

"What?"

"I heard from the medical examiner," King said. "Dick—Richard"—*So strange to call him that*—"spoke to her."

At least he had her attention now.

"And?" Rita asked.

"And it looks like Nova was killed somewhere else. She was dead before she was thrown off the balcony."

Rita scowled. "That isn't possible. We heard her scream."

King hadn't been sure how she'd take the news. If she would react in anger, or if she would be upset. Instead, she looked tired, so very tired.

"Can anyone else corroborate that they heard the scream?"

"At least half a dozen others said so during the initial interviews. Ask Herb yourself if you don't believe me." Her tone had turned indignant.

"I never said I didn't believe you," King said.

"It doesn't matter. They'll find a way to put this on me."

"Not necessarily," King said, "though I suspect the family might sue you for one reason or another."

"Which I can't afford," she replied simply. "I can't even afford you. But Richard insisted."

Because Dick's a good friend.

"We need to get the timeline straight so we can solidify your alibi," King said. "Were you with anyone leading up to the time of Nova's death? Did anyone see you anywhere? Can we prove without a shadow of doubt that you didn't have the opportunity to do this?"

She thought about it. "*Right* before she fell—or was thrown, as you say—I was with Joanna, the head housekeeper."

"Where were you standing?" King asked.

"Outside, near the garden. She was complaining about the state of the bougainvillea on the south wall, and I promised that I would get ahold of Michael and speak to him about it," she said. "We heard Nova—we heard her scream and then— the patio."

"Did you go anywhere else that day?" King asked.

"I went to the post office that morning. At least half a dozen people saw me in there."

"We need to get a statement from Joanna, confirming your alibi," he said.

"She will be in by two today."

King felt like he needed to give her hope, if only the smallest shred of it. "It helps that there was no DNA evidence on the body from you, so they can't accuse you of hitting her or pushing her."

"Lucky for me," Rita said. Only she didn't sound like she felt lucky at all.

She sounded miserable.

"Perhaps I can ride out to Michael's place and get a statement from him. You said he arrived right after Nova was found?"

"That's right. I'll give you the address," she said. "And if you see him, please tell him to come to work."

"You haven't seen him?"

"He asked for a week off after Nova died. I told you they were—"

"That's right. Sorry for making you repeat yourself."

"If there's nothing else..." She turned to leave.

"Just one more question," King said. "Then I'll let you get back to work."

She didn't humor him with the smallest of smiles. "Go on."

"Do you have any idea who would do this?"

"No, it doesn't make sense. She was just a kid. Lovesick and stupid, but just a kid."

"No one at all? An ex-boyfriend? Someone in her family?" Because King knew the sad truth was that most murdered women were killed by someone they knew. "Anyone?"

"I can't think of a single person in my staff who would have it in them to do such a thing." She looked off in the direction of the garden, at the trees swaying in the breeze. "But..."

King wondered if she wanted to say, *But there are the ghosts*, yet couldn't bring herself to do it.

"It has to be Harrison Glen," she said finally. "I doubt he'd come over here and dirty his hands himself, but he knows plenty of people in town who would do anything for a large enough check."

"Harrison Glen owns the other plantation house, is that right? He's your competitor?"

Rita's gaze fixed on something in the distance. "You know, he came to me after Johnny was gone, tried to buy me out. He lowballed the hell out of me. Guess he thought, here we have a pathetic woman, all on her own. She can't even save her marriage, let alone—"

She broke off, her face turning red.

King waited, giving her the space she needed to finish.

Finally she said, "I turned him down. He's had it out for me ever since. He's no better than everyone else in this damn town. I should just sell this place and get the hell out of here. I don't know what's keeping me here anyway."

A sudden swell of pity for her washed over King. "It will get better, Rita."

"If you say so." She practically rolled her eyes. "Excuse me."

He had no reason to call her back, no pressing questions that he needed her to answer. He had no choice but to let her go.

KING SPOKE TO THE TELLERS AT THE POST OFFICE, confirming that *yes*, they had seen Rita the day Nova died and could vouch for her whereabouts earlier in the day. The window of time in which she could have killed the girl and dragged the body to the fourth floor of the manor was getting smaller and smaller. Now he needed only to speak to Michael, the gardener, and Joanna, the housekeeper. Hopefully, together they could clear Rita of any wrongdoing.

It wouldn't improve her financial situation, nor improve her relationships with the people in town, but it would be something.

While at Freddie's eating brunch, King managed to get directions to Harrison Glen's plantation house, which was called the Basswood Mansion, or, he quickly realized, just Basswood.

He texted Piper and offered to bring her back some food, but she said that Lou had taken her to eat already and if it was all right with him, she would start interviewing the staff using the questions he'd left for her.

With Piper settled and on task, King took his time finishing brunch—another salty but delicious BLT with home fries and a generous glob of ketchup. Once his belly was full, he ordered an extra-large coffee to go, which he drank black as he navigated the narrow, weed-choked streets of Vicksburg in search of the Basswood Mansion.

He saw the great house long before he found the driveway for it. Unlike Margo Manor, which lay hidden behind a shield of secretive trees, Basswood stood in plain view. Proud and ostentatious in its demeanor.

The white exterior shone in the sunlight, its black shutters pristine. The lawn was perfectly maintained, cut at a diagonal pattern that King hadn't seen for decades, not since he was married and living in the suburbs many moons ago. Those gorgeous diagonal cuts that seemed to turn the grass into an inviting chessboard brought back old nostalgic feelings for him.

The quarter-mile driveway leading to the mansion's door had not a single pit or groove in its blacktop surface, and its parking lot lines were freshly painted and straight as arrows.

When King put the Buick in park, a footman was already at his door, opening it.

"Welcome to Basswood Mansion, sir. We've been waiting for you," he said in a clear, enthusiastic voice.

"Thanks," King said, unsure what the appropriate response to such a hearty greeting was.

A man with a bright smile and round belly stood on the large porch, eyeing King's approach with unmasked curiosity.

"Welcome to Basswood, sir," he called out, offering a hand once King was within reach. "My name is Harrison Glen."

"Just the man I was looking for," King replied, amused by the man's accent. He was most certainly a local, the way he drew the words out as if to savor each syllable. Yet there was something theatrical about it, almost as if he were exaggerating it for full effect. "I've been hired on behalf of Rita Golden to help with the investigation regarding Nova Perry's death."

Glen frowned. "Yes, that's a terrible thing that happened there. She was just sixteen, wasn't she?"

"Seventeen," King corrected, but felt like an asshole doing so. No amount of accuracy changed the fact that Nova Perry had been too young to die.

"I see. I don't know how much help I'll be to ya, but if you'd like to come in and have a glass of tea with me, I'd be happy to answer your questions the best I can."

As King was led through the large doors, down the hall, and into Harrison Glen's office, he was reminded how this house was, in every way, an improvement on Margo Mansion. Unlike Margo Mansion, there were no signs of wear and tear. No signs of neglect or decay.

King found himself disliking Harrison for reasons he couldn't explain and feeling protective of a woman who, just twenty-four hours before, he'd been convinced was the most unlikable woman he'd ever met.

How infuriating it must seem to her, he thought as he accepted one of the plush high-back chairs that didn't have so much as a scuff on them. *He makes it look so easy. To keep such a place.*

And if King had been struggling as much as Rita was, this man's success would have certainly chafed.

A woman in a maid costume entered the room with two tall glasses of iced tea on a silver platter. She placed it on the desk with a little dip of her head.

"Thank you so much, Evangeline," his host called out in that robust voice.

"You're welcome, Mr. Glen," she said, and then she was gone.

When King didn't pick up the glass, Harrison said, "Oh,

you won't want to miss this. Evangeline makes the best sweet tea in the whole state of Louisiana."

"Nova Perry was murdered," King said.

He told himself he hadn't blurted this because of the absurdity of the man's behavior, but that he'd only wanted to get a genuine reaction from him.

Harrison's eyes narrowed. "Now who told you that?"

Interesting. *He's suspicious. But of who? Me?*

"The Baton Rouge medical examiner," King said.

"Oh my." Mr. Glen put his tea down on a coaster as if it had soured in his hand. "This is gonna break Bill's and Nancy's hearts. Bill and Nancy are her parents, you see. Have you already spoken to them?"

"No," King said. "I will leave that to Herb."

"Right," Mr. Glen agreed. "They're on good terms with Herb. We all are. It will be better to hear such terrible news from a friend."

King searched Glen's face. He looked disturbed more than anything else. King detected no guilt in his eye movements. No false joy or feigned indifference. If anything, he looked like a man who'd been trying to tell a favorite joke, only to find the audience had not laughed at all.

"May I be forward with you, Mr. Glen?" King said.

"Why yes. Absolutely." Worry creased the man's face. "Of course."

"I came over here to find out if you paid anyone to kill Nova Perry."

Glen's eyes bulged, his chin quivering as his mouth opened and closed, at a loss for words. King was fairly certain that soft wheezing sound was also coming from the portly man, and not some appliance in the adjacent kitchen.

"Why in the world would you think I'd kill Bill and Nancy's *child?*"

And then King saw it. Genuine hurt. Disappointment.

"Who told you I could do such a thing? No, don't tell me. It was Rita, wasn't it?"

"I didn't say you did it. I said, maybe you hired someone else to do it for you. Maybe you hoped the girl's death would ruin Rita's reputation."

"Her reputation!" he bellowed. His face was growing redder by the minute. "*Her* reputation. How in God's name could *I* ruin Rita Golden's reputation? *I'm* the one who told the Perrys not to let their daughter work with a murderer to begin with, because if anyone in this town has killed anybody, it's Rita herself. Not one of us—not **one**, Mr. King—believe for a second that Johnny up and left that estate in that woman's hands. And mark my words, if he saw the state of that place now, he'd be turning in his grave, I tell you."

"You told the Perrys not to let Nova work at the manor?"

"Yes," he said, chin quivering. "But they didn't listen to me. I even told them I'd give the girl a job here, at Basswood, if she wanted. She could've worked in the kitchens with Evangeline and the girls, but they claim Nova *wanted* to work at Margo. Lord knows why."

"What reason would Rita have to kill Nova Perry?"

"Come now." Harrison Glen clucked his tongue. "The only reason she would've hired you and asked you to run interference is because this whole town already knows what she's capable of. Maybe she got off on a *technicality* over Johnny, but a second murder on her property, and a child at that? No offense, Mr. King, as I am sure you are a very talented man, but it's going to take a lot more than one private detective from..."

"New Orleans," King offered.

"From *New Orleans* to save that woman. She's been digging her own grave for fifteen years."

King wanted him to be wrong. It was his arrogance. His self-entitlement. It was also the way his eyes had traveled up

Evangeline's legs when she'd put the tea on his desk. King had a very good idea why the Perrys hadn't wanted to let their daughter work for such a man.

"But *why* would she kill Nova Perry?" King insisted. "As you say, she was just a girl."

Glen clucked his tongue. "Lord knows what goes on in that woman's head. Maybe she looked like the woman Johnny tried to run off with. Maybe she wanted to renew the rumors."

"What rumors?" King asked.

"The rumors about that place being haunted. If Rita survives this investigation, demand for Margo Manor will certainly go up. Tourists round here love a good haunting."

"She killed a girl for sales?" King asked, his tone flat. "And you believe she killed her husband for sales too?"

Glen clucked his tongue for a third time. Each was worse than the last, the sound grating on King's nerves. "Find that man alive and I'll get down on my hands and knees and kiss both of Rita Golden's feet. Until then, I will hold fast to my belief that she's buried him out there somewhere on her acreage, or if she's smart, she threw his body into Gator Hollow and was done with it. Though Herb dragged every body of water he could find when Johnny went missing. That's why I think she buried him."

This man's voice was giving King a headache.

Time to play bad cop.

"Did you have any run-ins with Johnny Golden? As a fellow mansion owner, he was your competitor, wasn't he?"

Glen's eyes narrowed again. "No. I can't say I did. I was friendly with Johnny. Everyone was."

"And if I spoke to the Perrys, would they also say you're on friendly terms?" King asked.

"They owe me a bit of money, that's true," Harrison Glen said cautiously. "But most people in this town do. I'm the one they come to when they're in a tight spot. Especially now that Johnny's gone."

King gave his most wicked smile. "Your office is very nice, Mr. Glen. Basswood looks to be in great condition. Would you say you've prospered since Johnny Golden's absence? Maybe you'd prosper even more if Rita Golden was out of the way."

The emotion left Glen's face. There was no humor nor amicability in those eyes now. They'd blackened. The good ol' boy King had sat down to tea with was gone.

"Pray tell, Mr. King, what do I stand to gain by framing Rita Golden for murder?"

King shrugged. "It just seems to me that putting Rita out of business is better for your own bottom line. With Margo Manor gone, you'd hold the monopoly on mansion weddings in this area, wouldn't you?"

"You said yourself that I'm doing just fine. Better than anyone in this town." Glen gestured at the office around them. "Do I *look* like somebody who needs to put Rita Golden out of business? That woman is running herself into the ground just fine without *any* help from me."

"Maybe—" King began, but Glen wasn't having it.

He spoke right over him. "The *only* thing I want from that woman is her gardener."

This stopped King's mind. He frowned and asked, "Michael Reed?"

"Yes, Michael Reed. That man is the only fool in thirty miles who knows how to keep a bougainvillea alive."

"Did you know that Michael Reed and Nova Perry were seeing each other?" King asked.

Given the earnest shock on the man's face, King didn't think so.

"He's much older than her. Something like fifteen years," Glen remarked.

Yet somehow I think that doesn't bother you as much as you'd like me to believe, King thought. But he could say nothing in this regard. There had also been a gap between him and Lucy.

"Maybe you tried to force Michael to come work for you. Maybe you threatened to hurt his girl if he didn't ditch Rita and come to Basswood."

"Michael was already working for me," the man sputtered. "Why would I kill his *girlfriend* to get him on the payroll if he was *already* on the payroll?"

"He worked for you?"

"Yes. For years," Glen added. "Under the table, of course."

"Of course," King echoed. "Do you have any way to prove this arrangement was consensual and not coercion? Any receipts?"

"Sure, Mr. King. You come on back with a warrant and I'll be happy to give you whatever you want," Glen said coldly. But sweat stood out at the man's temples.

King took this mention of a warrant as his cue to end the conversation.

"If that's the case, then thanks for the tea. I'll show myself out."

King hadn't even made it to the end of the driveway when he saw Herb's police car swing into view. Herb waved, slowing down. King did the same until they were parked facing opposite directions, their windows aligned.

"Mornin', Mr. King. My Birdie says you were in for coffee and a BLT earlier," Herb said with a smile that didn't reach his eyes. "Gary sure knows how to fry bacon, don't he?"

These small-town folk and their niceties, he thought. *It's all just for show.*

"He does," he said, hoping he was camouflaging better with his own smile. "You have business with Mr. Glen?"

"And you," Herb said, nodding. "We just found Michael Reed's body out at his place."

"Michael Reed. The gardener?" King's heart sank.

"That's the one," Herb said with a dip of his head.

"Murder?"

"We don't think so," Herb said. "But we didn't think that for our little Nova neither, did we? Your friend from New Orleans seemed like a nice fellow. He called to see how we were getting on and to pass along the report from the medical examiner. I guess he's friendly with the folks in the Baton Rouge office, is he?"

"Probably. He gets around," King said, as if they should really be discussing Dick at a time like this. "Can I ask about the condition of Michael's body? Any idea of the cause of death?"

"Well." Herb looked out over his steering wheel in the direction of Basswood. "From what I'd seen, he put his Glock in his mouth."

King's heart sank again. "Did he have a history of mental illness? Depression?"

Herb frowned. "No, we don't have anything like that around here."

Around here? King was fairly certain that a man could get depressed anytime, anywhere, for any reason at all. The idea that somehow a Vicksburg man was immune to the experience seemed wholly ignorant.

Slowly, King said, "I can't imagine a happy man would shoot himself in the head."

"It's strange, certainly. And my Birdie says misfortune always travels in threes. That's what we should be worrying about. A third body's gonna turn up somewhere."

"Were you aware that Nova and Michael were seeing each other romantically?" King asked.

Herb clicked his tongue. "Michael wasn't dating no child."

"How old was Mr. Reed?"

"Thirty-two. Nova was barely seventeen," Herb said. "Who told you they were sweet on each other?"

"I always protect my source," King said. "A little bird also told me that Michael was working under the table here at Basswood."

"That ain't no secret. Everybody knows everyone else's business in this town." Herb swatted at a mosquito, which escaped through the open window. "It's why I came. Harry's gonna be mighty put out to lose Michael. He was a hard-workin' guy."

King didn't feel any sympathy for Harrison Glen's loss.

Though Michael Reed's possible suicide did beg some serious questions.

If Harrison Glen *was* trying to put Rita Golden out of business, would he have killed Michael to cover his tracks? Maybe Michael knew of the plan and had confronted him when he suspected Glen was responsible for Nova's death? Or hell, maybe Michael killed her himself, in a crime of passion, or on Glen's orders, and then felt so guilty he took his own life?

Or I'm overthinking this, King thought. *Maybe Michael was just a lovesick man who couldn't handle losing her.*

"It's a shame, what's happening here," Herb said, putting the police car in drive, his gaze turning in the direction of Basswood's great house.

"It really is," King said.

A shame I don't know more.

17

When Lou stepped from the shadows pooling in the corner of Konstantine's office, she already knew he was in a bad mood. It was in the set of his shoulders, the furrowed brow, the way he scowled at the computer open on the desk in front of him.

She went to him, leaning her hip against the edge of the desk. "You look terrible."

There. She saw his expression before he could properly conceal it. This had been a test to see where his true feelings really lay.

"You didn't sleep well, did you?" she asked. "And you blame me for that?"

"No." His scowl softened. "No, *amore mio.*"

He shut the computer and rubbed his eyes.

"Forgive me."

When he leaned back in his chair, she threw one leg over his, straddling him. She slid her arms around his neck, placing a kiss first on one eye, then the other.

"*Così bello,*" he cooed, and wrapped his arms around her waist. "I could fall asleep like this."

Lou let him rest his head against her while she pushed her fingers through his hair.

She thought he was asleep—or nearly—his arms softening around her, when the door to his office opened and Stefano appeared.

Stefano saw them and froze, a cigarette halfway to his mouth.

Lou held his stare unflinchingly. She didn't look away, nor did she remove herself from Konstantine's lap.

"Yes?" she asked.

He was frowning at Konstantine. He pointed at him with the unlit cigarette. "Have you killed him?"

"No," Konstantine muttered. "*Vai via.*"

Stefano gave a little dip of his head. "*Scusami.*"

They were alone again.

"Should I take you home?" she asked. "We can nap together. For a little while."

Given his mood, she shouldn't promise too much.

"Yes, I'm no use like this anyway."

It was easy to pull them from his office to the villa. It was only minutes before they were beneath the sheets, in their large bed, their bodies entwined.

"Will you really stay?" he asked when he saw that she had not changed into pajamas as he had. "Is this a trick?"

"I said I could only stay for a little while."

"Why? What do you have to do today?" he asked.

The pout amused her. Who knew this was the same man who ordered torture on betrayers, led his men through war, and destroyed his rivals. That pout made him seem more like a child than a conqueror. She liked it.

"Gator hunting," she said.

His frown deepened. "What?"

"I think there's a body in a swamp. I'll have to go in to find out. Do you know what a swamp is?"

She tried to explain it to him.

The more she spoke, the more he wrinkled his nose. "It sounds gross."

She lifted one shoulder in a shrug. "I've waded through worse."

"Still."

"What about you?" she asked.

"There is nothing I can do without sleep," he said. "I need sleep to make good decisions."

"Then sleep," she told him, and pulled him close.

With his head against her chest, his doze gave way to slumber. His chest rose and fell with the ease of the exhausted. Lou refrained from playing with his hair, worried it might wake him.

As they lay together, she listened to the sounds of their villa. To the hum of the refrigerator. To the air-conditioning clicking on downstairs. To the washing machine turn.

Then there was the city outside. A gull screeching above the Arno. Smaller birds she didn't know chirping and dancing on the rail of the bedroom balcony. She could even hear the people and cars moving in the streets below, to a certain extent.

Home, she thought. And, for a while, slid into sleep herself.

She woke first and found that night had fallen while she'd slept. Konstantine remained still, his breath easy.

The birds had gone home for the night, replaced by frogs croaking at the canal's edge, their song floating up to her.

Lou checked her watch and saw she had only two hours before dark in Louisiana. If she wanted to search the swamp today, she had to go now.

Slowly, carefully, Lou slid from the bed, trying her best not to wake Konstantine.

She managed it. Pulled on her boots, her leather jacket, her shades.

With her hand on the closet door, she gave him one last look, then stepped through the dark.

A lush scene rose up to greet her.

There were enough shadows beneath the trees to allow Lou direct access to the swamp—much to the residents' dismay.

Her appearance elicited several splashes from those who'd been peacefully enjoying the early evening the moment before they found their homes intruded upon.

As Lou stood beneath the tight canopy of trees, the heat settled along her skin, giving her the distinct impression of having stepped into a sauna fully clothed. From the embankment, she searched the waters, allowing her compass to spin.

A full minute passed before it locked on something.

Of course, it had to be in the center of the black waters, the furthest point from either shore.

Lou took one tentative step off the mossy embankment into the water. She took another step, then another. The water rose from ankle deep to thigh high. A couple more steps and it was sloshing against her waist. Something in the water darted from her path. She felt the brush of...a tail? A body?

It was unpleasant, but she didn't feel the need to escape. It reminded her of something her father had said to her when she'd screamed at a spider as a child.

It's more afraid of you than you are of it.

She had doubted him for the longest time. But now that seemed to be true. For most things.

The mud below the surface pulled at her boots with each step, but she reached the center of the swamp, the water chest high.

Her compass tugged.

Here.

Something was here, at her feet.

Before diving, she glanced around, looking for any trouble. Beside the mossy shore, twenty feet off to her right, she saw the luminous eyes of an alligator.

But the waters remained still. Those eyes showed a certain intelligence, but little interest in her.

Lou took a deep breath and sank. She kept her eyes closed, the water cool against her eyelids, her cheeks, her mouth. She reached out, groping.

Down, her compass said.

Her fingers brushed the mud and she realized that whatever she was looking for was buried in the muck.

With gentle movements, she began to dig, using her fingers to claw at the mud for whatever might be concealed beneath.

Her lungs began to burn and strain from the effort. She'd *just* decided to surface, take a breath and try again, when her nails scraped something.

Her compass pulled, confirming her find.

This is it.

She'd expected to find bone. A skeleton half buried in the mud worn smooth by the passing years.

But what she touched felt like metal, cooled by the water. And its shape was strange. Imperfect. It had edges like a rectangle, but one side was curved, and irregular even in that curvature.

She traced the edge of it, using her fingers to clear away the mud as she went. The suction created by the mud and water worked against her, holding the object down even as Lou labored to free it.

Head pounding from a lack of oxygen, Lou pulled hard, and the object finally came free in her hand. She pushed herself to standing, gasping.

Using one hand, she cleared the water from her face.

In the other she held—

A jaw, she thought.

Yes.

Lou was almost certain that what she held in her hand was a human jaw. Or at least part of one.

Except that only part of the bone itself had survived. And the reason why it hadn't felt like human remains to Lou was because there was a metal plate, affixed to the bone itself.

She stood there breathing, admiring the bone and trying to inhale enough air to chase away the burning in her lungs and pounding in her head.

Anything else? she wondered.

But her compass didn't urge her to dive for a second time.

This was it. Whatever this was—a jaw or some other piece of bone—it was all that was left of Johnny Golden.

Lou carried her find tightly in her grip as she waded back to dry land. At the water's edge, she grasped the moss and hauled herself out.

Dripping, she looked back to see what, if anything, was behind her.

There was nothing but the waters rippling and sloshing from her movements.

Alligator eyes shone in the dark.

It was hard to tell if they were curious as they watched Lou's departure as much as the approaching night.

18

King was certain he'd enjoy this garden more, with its large rose blossoms and fragrant hibiscus, if sweat weren't dripping into his eyes. He patted his forehead for the hundredth time with a damp handkerchief.

"Where is she?" he muttered.

When he'd asked Rita what time Aubree Owens was coming in, Rita had told him to go to the garden. Only Aubree wasn't here. And King had been walking the path between the hedgerows and sweating for almost ten minutes now.

Under the unforgiving summer sun, ten minutes felt like a *very* long time.

He heard her before he saw her.

Someone was crying. Crying in that muted way, as if the crier didn't want to be heard.

King followed the sound, weaving through the flowers and shrubs until the hedgerow broke open on a patio he hadn't seen. He'd been under the impression, given the shape of the hedges, that the garden didn't extend this far.

But here she was.

Aubree Owens.

She was sitting on the ground, her back against a stone bench, her face covered by her hands. Her brown hair fell down around her shoulders in waves.

"Excuse me, ma'am," King said softly. "Are you all right?"

The woman looked up. Her eyes were red-rimmed and her nose red. King suddenly wished he had something to offer her besides his sweat-soaked handkerchief, which was out of the question.

"I'm sorry," she said, her lip quivering. "I didn't realize anyone was here."

Even through the mess of her tears, King could see she was very beautiful.

He suspected it was the Bambi eyes. Large, round, and blue.

"Are you Aubree Owens, by chance?" King asked.

She looked startled. "How did you know?"

"I'm Robert King. Rita Golden hired me to help her sort out this mess." King gestured toward the house. "I'm very sorry about Nova."

Something passed across her face, but it was too quick for King to catch.

"It's terrible," Aubree said. "You know, I was her age when I started working here."

"Were you? How long ago was that?"

She gave him a shy smile. "Are you trying to find out how old I am, Mr. King?"

He shook his head. "No. I'm sorry. I—"

"About fifteen years," she said. "I'll be thirty-three in September."

"Happy early birthday," he said.

Her smile crumpled at the corners. "Thanks."

"I know this is a difficult time for you, given everything

that's happened, but I'd like to ask you a few questions, if that's all right. I think you could really help me to understand what's going on, and more importantly, what I can do to help."

She sniffed. "All right."

She began to get up, and King extended his hand even though he was very aware of the dampness of his palm.

She accepted his aid nonetheless. "Thank you."

Side by side, they took a seat on the stone bench beneath the tree, King doing his best to put a polite distance between them. The shade offered a welcome reprieve from the sun. The back of King's neck, which was beginning to feel red and tender, felt especially relieved.

"Were you on the fourth floor with Nova when she fell?" King asked.

"Yes, I was. I was cleaning the bathroom in the second suite. I didn't even know she was still up there. When she screamed, it really startled me. I thought—"

She broke off.

"It's all right," King said. "Whatever you want to tell me, I'll believe you."

"It's just, I thought it was a ghost," she said, looking embarrassed. "I thought a ghost had screamed because I was alone."

"And why did you think you were alone?" King asked. "Wasn't Nova supposed to be helping you?"

Aubree hesitated. Then she asked, "Are you going to tell Rita anything that I say?"

"I don't have to, no," King said. "Especially not something that you tell me in confidence. But if it has to do with Nova's death, I must warn you that it could come out in court if we get that far."

"I suppose it doesn't really matter. I'll just tell you."

Aubree sighed, trailing her fingers through her hair.

"I thought Nova had left because it wasn't the first time she'd ditched me like that halfway through a cleaning."

"You're saying that Nova often left before you were finished?"

"Yes."

"Didn't that bother you?" King asked.

"It did. At first. But then I thought, oh, she's just a kid. Cleaning is hard work and it's really hot up there. I wanted to give her a break. Then I found out she was leaving not to take a break but to meet up with Michael."

Aubree frowned, her irritation and disapproval evident.

"I tried talking to her about it, but she insisted that she wasn't meeting up with him. I was a fool and believed them. I saw them together. I asked her again and she still denied it."

"Was this the day she died?"

"It was, actually," Aubree said. "I thought she'd bailed on me because she was mad that I kept asking her."

"Then you heard the scream," he said.

"That's right."

"What about before that? Did you see anything? Hear anything unusual?"

She thought about it, gazing out over the rose bushes without really seeing them. Dappled sunlight danced prettily on her cheeks.

"No," she said finally. "Nothing that I wasn't already used to."

King considered how to frame his next question respectfully.

"Are you talking about ghosts?" he asked.

"I don't know if it's ghosts, to tell you the truth," she said after a pause. "But there's something about that house. It gets into your head somehow. It's like it remembers things. Terrible things. And it whispers those terrible things to you while you're inside it."

The hair on King's arms rose.

Aubree laughed, a sound so at odds with the expression she'd worn just the moment before that King was startled by it.

"I sound as crazy as her, don't I?" She shook her head. "I'm sorry. I shouldn't say that. I don't mean Rita any disrespect."

"You think Rita is crazy?"

Aubree bit her lip. "I think that whatever she is, she's gotten worse since Johnny...left."

King noted the pause in her words.

She's being very careful in what she says to me. She's probably worried this will get back to her boss and she'll get into trouble.

What had Aubree *really* wanted to say? That Johnny abandoned Rita? Died? Was murdered?

"What happened after you heard the scream?" King asked.

Aubree laughed again. "I'm not ashamed to admit I ran away. I ran right out of that bathroom into the hallway. I thought the ghost was in the bathroom, you see. But then when I was in the hallway, I saw that the balcony doors were opened, and seeing them open like that, it shocked me. It *really* shocked me. Rita is very strict about keeping those doors locked. She would never leave them open. The balcony isn't safe."

"What did you do when you saw the doors open?"

"I thought the ghost had opened them," she said. "I heard a scream and I thought the ghost had thrown open the doors and so I ran. I ran down all those stairs and right out the side door, and that's when I saw her, there on the pavement."

Aubree looked at the patio beneath their feet, her eyes wide and unseeing.

King gave her a moment alone with her memories.

Finally, she said, "That's when I realized what had

happened. That the scream had been Nova and that she must've opened the doors and jumped."

"And you don't think someone pushed her? That Rita hurt her, maybe?"

"No," Aubree said fiercely. "No, because I saw the keys to the balcony right there, on the ground beside her."

King arched a brow. "You saw the balcony keys beside her body?"

"I did. And I took them. I couldn't tell you why I did it. I keep asking myself why and I don't have a good answer. But I saw them there and my first thought was, 'Oh no. I have to put those back before Rita sees them or Nova will be in so much trouble when she wakes up.'"

Aubree turned to him.

"Only she didn't wake up. And now I know that sounds stupid. She was dead. She wasn't going to get into trouble. I don't know what I was thinking."

"You were afraid of the girl getting in trouble, and you were in shock from your scare," he said. "I think your reaction was perfectly normal. But if I may be honest with you, Aubree, it seems like you're pretty worried about Rita's reactions to things. You're worried she'd get mad at Nova for cutting out early, or get mad at her for taking the keys. Is Rita a harsh boss, would you say?"

Another hesitation. Then she said, "She's particular. She likes what she likes. And she's got a lot of weight on her shoulders."

King took that as a yes.

"Do you know of any reason why anyone would want to hurt Nova?" King asked.

He'd expected her to say no. To adamantly declare that of course not, Nova was just a girl.

But she didn't. Instead her jaw set tight.

"These things happen," Aubree said. Her tone sent a

shiver down his spine, like ice on the back of his neck. That voice was so at odds with her beautiful, soft face it filled King with unease. "I don't know what else to tell you."

I'M LOSING IT. ABSOLUTELY, ONE HUNDRED AND TWENTY *percent going cuckoo*, Piper thought. The only question was why. She couldn't tell if the heat was starting to get to her or if it was the stress of having no internet and no phone. Or maybe it was this creepy wallpaper that was freaking her out. At a distance she'd thought the symbols were something elegant, like a fleur-de-lis, but no. Once she put her eyes right up to it, she realized it was a panther tearing a deer's guts out.

"Gee-*zus*," she murmured.

"It was my husband's family crest," a voice said.

Piper jumped.

She turned to find Rita standing behind her, her face washed and eyebrows freshly redrawn.

"Cool," Piper said with feigned enthusiasm.

"It's macabre," Rita agreed, going to a wall and pressing one long red nail to its surface. "It meant overcoming adversity. A nice, useless sentiment."

Piper wasn't sure how much *adversity* a deer could offer a panther, but she kept her mouth shut. Mostly because she had the distinct impression that Rita didn't like her, and Piper was absolutely sure she'd done nothing to this woman. Secondly, because she believed that Rita had killed her husband. She was just trying to figure out how to prove it.

Maybe that's *why she doesn't like me*, she thought.

Fair enough.

"I've gathered the house staff in the salon for you so that you can conduct your interviews. The detective said it would be easiest if I sent everyone to you."

"Thanks," Piper said, trying to add some warmth to her

tone. She didn't think she was successful. Her smile felt tight and miserable on her face.

"Could you point me in the direction of the salon?"

"First floor, last door on the right," Rita said. "It's just beside the front entrance."

Piper found the salon after only two wrong turns.

Someone'd had the decency to leave the double doors open so that Piper could spot the group of gathered employees easily.

One glance around the room, decorated in deep reds and dark woods, told Piper that most of the staff were older than her. Hopefully, no issues of authority would crop up.

When in doubt, smile, Dani had told her once, and if Piper's girlfriend was anything, she was smart.

So Piper smiled.

"Hi, everyone. My name is Piper Genereux and I'll be conducting a short interview with each of you. If you'd be so kind, when I call your name, if you can step into the hallway here with me, and I'll ask y'all to have a seat."

She pointed at the two armchairs facing one another, their high backs pressed against the staircase behind her.

"I'll also close these doors for a bit of privacy during each interview, if that's all right with you."

"Fine by me," a maid said. She'd been fanning herself with one of the Margo Manor brochures. "It's cooler with the doors closed anyhow."

"Great." Piper looked at the list of names provided by Rita that morning, slid under her door so that, no doubt, she didn't have to speak to Piper. "Let's start with Edy Roux."

A round woman with a considerable backside stood and gave a little wave. "That'd be me."

She exited the salon and took a seat in an armchair, and Piper closed the double doors behind them.

What followed were sixteen interviews with striking overlap. Nearly all of the staff at Margo Manor had a similar account of the events of that day, but also in their opinion of Rita.

Yes, she was particular and demanding. *Yes*, her expectations were high.

But equally true was the fact that she paid better than anywhere else in town. They also seemed to like that Rita kept to herself, minding her own business, unlike the other townsfolk with their penchant for gossip.

"Do you think she killed her husband?" Piper asked each employee in a low tone.

All she got for her trouble was indifferent shrugs.

It seemed like no one really cared if she'd killed Johnny Golden or not. Or at least, that fact seemed to have little to no bearing on their current circumstances.

King had instructed Piper to find out who had officially found the body, and it turned out that an elderly housekeeper, Joanna, had been first. The moment before she'd been talking to Rita, and then they'd heard the scream and Joanna went to see what it was and found Nova, there on the ground. If she had been traumatized seeing a young girl busted open on the pavement, she didn't seem like it.

She seemed bored, more than anything, of Piper's interview tactics.

During the course of their interview, Joanna did admit that she saw the maid, Aubree Owens, bend and pick something up off the ground beside the girl's body, but couldn't say whether or not they were the balcony keys.

"In truth, she's always pocketing things here and there. We've all seen her do it. It's what them doctors call a *compulsion*. I reckon she'll get fired for it sooner or later."

"None of you have reported her thieving to Rita?" Piper asked, scribbling in her notes.

"It's not my business," Joanna said with her brows raised. "And my mother didn't raise no tattletale."

Funny you should be telling me then, Piper thought, and wondered if perhaps it wasn't that Joanna and the others didn't want to tell on Aubree. Rather, they just didn't care enough for Rita to give her the truth. They had more allegiance to the local than to the interloper.

"Do you have any idea who could have done such a thing to the girl?" Piper asked them.

Joanna dipped her head once in solid confirmation. "Course I do. It was the ghost."

Here we go, Piper thought.

Overwhelmingly, nearly every one of the staff members had been convinced it was the ghost. Two—to their credit—had said they weren't sure what happened, but the other fourteen remained certain this was just one more stream of bad luck to visit a great house that had been cursed for hundreds of years.

The theories abounded. Some thought Nova must've looked like the slave's long-lost love and he pushed the girl in order to unite them again in death.

Others thought that maybe it was the daughter of the slave owner, who, seeing Nova's beauty, was jealous enough to push her over the rails.

Still others thought maybe ghosts just got jealous of the living from time to time and wished ill will on them.

If Piper had not seen Johnny Golden standing in Rita's office somberly, she would have been inclined to pass this off as small-town superstition. But the staff had been adamant they'd each had their own unexplainable experience or two, and Piper knew what she'd seen with her own eyes.

Only, she didn't think it had been Johnny who'd pushed the girl off the balcony. All of his attention seemed to have been on Rita. And Piper had no idea how killing one of her maids would have given Johnny any sort of peace or vengeance.

Piper was trying not to think too much about the unexplained encounters the staff described while working at Margo Manor, lest she work herself up into a panic. They explained that in the winter months, when the dark came sooner than most of their shifts ended—that was the worst of it.

Floating lights could be seen moving along the upper floors, even from the windows outside.

Banging in the walls. The sound of a woman crying, but no matter how much the house was searched, no one could find her.

Footsteps running overhead as if someone were above them, only no one was.

Doors slamming loudly and suddenly.

Dark figures looming in the corners of rooms.

One maid even reported that a screech rang through the house. The sound was so terrible and loud she thought her eardrums had split. She claimed her ears rang for three days after that.

Piper asked if there could be any other possible explanation for these experiences, and every single member of the staff insisted *no*.

They knew what they'd seen. Knew what they'd heard.

Knew what they'd felt.

Once all the staff had been interviewed, Piper wandered out to the parking lot and tried, unsuccessfully, to get a message through to Dani. She tried for fifteen minutes before giving up in exasperation, throwing her hands into the air.

The sooner we get the hell out of here, the better, she thought.

A chill suddenly ran up Piper's spine. It was as if someone had placed an ice-cold hand on the back of her neck. She froze, turning slowly toward it. She half expected to find someone behind her, but there was no one.

There *was*, however, a figure in the window, no mere shadow this time. Only it was the second floor, *her* floor. At a glance she could almost convince herself that it was one of the maids, but no.

It couldn't be.

The young woman standing at the window wasn't wearing the black uniform that Piper had spent the better part of the day looking at. She wore a long white dress. The collar was high, hiding the girl's throat, and her hair fell down over her shoulders, framing her face in soft waves.

She couldn't have been more than fifteen. Sixteen.

And she kept fading in and out. More than once, Piper could see right through her to the plant stand on the other side of her, against the wall.

Then, when she was reduced to little more than a dark smudge in the glass, she moved away from the window for the last time, disappearing completely in a momentary flash of light.

Piper threw up her hands and groaned at the sky. "Great. *I'm* not going to sleep *at all* tonight."

19

Lou found King standing in the garden outside Margo Manor. He was looking at the balcony, then at the garden, then at the shed tucked neatly out of sight beneath the sprawling branches of a live oak. If King hadn't been looking at the shed, Lou thought she wouldn't have seen it herself, as it was hidden almost entirely by the thick shadows surrounding it.

She watched as King traced the garden's footpath. She didn't want to step into the light lest she be seen by any of the workers.

If she was seen, King would have to explain who she was and what she was doing lurking on the property. Finally, he reached the edge of the garden closest to her, and she called his name.

He looked up, the frown creasing his face softening. "Hey, Louie."

He came over to her, disappearing beneath the large branches of the tree, removing himself from the line of sight of anyone who might be looking out the mansion's windows.

She showed him the jawbone.

He took it, the frown returning. "What am I looking at here?"

"It's Johnny Golden's jaw," she told him.

His eyes widened. "Where did you find it?"

"In a swamp. Bog. Bayou. Honestly, I'm not sure what the difference is between them. Underwater in the muck," she said, which was as accurate of a description as she could give.

"Nearby?" he asked, turning the jaw over in his hand. He was inspecting the metal plate fixed into the bone as if trying to read something inscribed there.

"I don't know," Lou said. "It's not like I took a car to get there."

"Right." He brought the bone up close to his face and squinted at it. "I'd ask if you were sure it's Johnny's, but I guess you are. I'll ask instead if you know who killed him."

The question alone was enough to send Lou's compass into a spin. She pointed in the direction of the current rolling through her.

King followed her finger, his gaze falling on Margo Manor.

"Rita?" He seemed genuinely hurt by the idea.

"Or someone else in there," she said. "But they're close, yes. Do you want me to get Rita? To be sure, I just need to—"

"No," King said, pinching his eyes shut. "Innocent until proven guilty. If we can't find enough evidence to prove it was her, it would be impossible to take her to court for killing him anyway."

"You could double-check that Johnny had a jaw plate," Lou offered. "Then you can work to see if she had any motives for killing Johnny. Financial. Infidelity."

Absentmindedly he said, "I'll do that. Thank you. I don't suppose you found anything else? Any other *parts?*"

"No," she said. "This was all that's left. Either the rest was eaten or it dissolved in the water over time. Maybe being in the mud preserved it."

"Maybe." He was looking at the house, his discontent evident.

"How are the interviews going?" Lou asked.

"I talked to the maid who was cleaning with Nova the day she died. Piper's talking to the rest of the staff. We'll need to compare notes at the diner for dinner. Then again, this town is too small to be discussing case details anywhere public. Any chance you could take us somewhere else? Far enough away from prying eyes and ears?"

"Sure," she said.

"Then I'll go get Piper and meet you back here," he said.

A few minutes after King departed from the garden, Lou caught sight of two women coming around the side of the house. She could tell just by looking at her that the one on the left with the goth-black hair teased up into a dome on top of her head was Rita Golden.

The woman beside her wore an all-black staff uniform, and if Lou had to guess, she was one of the maids. Her face was puffy from crying.

To Rita's face, the maid smiled halfheartedly, nodded in agreement, and she kept a polite distance from Rita while the woman spoke. But the moment Rita turned away, the maid's smile fell, her expression growing cold. It was far more than annoyance or dislike on the other woman's face.

Whoever she was, she *hated* Rita.

Not everyone thinks you're as innocent as King does, Lou thought.

Maybe it didn't matter.

Who killed Johnny Golden? Lou asked.

Her compass snagged, locking on to its target without hesitation.

So she'd been right. Rita Golden *was* Johnny's killer.

The only question that remained was *why* had she killed him?

Lou wouldn't judge.

As a killer herself, she understood that sometimes a woman had her reasons.

LOU TOOK PIPER AND KING TO HER FAVORITE BURGER place in Chicago, a diner-type establishment that delivered huge burgers piled high with toppings and a knife shoved through the bun to keep it all pinned in place.

"Don't tell my vegetarian girlfriend," Piper said, lifting her enormous burger off her plate, "but sometimes I just want to eat a pound of meat, you know what I'm saying?"

Lou snorted. Piper's mood had lifted noticeably as soon as Lou had carried them away from that mansion in the bayou.

King had made a call as soon as they sat down at the table and was still on the phone after their plates had arrived. Now he popped a fry into his mouth as he continued to listen to whoever was on the other end of the line.

"Yes," he said. "Yes, I understand."

Piper was halfway through devouring her burger when he ended the call.

"According to Herb, it was well known that Johnny broke his jaw in a car crash back in high school. He slammed his face on the steering wheel after running off the road and hitting a tree. The air bag didn't go off."

"What else did he say?" Piper asked, her cheeks bulging.

"Nothing," King said, returning his phone to his pocket. "And I was scared to ask for more when it took me ten minutes just to get the whole story out of him. That man sure loves to talk."

"So it *is* Johnny's? The jaw?" Piper asked, wiping ketchup out of the corner of her mouth. "It was totally Johnny's jaw that Lou dug out of that swamp. You know this means Rita killed him."

"We do *not* know that," King said, picking up his burger. "There are other suspects."

"She killed him," Lou said.

King sat back in his chair. His eyes were pinched closed as if he refused to look at either of them. After a moment, he exhaled slowly.

"Even if you're both right, even if Rita *did* kill her husband, we don't know why," King said. He gestured at Lou. "You know better than anyone that sometimes it's in self-defense, and given how the town treats her, she might have been too scared to go to the police or anyone for help if he was, say, beating her."

Lou conceded the point with a shrug, her leather jacket shifting on her shoulders.

"And I will remind you both *again* for the hundredth time, we are not here to prove that *Rita* killed her *husband*. We are here to find the person who killed Nova Perry."

"All of the staff were convinced the ghost did it. They say they even have evidence," Piper said, before biting her pickle slice in half.

King looked at her, incredulously. "What evidence?"

Lou listened with mild interest as Piper relayed all the incidents of floating lights, strange sounds like crying, banging, and knocking. Doors slamming. Dark figures looming in corners of rooms and at the edge of one's vision.

"None of that is evidence," King said, clearly unimpressed. "It's hearsay. Speculation."

"But what if she—"

"She was killed by a person," King said with growing irritation. "Someone hit that girl in the back of the head hard enough to crack her skull and then threw her poor body off the balcony."

Lou and Piper exchanged a look but neither of them said more. It was clear they were pushing him too far. King was a man of reason. They weren't going to convince him to believe in ghosts. They couldn't even get him to believe that maybe Rita killed her husband for personal gain.

King's face softened. Clearly he felt bad for losing his patience. He ran a hand down his face and took a drink of water.

"Now. Tell me what the staff said. Leave out the ghost stuff."

Piper filled King in on the interviews, and then King filled them in on his visit to Basswood and his run-in with Herb.

Piper shoved the last bite of her burger into her mouth and drank half of her soda in one go.

"That makes three murders that we know of in connection to the manor," Piper said. "Something is off about that place, man. Come on. You have to feel it. It has bad vibes."

"I never said it didn't," he said, and Lou noticed for the first time how dark the circles under his eyes were. Maybe Piper wasn't the only one who couldn't sleep while inside the manor's walls.

"All I'm saying is that we need to remain focused on why we're here. Do either of you understand what will happen if we pull the trigger on this and have Rita arrested for Johnny's death?"

Neither Lou nor Piper answered him.

"They'll arrest Rita. They'll shut down the manor and comb it for evidence. All the workers will be sent home and the premises closed off to outsiders, even us, until it's cleared by the authorities. We will lose all access to our crime scene, our witnesses, not to mention, we'll lose any hope we have at getting justice for Nova Perry."

"Oh," Piper said, her gaze falling to her now empty plate.

"And who's to say that Rita didn't kill the girl too?" he went on. "We could also lose our chance at prosecuting her for Nova's murder because Johnny's case would take precedence. And if there isn't enough to convict her—which right now there isn't—we could lose both cases then and there. I want justice for Nova—don't you?"

"Yes, of course," Piper said, wiping her mouth with a paper napkin. "She was just a kid. She didn't deserve what happened to her."

"Exactly," King said, taking a bite. "I'm glad we're all on the same page."

Lou said nothing. She didn't feel the same pressure they did because she never played by the rules. If she wanted justice, she simply took it into her own hands.

"We do this right," King said. "We build Nova's case properly, and if we find something to pin on Rita as we go along, so be it. But we can't, even for a *second*, forget who we are really serving here."

Piper bounced her straw up and down in her milkshake and said, "All right, boss. Tell us what to do."

Somehow Lou fell asleep. She wanted to blame the constant shifting of time zones, the back and forth. And if she was being absolutely honest with herself, she supposed Konstantine wasn't the only one who struggled to sleep when they were apart.

However long she had been asleep, it ended the moment a horse kick of anxiety hit her in the guts. Her eyes opened. She sat up, finding herself in the unlit room, the four-poster bed reminding her immediately where she was. Piper snored softly beside her, one arm thrown over her face as if to block unwanted light. Though the room was far too dark for that.

A tug shimmered through Lou's abdomen again. Fear.

Someone was very afraid.

She gave Piper one last look.

Sorry, she thought. *I'll be back before you know I'm gone.*

Lou slipped through the dark, putting her feet on the ground beside the large, elegant bed in Margo Manor only to find herself rising from an empty hospital bed in Florida. She was alone in a dim room, the smell of antiseptic and wilting flowers rushing up to greet her again.

She pushed herself away from the bed and crossed the tiled floor cautiously.

At the door, she peered into the hallway, but saw no one.

Her compass urged her forward. She crossed the hall into the opposite room to find a figure standing in the halo of a small lamp, her hunched form illuminated by the light.

She was leaning over a bed with something in her hand.

Lou rushed forward and seized her arm without thinking.

The old woman squealed, drawing back, raising her forearm in self-defense as if she were expecting a strike from Lou.

Lou froze, realizing her error.

The old woman didn't hold a weapon. She held a mirror.

"Sweet Jesus," the woman hissed, placing her gnarled hand over her heart the moment Lou released it. "I thought you were the bad one."

Not a killer, Lou confirmed with her compass. Just a terrified old woman.

Lou recognized her. Moira. Moira Bradley. The woman she'd found before.

"I thought you were going to hurt him," Lou confessed.

"Hurt him! No. I wanted to make sure Philip was still breathing. Now that my sweet Dorothy is gone, he's the only friend I have left in this place."

"I'm sorry I grabbed you," Lou said.

The woman's eyes widened, her cataracts reflecting blue across the milky surface. "If you thought I was going to hurt him, then you must know about the bad one too. I thought I was the only one."

"The bad one?" Lou asked.

"Oh, it's you." Recognition sparked in Moira's face. "Yes, my friend Dorothy liked to wander the building at night, you see. She said she always woke up hungry and that she was old but not an invalid, and if she wanted a peanut butter and jelly sandwich, by God, she was going to have one."

Lou threw a nervous look at the doorway she'd come through, but the hallway remained dark, still. She wasn't sure how much time they had before they'd be interrupted.

"But Dorothy saw something the last time she was up. When she was wandering the halls, she *saw* something."

"What?" Lou asked.

"I don't know. She was too scared to tell me."

"Did you believe her?" Lou asked.

"Of course," Moira said. "Of course I did. And now I'm scared. I'm not too proud to admit I'm scared. Scared for me and scared for Phil. Though who would want to hurt a bunch of old people in their beds, I don't know. What could they possibly gain?"

Lou looked at the unconscious man reclined beside her. Phil didn't appear to be scared of anything.

"He sleeps like the dead," Moira acknowledged. "But I'm like Dorothy. I have a hard time resting at night."

"Do you want to leave?" Lou asked her. "If you aren't safe here, if someone is hurting people, I could take you somewhere else."

Moira laughed, a tight, bitter sound. "Where would I go? All of my children are dead and my grandchildren put me here. They don't want me. And what about Phil? His wife died here and he's dead set on dying here himself. He won't leave. Who will look out for him if I go?"

Lou didn't have any answers to these questions.

Moira began to cry. "I miss her so much. Dorothy. My poor Dorothy."

She ran her twisted fingers under her nose.

"I'll find the person who did this," Lou said. She placed one hand on the woman's back, and Moira folded into her embrace.

Lou held her while she cried, noting how thin the woman felt in her arms. All skin and bones.

"I'll take care of it," Lou said into her wispy hair. "I promise."

20

—————

A bang shook the bed and Piper woke with a start. She bolted upright, looking around the dark, warm room for the source of the sound. There was nothing. Only the shadows shifting menacingly across the field of her vision.

"Lou?" Piper reached out and touched the coverlet beside her. The place where Lou was supposed to be was empty. She wasn't there. The covers were rumpled and thrown back.

"Lou!" she hissed again.

Another bang echoed through the walls. Piper's breath hitched. Beneath her door a light passed, slow and ominous.

It was followed by a soft whisper.

Piper's first instinct was to hide herself beneath the covers. To throw them over her head and reject anything that might be happening.

Only, the thought of removing the blankets to find a nightmarish face pressed into hers was so terrifying that she couldn't bring herself to do it.

She rose from the bed, slowly. She pressed one bare foot to the floor, then the other.

She crept to the door with her heart pounding. One hand braced against the jamb, she pried it open slowly, peering out into the hallway.

It was Rita, in her pajamas, holding what looked like a gas lamp in her free hand. She was holding the light up to the portrait fixed to the wall.

She was *talking* to it. The portrait.

"Stop it!" she hissed through gritted teeth. "I'm begging you."

Piper's pulse was so thunderous in her ears she was certain that Rita could hear it. But Rita turned away, rushing down the hallway toward the stairs as if in pursuit of someone.

Piper looked from her empty bed to the disappearing light telling her where Rita had gone.

"Am I really going to follow this lady?" she asked herself. "Am I going to leave the safety of my bedroom without my badass bodyguard and follow a crazy, husband-killing woman through this super-creepy house at night?"

But she was already slipping on her house shoes and stepping out into the hallway.

Part of her felt she should call Lou to her. Maybe she'd gone out hunting or something had come up. But *surely*, if Piper called to her, Lou would come back. The only problem was Piper wasn't sure she wanted Lou to materialize right now as she followed Rita into the dark. She wasn't sure, given how keyed-up her nerves were, if she could stifle a scream in time.

Perhaps more discretion was required if she wanted to see what Rita was up to.

If I get mauled by a ghost or even just bonked on the head by Rita and thrown into the swamp like Johnny, I'm gonna be so mad at you, Lou-blue, she thought as she rushed down toward the fleeting light.

It was a tricky dance. Staying far enough away from Rita

to remain hidden by the pooling darkness but also close enough to keep the light in her field of vision.

Piper pressed herself against the old wallpaper, her hand trailing along it as she tiptoed over the carpet, first speeding up, then slowing down to keep Rita at an equal distance. Piper was struck by how small Rita looked in the halo of light.

Piper inched up a staircase after her, her breath loud and her heart like a war drum.

She lost sight of her for a moment when she turned a corner but found her again on the fourth floor, talking to the walls. Or at least it *looked* like she was talking to the walls.

"Please," she begged, her face twisted. Piper couldn't tell if the expression was horror, misery, fury, or some mixture of the three. "I'm begging you, *please.*"

The house began to rumble.

Piper could feel the vibration in her feet.

What the hell is that?

It was like something was rattling the floorboards from beneath. Then a screech rang out, sharp like nails down a chalkboard. It made Piper's skull and teeth ache. She pressed her hands against her ears to muffle the sound.

Rita slammed her fist against the wall several times in quick succession. "Stop, damn you! Stop it!"

A shadow began to break away from the corner opposite Piper. It grew larger, more distinct, moving toward Piper. A scream built in her throat and she felt faint from the mounting panic consuming her.

The shadow reached for her and Piper screamed.

Not just a small yelp of surprise.

Piper Genereux *screamed* bloody murder.

At the top of her lungs, throat burning, chest compressing, she screamed as if the shadow were going to swallow her soul.

Only it didn't.

It slammed its hand over Piper's mouth and yanked her through the dark.

Then Piper was in her room again, with a very confused Lou looking at her, both of her eyebrows raised.

"Oh my *god.*" All the breath left Piper in one relieved whoosh. She felt faint on her feet. "You have the *worst* timing."

Before Piper could even ask Lou where she'd gone or why did she *insist* on appearing in a haunted house like that—did she really have no idea how terrifying it was?—footsteps pounded on the stairs, hurrying in their direction.

"Get in the bed. Pretend to sleep," Lou told her. Then she was gone.

"Wait!" But there was no time.

Piper saw the light. Rita's light. And realized how soon the woman would be at her door.

She threw herself into the bed and pulled the covers up to her chin.

The door to her room opened and Rita's light flooded in. Piper waited, still beneath the too-hot covers, heart hammering.

The light grew stronger as Rita approached her bedside and stood over her.

Piper turned toward her, pretending to wake. "What? What is it? Is it time to get up?"

At least the proximity of the light made her squinting authentic. She could really only get one eye open.

Rita said nothing. She only waited.

"What is it?" Piper said again, hoping she seemed annoyed and not guilty. "Is something wrong?"

Only Rita never answered that question. She simply left. The light that had been so bright at her bedside a moment before dimmed, floated away, until there was only darkness in her bedroom once more. She waited for several full breaths before sitting up.

"Whew, that was close." Piper released a tense breath. "Lou?"

Lou stepped forward from the darkness in a very human way. That's when Piper realized she hadn't disappeared, she'd only hidden. Maybe she'd wanted to stay close in case Rita tried to do anything.

"Do you think she knows it was me who followed her?" Piper asked.

"Who?" Lou asked.

"Rita." Piper gestured at the bedroom door and the light that was disappearing.

"That wasn't Rita," Lou said plainly.

"*Excuse* me?" Piper said.

"That wasn't Rita," she said again.

Why the hell is she smiling like that?

"What do you mean it wasn't Rita? I saw her."

"Did you?"

The question stopped Piper's mind. It was true she hadn't seen the person's face. Only that bright, intense light, which she'd assumed was Rita's lamp.

"I'm going to need you to explain this to me," Piper said calmly.

Lou leaned her weight against one of the bedposts. "It wasn't a person. It was only a light."

Piper took a moment to consider this and whether or not Lou might lie to her for a laugh. But Lou looked serious. In fact, she looked elated.

"I've always wanted to see a ghost," she said.

"No." Piper threw the covers back. "Fuck this."

She was out of the room, down the hall, and shoving open King's door a second later. She turned on the light.

King was already up, trying to get his pants on. He was struggling to hide his tighty-whiteys from them.

Piper couldn't care less.

"What is it?" King asked. "Who screamed?"

"I did," Piper said.

"Why? What's happened?"

"I screamed because Lou keeps popping up in the dark and scaring the living shit out of me. But you know what? *You know what?* That's not even my real problem here. The problem is that this mansion is haunted, I keep seeing ghosts, and I don't give a shit if you're too rational to believe me, but I'm not sleeping in this freak show for one more single night unless you get Mel out here to talk to these—these—*people* and make sure that we are all on the same page that I am *not* to be possessed or eaten or forced into the light or—"

"I didn't realize ghosts ate people," Lou interjected.

Piper threw up her hands. "Whatever! *Whatever* they do, I want to make sure they know they are *not* to do it to *me* or I'm going back to New Orleans and you're on your own with this one, man."

King finally had his pants on and the top button secured. He paused in pulling a polo shirt over his head.

"I feel like I've missed some things," he said.

"You think!"

Piper recounted the night from the moment she woke to the banging on the wall and followed Rita's light to the fourth floor. The way she talked to the walls, the portraits. How upset she seemed. She ended, of course, with the moment a ghost stood over Piper's bed.

Every time she thought about it, how there had been no face because of the glowing light, Piper shivered.

Maybe the light was *its face.*

Goosebumps rose on Piper's arms.

King was incredulous. "You're sure she didn't just come

check on you? I mean, that's what I was doing. I'd heard you scream and so I was trying to get dressed so—"

"Right!" Piper said, with a triumphant point of her finger. "See? How could Rita get all the way down to my room from the fourth floor when you couldn't even get your pants on and come next door?"

Now that Piper thought about it, she wasn't sure why she'd first believed it had been Rita at all. The woman could've never reached Piper's bedside in time.

King didn't look too pleased to be reminded that he'd been in his underwear when they'd arrived.

"I saw it," Lou said. "It was a floating light."

King pursed his lips. Piper tried not to take it personally that he was more likely to believe Lou than herself.

"I'll call Mel tomorrow and see if she'll come out," King said finally.

"I can go get her," Lou offered.

King nodded. "That would help, thanks. The only question remaining is whether to bring Mel at night and keep her hidden from Rita or bring her during the day and say she's a consult. I guess that depends on Mel's schedule."

"You can work out the details," Piper said, her adrenaline falling. "I just wanted to be perfectly clear what we're dealing with here because I'm not going to spend the rest of eternity living in a possessed doll or something worse."

"Can you make it through the night?" King asked. At least he had the decency to show her genuine concern now. "Lou can take you back to New Orleans now."

Piper was tempted. It certainly would not be the first time she'd longed for her own bed. But the truth was, she was also scared for King. He was way too rational for a situation like this. Rational people would only believe what was right in front of them. They were no match for freaky stuff.

He was *definitely* going to end up as a possessed mannequin or something if she didn't keep an eye on him.

But most importantly, the first rule of surviving something scary was to stick together.

Stick together, no matter what.

And that's exactly what Piper planned to do. No man—no matter how dumb about ghosts he might be—was to be left behind.

"I'll stay," she said at last. "But only if Lou promises *not* to leave me alone in the dead of night again. What the hell were you doing anyway?"

"Someone needed me," she said simply.

"Yeah, well *I* need you. So stay with me until you see the sun come over the horizon. Or feel it in your bones. However it works for you."

Lou snorted. This annoyed Piper. She was having way too much fun with this. Between her and King, Piper was starting to feel like the only sensible person in this house.

"Try to get some sleep, you two," King said.

Piper waved her hand, returning to her room with only one suspicious glance up and down the hall before closing the door behind both her and Lou.

As soon as the door was shut, Piper flipped the switch on the wall, flooding the bedroom with light.

"*This*," she declared, "will be staying on for the rest of my stay here. Thank you very much."

21

———

King tried to call Mel from the parking lot first thing the next morning, knowing she would be the most available in the hours between waking and before Melandra's Fortunes and Fixes opened. When he couldn't get enough reception to connect the call, he climbed into his Buick and drove to the end of the manor's driveway, parking it on the side of the road in the shade of a large tree.

No sooner than he had thrown the Buick into park did he receive three text messages one after the other. One from Mel asking if they'd arrived all right and inquiring as to how the small-town folk were treating them, and two from Beth. One confirming her return to New Orleans and a second commenting on his radio silence.

He responded to Beth first, explaining where he was and why he hadn't been able to text.

Mel he called, and she answered on the third ring.

"One second, Mr. King," she said. "Just let me finish drying my hands."

"No hurry," he told her. Something in his chest loosened at the sound of her voice.

"All right," she said. "Thank you for calling me back. I was worried when I couldn't even get a response from Piper. I know how attached that girl is to her phone."

"It's the reception out here," King told her. "Or lack thereof."

"I figured," she said. "How goes the case?"

He hesitated.

"Whatever it is, spit it out," she said.

"Are you free tonight or tomorrow evening?" he asked.

"I can be, if it's important. Why? What's that I hear in your voice? Something got you worried?"

He couldn't tell her because he wasn't even sure himself. Doubt? Maybe even a little fear or concern that perhaps by agreeing to help out a friend, he might have gotten himself in over his head.

"How do you feel about ghosts?" King asked at last.

"I haven't spoken with them myself, but Grandmamie did," Melandra said simply, as if this were a perfectly normal question. "And she wasn't a lying woman, so don't ask me if this is a joke."

King knew better.

"Piper says the manor is haunted, and she thinks Rita—Rita being the woman who Dick asked me to help—killed her husband. His ghost is following her around. I think. And something about floating lights."

After a long pause she said, "If that's true, Detective Dick White will be disappointed to learn his friend is a murderer."

It took King a moment to realize that the doubt in Mel's voice had nothing to do with the ghosts. It was focused solely on the question of Rita's innocence.

"You think Piper really saw the ghosts?" King asked.

"Our girl isn't a liar as long as we've known her," Mel said firmly. "She might exaggerate a story to get a laugh out of you, and she might omit something in order to protect someone she loves, but lie? No. If she's seen a ghost and has been bold enough to admit it to you—*you*, Mr. King, then I suspect she's seen a lot more than a ghost."

King rubbed his forehead with his fist. "She wants you to come out here and talk to them."

"To who?" Mel asked.

"To the ghosts. She thinks you can tell them not to possess her or something."

Mel chuckled. "I don't know what I can do. Like I said, it's beyond my natural talent."

"I think she's just looking for reassurance that it's safe enough to stay here and close out the case. I could use her help, but I guess she doesn't need to stay. I don't want her to if she feels uncomfortable. Maybe I should just send her home."

"She won't leave without you. If she really thinks the place is dangerous, she's probably staying to look after you."

"Me?" King scoffed. "I can look after myself."

"We can't change our natures," Mel replied.

King wondered if she was talking about Piper—or himself. There was also a part of King that wondered if Piper's nature came from having the mother she had. She'd grown up caring for and protecting her druggie mom. Maybe instincts and conditioning like that never really went away, and those around her would just have to accept Piper's protective nature.

"I think it's best if I come to you," Mel said at last. "Give me a couple of hours to get some things together and then I'll be ready."

"When should we send Lou to get you?"

"Is there a time when the ghosts are most active?" Mel asked.

King regarded the great house in the rearview mirror with a certain growing disquiet. "After dark, apparently."

"Then come get me tonight, after dark. I'll be ready."

22

Lou found Konstantine asleep at his desk. His laptop was open, the screensaver flashing. His cheek rested on a stack of papers, his mouth slightly ajar. Lou watched him, admiring the curve of his jaw, the fullness of his lips. She wanted to bite him on the back of his exposed neck and see him wake in surprise.

Lou went to him, placed her arms around his waist, and pulled him through the shadows. His eyes didn't open even after she put him on their bed.

She bent and began unlacing his leather shoes, pulling them off. Then her hands were on the button of his pants. Desire rippled through her, but she pushed it aside. His eyes had fluttered briefly but had stilled again. His breath evened out.

If she had to guess, she would have thought he had not slept at all since she left. At least she had managed a few hours in the large bed beside Piper, whose grip on her arm hadn't weakened all night long. It was as if she hadn't trusted Lou not to slip away again.

With Konstantine in his silk pajama pants, it was her turn

to strip down. She would be lying if she denied how good it felt to be in her own bed. Beside him, the tension in her shoulders and neck eased. Her eyelids grew heavy.

They slept.

She woke to a voice. Someone was calling in jubilant Italian from the street outside. A burst of laughter floated up to her as her mind sharpened with wakefulness. A moped rumbled by.

Their bedroom had collected darkness while they slept, filling up until no color remained.

"*Amore mio*," Konstantine said, his arms going around her. "Don't go."

She chuckled low in her throat. "I'm hungry."

He peeked one eye open and then the other. "Me too. Should we go to a café?"

Twenty minutes later they were sitting on a terrace overlooking Ponte Vecchio. Konstantine's face still wore the signs of sleep. His eyes were puffy. His jaw unshaven. He was impeccably dressed as always. He was too much of an Italian to go out into public as Americans did, sometimes in their pajamas and house slippers, an idea that seemed to genuinely horrify him.

Lou was halfway through her steak and side of olive oil–drenched cavatappi when she asked, "Did you find any reports of elder abuse at Hellman?"

"No," he said, rubbing his eyes. He finished his water and motioned for the waiter. When she appeared, he said, "*Un espresso, per favore.*"

"Did you make a list of who is working there yet?"

"You suspect an employee?" he asked. "No longer Jesse Elmer?"

Until Lou had her hands wrapped around the culprit's throat, she would suspect everyone. "When you make the list, focus on the night shift. One of the residents said that

Dorothy saw something when she was walking around at night."

He frowned. "Dorothy?"

"The woman who was killed. Dorothy Brown." Lou had read her obituary in the paper.

"Okay," he said, and thanked the waiter when the espresso was placed in front of him. "*Grazie mille.*"

"We could also check the work history of everyone on the night shift and see if there was elder abuse at their previous work locations. It's possible that someone was caught and fired and now they're being more careful. And maybe someone has domestic charges too. If they're hurting someone at home, maybe they've started hurting people at work too."

"*Sì, sì,*" he said, throwing back the espresso the way Lou had seen American frat boys take shots. "I know how to do this, *amore mio.*"

"I saw a ghost," she said.

Truly, it was a test to see if he'd been listening to her requests for information on Hellman House or if he'd only been humoring her until the caffeine kicked in.

He choked. "*Cosa?*"

"I saw a ghost last night. A glowing ball of light."

She told him of the encounter, amused at the way his brows rose as she spoke, climbing higher and higher with each detail. They didn't come down.

"Wow," he said once she'd finished. "*È molto interessante.* This world really is full of magic."

He placed a hand on her thigh beneath the table.

"But I already knew that."

"You must be feeling better," she said, acknowledging the flirtation.

"*Sì. Il caffè è vita.*"

She snorted. On its own current, Lou's mind floated toward Rita, wondering again what her reasons might have been for ending her husband's life.

Piper might be convinced that she killed him so he wouldn't leave her, but Lou had another feeling.

"Will you do something else for me?" she asked him finally.

"I would do anything for you. Especially after the way you purred into my ear when we were in the shower."

She placed her hand over the one holding her thigh.

"Rita Golden. It's the case King and Piper are working. I know she killed her husband, Johnny Golden. This happened about fifteen years ago, in Vicksburg, Louisiana. Can you find out if she had a *reason* to kill him?"

"*Sì, amore mio.* I'll find what you want. It will be easier now that I've had some sleep."

"And some coffee," she said with a smile.

"*Esattamente. E un po' di caffè.*"

MELANDRA LOOKED AS IF SHE WERE WAITING FOR THE BUS. When Lou stepped from her unlit bathroom into the woman's apartment, she found her sitting on her sofa, her purse clutched in her lap. The ruckus of Bourbon Street raged outside her window. Music pouring from the liquor-drenched bars filled the air and obnoxious laughter cut through all of it with impunity. Lights flashed like a disco ball, dancing across Mel's cheekbones where she sat perched and waiting.

She turned off all the lights for me, Lou realized. Why else would she bother to sit in the dark like this? *How thoughtful.*

Lady rose from her place on the floor and came to Lou,

tail wagging. Lou knelt and gave her a good scratch behind the ears.

She kissed the dog's snout twice before asking Mel, "Ready?"

"Yes, ma'am." She stood and extended her hand toward Lou. The bangles on her wrist jingled as she did.

Lou opted for her arm instead, gently grasping her elbow before the room fell away and the garden rushed up to fill its absence. The thick chorus of cicadas and crickets greeted them.

"Listen to that. I forgot how loud nature can be," Mel said, breathing deeply. "And it smells so nice. The French Quarter can smell like an ashtray full of piss on most nights, but this—"

She took another deep breath.

King and Piper separated themselves from the large hedgerow bisecting the garden.

"Why are we out here?" Mel asked, stepping away from Lou.

"The girl fell from that balcony onto the patio," King said, pointing over his left shoulder. "I thought that might be a good place to start to see if you get any—"

He didn't seem to know how to finish the sentence.

"Impressions," Piper said, and she was already wrapping her arms around Mel and squeezing.

Mel gave her an affectionate pat on the back. "Have you seen any ghosts outside?"

"No," Piper said. "Johnny Golden was in the office, standing behind Rita. And there were two people, I think, in the windows? One was like a shadow and the other was definitely a girl, but I don't think either was Nova Perry. The one I could actually see had, like, old clothes. Victorian, maybe? Something like that."

They led Mel to the patio beneath the balcony.

She looked up at the side of the manor against the backdrop of the starlit sky, then down to the patio again. "It's hard to see in the dark with these old eyes."

"Yeah, but do you *feel* anything?" Piper waved her hands encouragingly. "Any malevolence. Evil? Maybe impending death?"

Melandra knelt and placed her hands on the stones. "No. Not here."

"She was killed before she was thrown," King said.

"Ah," Melandra answered. "We should go where you've seen the ghosts. Probably not the office, if the lady of the house is still up."

"Well, there's the second-floor window," Piper said. "Oh, and my room."

Melandra took several steps back so she could see the glass doors of the balcony. "Let's start with the second floor, and then the fourth is where she was killed, correct?"

"Probably," King said. "I think it would've been hard to kill her and carry her around the manor without anyone seeing her."

"Where's Rita now?" King asked Lou.

Lou stretched her compass out, searching, trying to gain a sense of where Rita was. "First floor, I think."

She waved in the general direction that her compass felt drawn to. She had a feeling it was the first floor because her attention wasn't pulled upward but focused instead on the window straight ahead.

"Somewhere toward the back of the house," she added.

"That's where the office is," King said. "The staff have all gone home but she lives here. Maybe she's up late working. She said her room was adjacent to the office. Maybe she's there."

"And I take it you don't want her to see me?" Melandra said, touching her head scarf.

"It would save us some trouble," King admitted. "But if it happens, we'll deal with it."

Mel turned to Lou. "How about you carry me up to the fourth floor."

"What about us?" Piper pouted. "You gonna leave us down here in the dark?"

"We'll wait in my room," King said. "Then you can meet up with us when you're done."

Lou placed a hand on Mel's arm again. The hot and humid night with its accosting chorus of insectile music fell away. They were alone on the fourth floor.

"Ooo, that heat," Mel whispered. "It sure is warm up here."

Lou had to agree, releasing Mel once she was sure the woman was steady on her own two feet.

Mel stepped away from her, placing a hand on the wallpaper. Lou kept a polite distance, her ears and compass trained on Rita, should she approach. Mel walked on, stopping every few feet and lifting her hand as if in question. When she turned to face one of the walls, Lou saw her eyes were closed.

"What is it?" she whispered. She could admit, if only to herself, that she was a little excited.

"I feel a draft."

Lou came to stand beside her. She felt it too. Cooler air pricked at the hairs along her face. It was more noticeable because of the relentless heat suffocating them.

"I feel it too."

"I didn't know you sensed spirits." Mel was unable to hide her surprise.

"I don't," Lou said, and stepped forward. Once, twice. Her hand traced the stream of air until she was up against the wall, her fingers searching for the source.

There.

She found a thin line. Working her fingers into the crack,

she pulled. The gap widened, and Lou was able to push it back an inch and then slide it completely to one side, revealing a gap wide enough to step through.

"Oh, I see," Mel said. "I guess that makes two of us who can't find a ghost."

Lou stuck her head into the passageway and the darkness was complete. "Should we see what's inside?"

Mel waved her hand. "After you."

Lou stepped into the narrow space between the walls, and Mel followed behind her.

She'd only gone five steps before conceding that her eyes couldn't adjust anymore to the lack of light.

She turned on her cell phone's flashlight.

The light shone, illuminating the rough and jagged planks supporting the walls from the inside. After fifteen feet the narrow passageway broke open, revealing a small room.

To find a room hidden behind a wall wasn't the surprising part.

The *surprising* part, Lou thought, was the shrine.

"Oh my. What is this?" Mel asked, placing one hand on her chest. "Do we know who he is?"

She gestured at the portrait showcased in the center of the shrine.

It was an enormous oil painting, at least five feet tall, of a young man with a babyface. The subject was posed for the viewer. His hand rested casually on his knee, his smile bright.

At his feet, items had been lain as if in offering.

There was a pocket watch. A ring. Silk neck scarves and handkerchiefs. A shirt.

Lou bent and read the tag on the shirt.

"How old do you think that is?" Mel asked, gesturing to the shirt. Her voice was filled with wonder.

"It's from Eddie Bauer," Lou said.

Mel laughed, part of it escaping before she could cover

her mouth. Once she regained control of herself, she whispered, "Not old at all. If so, that means someone might have been here recently."

Lou noted the colorful packages of candy. A box of chocolates. A bottle of Hennessey. "Looks like it."

"Might I suggest that we not linger then?" Mel asked. "Lest his admirer come back and find us here."

She gestured at the painting.

A photograph on the floor next to the candy caught Lou's eye. She bent down, shining her light on their glossy faces.

In the photo, a man stood beside his gleaming truck. He had his arm around a woman, but her face had been burned out of the photograph. From what was left of the woman's hair, Lou wondered if it had been Rita.

"I think this is him, too," Lou said, offering it to Mel.

Mel turned the photograph over in her hands. "Printed on paper. This can't be more than twenty or thirty years old, but I'd say even newer. It's well preserved. No water damage or anything."

"Should we take it back to King? Maybe he knows who it is."

"We *should* go," Mel said. "That's what we should do. And no. If we take anything, they'll know we were here."

Lou returned the photograph to where she found it and stood. They retraced their steps down the narrow passageway.

Together they maneuvered the wall into place, waiting until it clicked shut, evidence of their intrusion erased.

Then they stepped back, inspecting their work.

"You really wouldn't know it was there, would you?" Mel said.

Lou was about to say no when a sound pricked her ears.

Footsteps on the stairs. They creaked under the weight of someone's approach, and without thinking, Lou pulled Mel through the dark. It didn't matter if it was the owner of this shrine or Rita herself. In either case, Lou didn't want to be found.

King's bedroom was markedly cooler than the fourth floor, but still warm.

Piper looked up first from where she sat in the armchair by the window, bouncing her leg anxiously. Lou didn't miss the way her fingers had turned white from gripping the rolled arms.

She was on her feet before Lou even released Mel.

"Well?" she asked. "What happened? Did you see anything? Feel anything?"

"Feel? Not much," Mel told her. She reached up and touched her braids self-consciously. "But we found something interesting. Would you happen to have a photograph of Johnny Golden?"

After a few taps on his phone, King offered them a photograph of his beaming face, taken from the local paper, honoring him for a sizable church donation.

"What do you think?" Mel asked Lou.

"It's him," Lou confirmed.

Mel proceeded to tell King and Piper about the secret room. How they found it, what they saw.

King's brows went up. "There's a shrine to Johnny hidden behind a secret wall on the fourth floor?"

"Full of stuff," Mel said.

"What kind of stuff?" Piper asked.

"It looks like things from the house, if I had to guess," Mel said. "I don't think Rita did this. She could admire any of the paintings of her husband on the wall just fine. No need to have a secret room."

Piper snapped her fingers. "What if the person who made the shrine is the same person who is trying to scare Rita? Banging in the walls. The screeching. They could be trying to freak her out. What if that's how they bang on the wall? From inside this secret room?"

King turned to her, still frowning. "I thought you were blaming the ghosts for that. Are there no ghosts now?"

"Oh, there's ghosts," Mel and Piper said in unison.

Piper pointed her finger. "Ha! I told you."

"I just don't know if they have it in them to build a shrine for a dead man or to cause the raucous you've described to me. It seems more likely that someone is trying to scare Rita out of this house."

King considered this. He leaned back in his armchair, rubbing his chin. "If Nova was killed to put pressure on Rita, then this could be the same person."

"Or this could be someone else who wants her out of the house," Mel said.

"The owner of Basswood Mansion did seem to hold some animosity toward her. And he was poaching her employees out from under her. It's possible that he paid someone else to bang on the walls and make the noises in order to scare her."

Mel shook her head. "I don't think it's someone who is being paid. There was a feeling of..."

She seemed to search for a word.

"Obsession," Lou offered.

"Yes, obsession," Melandra agreed. "Whoever made that shrine is genuinely obsessed with Johnny."

"If that's true, they'd have reason enough to torment Rita. If this obsessed person believes Rita killed him, that's motivation enough to try to run her out of it." King looked at his watch. "It's almost nine."

He turned to Lou.

"Is there any way you can follow your compass to the person? To this *shrine maker*?"

Lou threw her mind out across the dark, searching, listening for something, anything, to snag. After a moment's hesitation, it did fix on someone, the connection locking into place.

"Yes," she said.

"We should *all* go, right?" Piper asked, shifting nervously from side to side. "I don't think any one of us should face a creepy, lovesick person alone."

Lou gave her a look.

"Except you. You'd be fine," she amended, and pointed at Mel and King. "But they need me."

"We'll go," Mel said. "Lou and I. You two are supposed to be here."

Both King and Piper looked apprehensive.

"You don't think I'll look after her?" Lou asked them.

King held up his hands in surrender. "I didn't say that. Just go get a good look and then come up and tell us who it was. Get a picture if you can."

"And don't take too long," Piper said, biting her lip. "You'll give me anxiety."

Lou was fairly certain Piper already had anxiety, but didn't say so.

"We'll be quick," she assured them. To Mel, "Are you ready?"

"I sure am," she said, and placed a hand on Lou's arm.

Then they were through. The mansion with its suffocating heat fell away, and in its place was a small white house with black shutters and a screen door that stood open.

The only problem was they weren't alone. At least twenty people, mostly dressed in black, were gathered in the yard outside the house.

"Oh my," Mel said as she looked around at the people mingling. "And here I was worried we'd be looking someone right in their eyes, one on one."

"Is it a house party?" Lou asked, keeping her voice low.

"A funeral, by the looks of it."

Funeral.

For who?

"I need to walk around," Lou said.

Mel hesitated. "What do we say if someone speaks to us?"

Lou hadn't been to a funeral since her parents had died. Aunt Lucy, her only other close relative, had been cremated. As far as Lou knew, her urn was resting on King's coffee table back in his New Orleans apartment.

"Just say a friend brought you," Lou said. "That usually does it."

"What if they ask what friend?" Mel pressed.

But Lou was already stepping away from her, moving toward the house.

Her compass directed each step.

She pushed past the people sitting on the porch, cigarettes dangling from their lips, smoke trailing into the air.

Into the house that also reeked of cigarette smoke, mingled with food. She smelled the garlicky pasta bakes and cheesy casseroles a second before seeing them spread out on the countertop in communal offering.

Still she pressed forward, toward the casket in the center of the room.

It was closed, Lou noted, with flowers resting on top of the polished lid.

Someone was crying softly.

"I just don't understand it. Michael was such a strong person. How could this happen?"

Lou stopped. She couldn't go any closer without finding herself pinned between the casket and the tight knot of people standing guard over it.

Her compass said that the woman with her back to Lou was the one she was looking for.

Did she make a shrine for Johnny? Lou asked.

The compass spun a confirmation.

Did she kill Johnny Golden?

No.

Did she kill the girl?

Yes.

So the obsessive shrine maker *did* kill the girl. King wasn't going to like that.

Still the conversation pressed on.

"Turn around," Lou murmured. "Turn around and look at me."

A gunshot went off, followed by a whoop of laughter and cursing.

The tension dissipated.

"God help us, Lloyd is drunker than a skunk again," the woman with red-rimmed eyes said. "He's gonna shoot off his own foot, or one of ours, by the end of the night, I tell you. Someone needs to take that damn gun away before it happens."

The woman finally turned.

Lou raised her phone and snapped a picture.

23

King wasn't happy. As he sat in the high-back armchair in his too-warm bedroom at Margo Manor, he squinted at the photo Lou had taken with her phone. It was useless. He thought all these new phones were supposed to offer cuttingly sharp snapshots with their fancy, space-worthy cameras.

"This is grainier than a polaroid picture," he lamented, turning the screen this way, then that.

She pointed at someone on the screen. "It was that one. She built the shrine and killed the girl."

"*That* one." King threw up his hand. "Would that be the black smudge on the *left* or the *right*?"

Lou didn't humor him with a reply.

He tried to check his growing irritation. "But you're certain it was a woman? They were all women?"

"Yes," Lou said.

"And no one said her name or called out to her?"

With a name he would at least have something to work with.

"No," she said.

King squinted at the photo again. Trying to enlarge it with his fingers made it worse. The women standing beside the casket only blurred more.

"This must be for Michael Reed," he said. "He was the gardener here. He was also working under the table for that bastard at Basswood."

"Do you think he really shot himself?" Piper asked from the opposite armchair. "Or did someone kill him and make it look like a suicide?"

"I don't know," King admitted.

"It was definitely a funeral, and I heard them talking about how they never suspected he'd take his own life," Melandra said. She'd been wandering the room, looking at the paintings on the wall. Now she stood before a gilded frame of a woman holding a small white dog on her lap, her shoulders bare. A lacy dress cut across her chest and flowed outward toward the view in sumptuous waves.

"I have to go," King said, giving up. He handed the phone back to Lou. "I have to see her for myself. And she built the shrine and killed Nova Perry? You're *sure*?"

"Yes," Lou said.

He rubbed his chin. "Maybe Nova was killed because she found the shrine. The killer wanted to hide her secret and her vendetta against Rita. Maybe when cleaning she stumbled across something she wasn't supposed to see."

"Funerals in a small town like this can run well into the night," Mel said, her eyes still on the painting. "Grand-mamie's wake ran until dawn."

"Then we should go now. Maybe the killer will still be there," King said, rising. To Lou he asked, "Will you take me?"

"What about Melandra?" Lou asked.

"I can stay for a little longer," Mel said.

"If Rita—" King began.

"She won't," Mel said simply, pulling the shawl across her shoulders tighter. "She'll have no reason to come to Piper's room. We'll wait there until you come on back."

It was fine. He wasn't sure why he was worried about Melandra. Rita might be a killer, but she'd have no reason to hurt Piper or Melandra, would she?

"We won't be long," King promised.

He felt Lou touch his arm a second before that horrible dropped feeling overtook him.

The stuffy bedroom with its antique furnishings fell away, and in its place bloomed a muggy night. The humidity licked his face like a cat's tongue. Crickets sang in the dark. Before he caught his breath, the mosquitos found him.

Lou released him, and he was in full view of a small white house with a low covered porch. Someone was shouting.

"I *won't* keep my voice down," a man said. "You should be out there lookin' for somebody, not here stuffin' your mouths with Debbie's little wieners!"

King turned toward the sound. A short man, no more than five and a half feet tall by King's measure, sloshed beer over the ground in front of him. His belly was round, and his eyes glazed from too much drinking.

"Now, Chris. Come on. This ain't no way to act. We ain't even put your brother in the ground yet."

This was Herb, the police chief, trying to talk him down. He wasn't in uniform tonight. Instead he'd opted for a nice pair of jeans, brown belt and shoes, and wore a white polo tucked in. His hair was damp and slicked to one side neatly, and his jaw freshly shaven.

"My brother! My *brother*—" Chris's voice broke. "My brother was a *good* man. And all of y'all are just standing around his house, acting like he actually kilt himself or some bullshit. He'd never! He coulda never, and every last one of you knows it!"

"Should we take him?" Lou asked at his elbow.

"That seems harsh," King said. "His brother just died. He's grieving."

The truth was King had gotten pretty trashed himself on the night of Jack's funeral. But he didn't want to bring up the death of Lou's father at a time like this.

If ever.

She turned to him. "I meant for an interview. If we take him somewhere private and talk to him, we might find out something about Michael."

"Oh," King said. Keeping his voice low, he added, "Maybe. Not yet. Either way, we'll talk to him before we leave. First I want you to point out this person to me."

He didn't want to say "Nova's killer" with this many ears around. As of this moment, no one was paying much attention to him, and he wanted to keep it that way.

Lou headed for the house, and as the front door grew larger in his vision, King's apprehension seized him. What if Herb or anyone else recognized him?

What if his presence caused a scene? What would he say to explain why he was here at the funeral?

But it was too late to turn back now. They were already crossing the porch, the weathered boards creaking under their weight.

The house was small. The entrance opened on a modest living room. Someone had moved a couch to the side to make room for the casket, but otherwise, King had a sense of how the man had kept his place while alive.

Tidy with cheap furniture but well maintained. Michael Reed was the kind of man who played caretaker to his home and life. King liked him a little more for that.

He understood now why Lou's picture had not turned out.

The lighting in the room was terrible. Clusters of people

clotted the space, making it hard to distinguish one body from the next as the shadows overlapped.

"Her," Lou said.

King followed the slight movement of Lou's hand.

He looked up.

His heart clenched.

"The blonde?" he asked cautiously. Hopefully.

Because please don't let it be—

"No, the brunette beside her. The one with the big blue eyes."

King's stomach flopped again, bile rushing up his throat.

"You're sure?" he asked.

"Absolutely."

King turned away, stepping out of the house and back into the moonlit yard before the woman Lou had singled out could see him.

Of course, that wouldn't change the fact that he'd seen her.

Aubree Owens.

Aubree Owens, a beauty and a liar.

Aubree Owens, obsessed with Johnny Golden.

Aubree Owens, killer of innocent teenage girls.

As he stepped outside, his shoulder connected hard with someone else's.

"Hey, watch where the—"

King didn't even have time to react. Lou pulled both him and the man through the shadows formed by the low-slung porch before either of them could protest.

Lou wasn't affected by the slip. She never was, as far as he could tell. At least King found his footing quicker than the drunk swaying in front of him.

It looked as if he were about to tumble over, perhaps face first into the lake now looming on his left. King's hand shot out at the same time as Lou's.

They both grabbed one of his arms, steadying him.

"Hey, hey! What the hell! I—" His face blanched. His words were cut off sharply by the vomit racing up his throat. He turned his head onto the shore.

King held the man up while he retched.

"Where are we?" he asked Lou.

"Nova Scotia," she said.

Nova Scotia?

He was trying to understand where Lou had brought them. It was remote, obviously. There wasn't a single artificial light as far as his eyes could see, and he hadn't seen evergreens this big since he'd gone to Yellowstone with his parents as a kid.

Chris groaned, and when King bent to check on him, he spotted something at the water's edge.

"Is that a tooth?" King asked, arching a brow at Lou.

"Nah, it's just my guts," the brother replied, obviously thinking King was speaking to him.

When he stood up, his eyes were clearer, if his stance no more steady.

"I'm sorry to bother you on such a difficult night," King began, hoping to keep the man's attention. No need for him to realize he wasn't at his brother's funeral anymore. That they were, in fact, thousands of miles away. "But I heard you mention that you didn't think that your brother's death was a suicide."

"'Cause it wasn't," Chris said. He wiped at his mouth with the back of his hand. "Michael would never hurt himself."

"I hope this doesn't sound too unforgiving, but can I ask *how* you know he wouldn't hurt himself?"

"I know my brother, man!" he said, staggering backward. Lou pressed a fist into his shoulder to prop him up but said nothing. King didn't think Chris had even noticed she was there. For all he knew, she could be a tree.

"My big brother loved people. He loved being here. He wouldn't hurt himself. He wouldn't because he knows how much it would break our momma's heart."

His voice broke, and King let the tears flow without interrupting him.

Wind pushed past them suddenly, cooling the sweat along King's forehead and hairline. It was a blessed relief.

Fall will be here before I know it, he thought.

Fall and his birthday.

Aubree's birthday.

Fucking Aubree Owens.

He'd eaten up her story during the interview. Her tears. How pitiful and overwhelmed she'd seemed. Her grief had seemed so genuine. So heartbreaking. Why had he believed it for a second?

"Chris, is it?" King asked gently, hoping that his anger with himself wasn't seeping into his words. He only hoped Chris wasn't well enough in his mind to notice.

"That's me. Who the hell are you?" he asked, swaying on his feet.

"I'm Robert King. I—" He couldn't say he was a friend of Michael's. He hadn't even met the man. "I believe you."

"You believe me?"

"I do," King said. "I don't think Michael killed himself. I work as a private detective, so why don't you tell me what you know and maybe I can help you solve this."

Chris looked hopeful for a moment before frowning. "I ain't got no money for—"

"I won't charge you," King said. "I think this is connected to another death I've been hired to investigate. Do you know about Nova Perry?"

"Yeah, I know her. She was a little stuck up, but she was all right for the most part."

"Were your brother and Nova in a relationship?" King asked.

Chris's face pinched. "What? No. It wasn't like that. Who told you that? Aubree?"

King's stomach turned again at the mention of the woman's name.

Chris misinterpreted King's pause. He threw up his hands. "Man, that woman is jealous as hell. I told Mikey that, but he don't listen to me for shit."

King cocked his head. "Why would Aubree be jealous of Nova and Michael?"

"I said they're not—"

King held up his hands. "No, I know. I'm just asking, if Aubree was jealous, why would she be?"

"'Cause Aubree and Michael is together. Was together. She don't like him talking to nobody. Not even his own family."

Lou arched a brow, but King ignored this. He was trying to remain focused on the man swaying in front of him.

"Aubree and Michael were a couple?"

"Yeah, everybody know'd that."

"Did Rita Golden know that?" King asked.

Chris frowned at King as if he'd just said something ridiculous. "No, why would she?"

Of course not. Because Rita wasn't one of them. They wouldn't keep her in the loop about their personal lives.

Did Rita think Michael was meeting up with Nova when it had really been Aubree all along? Did Aubree and Nova make an agreement? Aubree would cover for her so that Nova could end her shifts early, and Nova wouldn't deny the rumors that she was sneaking off with the gardener?

Then what had gone wrong?

"Can you think of anybody who'd want to hurt Michael?" King asked.

Chris hung his head. "Nuh-uh. No way. Everybody loved Mikey. He helped a lot of people out around here, and sometimes didn't charge them more than a beer for it neither."

"And you can't think of any reason why he'd shoot himself?" King pressed.

"I said—"

"I know what you said," King said, holding his hands up again, trying to soothe the man. "I just want to make sure I see the whole picture. Michael didn't have a history of depression, anxiety."

Chris looked ready to take a swing at King. "My brother was strong. He was a good man."

How could King explain that a man could be good, strong, and still want to die?

"But..." Chris hesitated. He ran his hand over his close-cropped hair several times, his eyes shimmering in the moonlight.

"Whatever it is, tell me," King said. "You never know what might help."

"We went to Margo the day Nova died. Michael said Nova needed a ride to her brother's ball game, but when we got there, there was Herb and all them police over from Slaughter."

"What did you see?" King prompted, hoping to lead Chris down memory lane.

"I seen her. Busted up on the concrete. It was bad. Then next thing I know, Mikey was yellin' at me to get back in the truck and talkin' crazy."

"Crazy how?"

Chris threw up his hands again. "I don't know. He was sayin' it was all his fault she was dead. That he killed her."

"He said that?" King repeated, his heart racing. "He said, 'I killed her.'"

"Yeah, but he couldn't have," Chris said, wiping his brow.

He didn't look so drunk now. "I'd been with him all day. When we pulled up, I'd been with him, I swear. There was no way he coulda hurt that girl."

An idea struck King square in the chest. He shifted his weight from one leg to the other. "Chris?"

"Yeah?" The drunk man looked up. He was taking in the lake for the first time. The clear sky and swollen moon.

"Was Aubree with you?" King asked.

"When?"

"When Michael told you to get back in his truck and left the manor, was Aubree with you? Did she get in the truck right away or did you wait for her?"

Chris shook his head. "Nah. It was just us."

"You're sure?"

Chris sucked his teeth. "Hell, man. Course I'm sure. I remember 'cause he was driving like a bat out of hell and I told him to slow down. I remember thinkin' that if Aubree was with us, he wouldn't be drivin' like that."

"Did he say anything else while you guys drove away?" King asked. He was two seconds from grabbing Chris's shoulders and shaking him.

"No," Chris said. "He just kept saying he killed Nova, but that's wrong. I know it's wrong."

"And where did you go?"

"He dropped me off at Mama's and said he was goin' home." Chris's eyes were shining with unshed tears. "That was the last time I seen my brother alive. The next day he was dead."

He pressed his palms into his eyes.

"I'm sorry," King said quietly. King had never had any siblings himself, but he knew grief. Lucy's death—the great love of his life—wasn't so distant in his memory. Sometimes, in his mind's eye, he saw her turn toward him, giving him one of her heart-stopping, devastatingly beautiful smiles. And of course there'd been his mentee, Jack. King might never forgive himself for Jack Thorne's death.

"I'm very sorry for your loss," King said.

Chris's eyes remained on the damp, moonlit earth at their feet. "I've had my brother my whole life. I don't know how I'm gonna live the rest of it without him here. It ain't right. I'm supposed to have him. Always."

"Can I ask you one more thing? Then I'll let you be."

He looked up, wiping his face with the backs of his hands. "What is it?"

"What kind of relationship did Michael and Aubree have?"

He frowned. "What do you mean?"

King did his best to clarify. "Was it happy? Did they get along? Or did they fight a lot?"

Chris rubbed the back of his head. "They got on pretty good. My brother's a laid-back guy, so he don't fight with people much. He's what Mama calls a peacemaker."

"So there weren't any fights that you can remember?"

"Well..." Chris scowled. "It's true that Aubree was the jealous type. If Michael talked to anybody too long or looked at another woman—not even in that way, just being respect-ful, you know?—she'd get mad about it. Crazy mad."

Crazy mad enough to kill someone? King wondered. Or had Michael made the mistake of saying something to her? Maybe something that had given Aubree the impression that Nova was a threat?

"Thanks for speaking with me, Chris. I know this wasn't the best time, but I'll do all I can to solve this."

King gestured to Lou, silently asking her to take him away.

She did, ending the interview with one side step through the dark.

King remained rooted where he was, his eyes cast out

over the placid lake. His heart racing, pulse pounding in his temples.

He felt Lou return rather than heard her. Louie Thorne was the kind of person you didn't hear unless she *wanted* you to.

"Did someone kill Michael?" King asked without turning around.

"The compass says no, or if they did, they're not alive," Lou said.

"You realize who killed Nova Perry, right? Aubree Owens. The other maid."

"I thought so," she said.

"If Aubree killed her, not Michael, then why would he kill himself?"

"Guilt," Lou offered. "He blamed himself for whatever Aubree did."

That's what King thought, his eyes fixed on the bright moon. "But *why?*"

24

———————

After returning Mel safely to New Orleans, Lou felt Konstantine's call to come home like a gentle tug through her abdomen. When she arrived, Konstantine was standing at the stove, his black sleeves rolled up, exposing his forearms. She especially liked the look of the dishtowel thrown over one shoulder. The kitchen smelled of garlic-soaked seafood, and a bottle of wine had already been opened, resting on the counter. She took a wine glass from its holder above the sink and poured herself a generous portion.

"What's for dinner?" she asked him.

"*Risotto ai frutti di mare*," he said.

She knew the word *risotto* and could see the fish for herself. In the pan adjacent, simmering in copious amounts of glossy butter, were scallops.

"Seafood risotto," she ventured. "I thought it was better to drink white wine with seafood?"

He gave her a look that bordered on disgust.

She smirked. "What's this?"

A stack of folders rested on the island counter beside the bottle of wine. Lou took one, opened it, and saw a photo in the upper-left corner of the sheet, followed by a long list of details about the featured person that filled the rest of the page.

"I researched the staff at your nursing home," he said, flipping the fish in the pan before turning to her. "But I haven't had time to sort through it all. I am sorry, *amore mio*."

It amused her that he preferred paper folders. Of course, she couldn't tease him about it. She was nearly thirty before she'd gotten a cell phone for the first time.

"I can sort them with Piper and Dani," Lou said. "Piper needs a night away from that house. It's getting to her."

"And to me," he said, taking her glass of wine. He pressed his lips to the rim in a way that told her what he was thinking.

She looked through a few of the files before saying, "What about Rita Golden?"

"I will do that next," he promised. "Though perhaps I should hold the information hostage until you return to me."

"That will only keep me away longer," she said. "The sooner they solve this case, the sooner I'll be back. All night long."

"All night long," he said, his lips red and wet from the wine. She took the glass away from him and kissed him, enjoying the taste of it.

"Maybe I can stay tonight," she said.

He visibly brightened. "Truly, *amore mio*? I don't mean a nap. I want a whole night of you beside me."

There were six hours between Louisiana and Italy. If they went to bed early enough, Piper wouldn't even notice she was missing. Lou would just have to discipline herself to keeping something akin to *normal* hours.

"I can stay for most of it," she told him.

No sooner than the words had left her mouth did he pull

her off her feet, his hands under her buttocks, lifting her and placing her on the island counter.

He was trying to undo his shirt.

"The scallops are going to burn," she told him.

"No, *amore mio*," he said. "I can—"

"They're smoking," she said. "Actually."

Swearing in Italian, he had no choice but to turn away from her and salvage his meal. Lou didn't mind. She poured herself another glass of wine and admired the view of his backside while he worked.

She offered to help plate the food and take it to their table on the balcony, but he shooed her away. She let him.

This time.

The truth was she simply wasn't as good at these domestic things as he was. She wouldn't dream of cooking for him when she'd barely just learned to cook for herself. But more than that, he seemed to enjoy it. *Really* enjoy it.

It seemed cruel to take away something he found so much pleasure in.

Once he'd put their plates on the balcony table, he went about the business of lighting the candles. There were six, sitting inside black lanterns affixed to the villa's wall and the balcony itself.

They ate in candlelight, overlooking the Arno River.

He refilled her glass twice without asking. When he leaned over to pour the remainder of the bottle, she asked, "Are you trying to get me drunk?"

He only smiled. "No. But we must finish this bottle. It's unhealthy to not finish a bottle of wine."

These Italians and their rules.

But she didn't complain. She was at peace.

He didn't rush her.

He let her eat her fill, slowly, as she liked. He let her linger and watch the moon make its way across the sky. He said nothing, did not ruin or fill the silence as she went to the railing and looked out on the lit streets below, to the cars and motorbikes passing. To the people walking arm in arm.

She took it all in and realized she'd never, not once in her life, imagined she could be here.

That she could be happy.

Happy.

It wasn't the kind of happiness that she found on the other end of a gun, with a target dead or dying at her feet. That was more of a release.

This was different.

This was unimaginable.

She turned toward him.

"What is it?" he asked, obviously curious about whatever it was he'd just seen cross her face.

"Nothing," she said. She picked up her wine, finished it, and put the empty glass back on the table.

She wrapped her arms around him, breathing into his neck and placing a kiss where the shoulder and throat met.

She held him. She breathed him in. "Let's go to bed."

Lou stayed with Konstantine for the full six hours, until the sun set in Louisiana. Then she stepped through their bedroom closet and into the parking lot outside Margo Manor. The last slice of sunset fell orange across the top of the building, brightening its exterior, as the trees swayed in a lazy breeze.

Piper stood ten feet away, holding her phone up in the air as if to capture something with it.

"Hey," Lou said, adjusting the stack of files in her arms.

Piper jumped, pulling her cell phone to her chest. "Sweet Jesus."

"What were you doing out here in the parking lot?"

"I was trying to get enough signal to text Dani an update, but it's not working," she said. "We didn't make much progress with the follow-up interviews today and King is in his room pouting. I think we'll be here for at least two more days."

She glared at her phone again, and after a minute groaned.

"Ugh, this stupid thing!"

Piper shook her phone and looked ready to throw it across the parking lot into the trees.

"Why don't we go see her instead?" Lou said.

"Yes!" Piper turned to her, looking at her as if for the first time. Then her excitement fell. She looked toward the manor hesitantly. "But that means King will be here alone with the ghosts."

"I'll keep an ear out," Lou promised. If what she used to tune into the movements of the world could be called *an ear*.

Relief washed over Piper's face. "Okay then."

She practically skipped into Lou's arms.

"I won't lie. I'm more than a little excited to get out of here," Piper whispered conspiratorially, as if someone—or something—could hear her.

I can tell, Lou thought.

She took only a moment to adjust the files in her arms and then reached out for Piper.

When they touched, the parking lot disappeared and Piper's apartment sprang into view.

Dani was on the sofa, glasses sliding down the brim of her nose as she typed on her computer. The laptop was balanced precariously on her lap.

She looked up as they stepped from the dark corner and did a double take. "Oh! Hey."

Piper was across the room, pouncing on her, before Lou could even get the files onto the coffee table.

"Oh my god, *babe.*" Piper fanned kisses all over Dani's cheek, her neck and shoulder. "*Babe.* I missed you so much."

A laughing Dani barely had time to close the laptop and slide it to safety on the couch.

"I missed you too."

She managed to give Lou a little wave behind Piper's back.

"Are you guys done with the case?" Dani asked, looking at the folders. "What's all that?"

"Not even close. King is still there, trying to figure out how he's going to get enough evidence to convict Aubree of murder now that her boyfriend has killed himself. And our one lead with him."

Dani pursed her lips. "Who's Aubree?"

"The other maid. King thinks she killed Nova. Nova's the girl."

"And didn't you also say that the person who hired you *also* killed someone?"

"Technically, Detective White hired us, but yes. The owner, Rita Golden, definitely killed her husband. Though I don't know if King is working hard enough to solve that case. Lou might have to give her the old *heave ho* if he tries to say that 'it's not our case.'"

"I have Konstantine looking into it," Lou told them. "Maybe she had a good reason to kill her husband."

Piper frowned. "If that's the case, I'm going to feel awful. And I'll be made fully aware of my eyebrow bias."

Dani held her while she talked. "I've uncovered a few interesting things while researching the place. Mostly it was just the lengths that Rita has gone through to try and keep herself afloat financially since Johnny left. From what I can see, she didn't see any financial gain from his death. Even when she inherited the house and the land, it was deep in the hole because of back taxes. Yet she's been working hard to pay everyone well despite her dire circumstances. It's admirable, actually."

"Y'all better stop praising Rita or I'm gonna feel like the bad guy here." Piper couldn't look happier curled up against Dani as if she were a sturdy piece of flotsam and Piper had been adrift at sea for years.

Dani pointed at the stack of folders that Lou had placed on the coffee table. "If you don't have any evidence or leads, then what's all that?"

Lou pushed her sunglasses up onto her head. "This is for Hellman. I need your help. If you're free."

It took ten minutes to convince Piper to release her hold on Dani so the three of them could gather around the coffee table and divide the folders evenly.

There were twenty-eight in all. Piper and Dani took nine each. Lou took ten.

To Konstantine's credit, he had been very thorough. He'd found everything from personal information on each of the employees, whatever they'd been silly enough to share on social media, to their financial history, criminal records, addresses, phone numbers, employers. Together, they quickly sorted through the piles, trying to find anything of note.

"I don't understand," Dani said, adjusting her glasses on her nose. She gave her messy bun a tug and looked up from the page. "Didn't you just say you used your compass to identify both killers at the haunted mansion?"

"Manor," Piper corrected. "Apparently there's a difference."

Dani ignored this, her gaze still fixed on Lou. "Why haven't you singled out the nursing home killer?"

"I've tried," Lou said. "First I found a man in a coma, Jesse Elmer. The second and third times it was a little old woman, Moira Bradley. All she had in her hand was a mirror. I don't think she was trying to hurt anyone."

"How many people have died at Hellman?" Piper asked.

"Ten in the last year," Lou said.

"That seems like a lot of dead old people," Piper said.

Dani frowned at her.

"I don't think they were all murdered," Lou said. "Many of the patients are in bad health."

"So you went every time you had a feeling but you didn't see anyone? *No* one?"

"No one that felt like a murderer," Lou said.

Piper's face lit up. "Oh my god, I watched this horrifying documentary years ago about a nurse who was killing a bunch of babies. She'd wheel them off the nursery and then smother them. She'd killed like twenty kids before they caught her."

A nurse, Lou thought. "I did see a nurse."

"Do you remember what she looked like?"

"No," Lou admitted. "I was trying to find an exit."

"Look at their photos then." Piper slid her stack of the folders over to Lou. "Maybe your compass will react to someone's face."

Lou opened each folder in turn and looked at the photographs. She went through twenty-two of them without so much as a twitch in her gut.

"I don't think this is going to work," she said.

When she reached the second-to-last file, it happened. She opened the folder and her stomach clenched.

It was a woman. Red hair, stern face. It looked more like she was posing for a passport photo than taking a photograph for her hospital ID. Lou recognized her.

"I've seen this one," Lou said.

She pushed the file over to them.

"No way!" Piper said. "A *third* woman. Are all three of our killers women this time? Holy shit. I think that's a record."

Dani read the file aloud. "Rachel Frisk. She's been a nurse at Hellman House for four years. She's twenty-six years old.

Single. No criminal record. Though she does have a couple of speeding tickets."

Piper turned the page toward Lou. "Konstantine wrote a little symbol here. What does this squiggle mean?"

"Oh, wait. I saw the key somewhere." Dani shuffled through the papers until she found what she wanted. Her finger slid down the page. "Here it is. It means that she worked on the night someone died."

"Does it mean six deaths if she's got six squiggles?" Piper asked.

"Looks like it." Dani met Lou's gaze. "Do you really think this is your killer?"

Lou stood up, pushing away from the table and the many files piled on top of it. "Let's find out."

DANI HAD INSISTED ON CHANGING OUT OF HER PAJAMAS and brushing her hair before being taken anywhere, even if it was eleven o'clock at night. Nothing Piper could say about how perfect and beautiful she was no matter what she looked like convinced her otherwise.

It was almost ten minutes before the three of them stepped from the shadows of Dani and Piper's apartment and into Moira Bradley's room at Hellman House.

Moira was sitting up in her bed, the soft light of a tablet flashing colors across her wrinkled face.

She gasped when the three of them stepped forward.

Lou moved into her line of sight. "It's just me."

Moira's hand relaxed against her chest. "Honey, I'm old. You can't be sneaking up on me like that."

"I'm sorry," Lou said. "But we didn't want the nurses to see us."

Moira tried to sit up taller in her bed, or at least, as tall as her hunched back would allow. "Did you find out who hurt Dorothy?"

Lou offered her the printout of Rachel's face, folded to reveal only the replica of her photo ID.

"Do you know this nurse?" Lou asked.

"I do." Moira placed her hand against her chest. "Do you really think she's doing it?"

"Yes," Lou said.

When her shock remained fixed on her face, Dani stepped to the woman's bedside. "Is there any reason why you *don't* think she would do it?"

"It's just…" She seemed to search for the words. "I don't know, it's just that she's one of the nice ones."

"What do you mean?" Dani asked.

"You know. Sometimes a nurse can get impatient with us. They treat us like children, but I have my own will, damn it. I don't want to do as I'm told as if I'm five years old."

"But Rachel never treated you poorly."

"No." Moira frowned. "Not at all. Oh dear."

The woman began to grope for the oxygen mask, and Piper was quick to put it into reach. They waited while she affixed it to her face and took deep, steadying breaths. Whenever they asked if they could do anything, she waved them away.

The only choice they had was to wait.

Finally, Moira's breath evened out and she handed the picture of the nurse back to Lou. She removed the oxygen mask and said, "I remember now. She was here. That night."

"Which night?" Piper asked.

"The night I said there was a dark shadow lingering over my bed. I was just about to scream because of how menacing it was when the light came on. But it was Rachel, asking me if I was okay."

Dani caught on first. "Is it possible that the menacing shadow *was* Rachel?"

"I guess it could be." Moira touched her throat. "I'd wondered how she'd gotten to me so fast, before I could even scream. I thought that maybe I'd just been lucky, that maybe she'd been right outside the door after checking on somebody else."

You did get lucky, Lou thought. *She must not have thought she could kill you before you screamed and didn't want to chance it.*

"This is so sad," Moira said, her face crumpling with despair. "Dorothy really liked Rachel. I'd hate to think that we're capable of being killed by people we *like*. What is this world coming to?"

"Do you like her?" Piper asked.

"No, but I don't really like anybody."

Dani suppressed a laugh.

Lou placed a hand on the woman's arm. "Moira?"

She looked up, meeting Lou's eyes. "Yes? What is it?"

"Do you want to help us catch Dorothy's killer?"

Moira's eyes widened. She drew back as if Lou might strike her. "How can I? Look at me."

"We just need Rachel to get caught. Then they'll know who did this," Lou said.

"Caught in the act?" Moira said. She placed a hand on her frizzy gray hair. "You mean you want to give her a reason to try and kill me."

"It's a good plan," Dani said. "And you'll be making sure there's justice for Dorothy."

Moira blinked. "Are you serious?"

"They're always serious," Piper said. "This is what we do. Hunt bad guys. Women. Bad women."

Moira held the oxygen mask in one hand and looked into each of their faces as if trying to decide whether or not this was a joke. Once she realized they weren't kidding, she laughed, a strained, wheezy sound.

She threw up her hand. "What the hell? I'm half dead anyway."

"Don't worry, Lou's not going to let her hurt you," Piper said with full confidence.

"She never fails," Dani added.

Moira looked to Lou as if to conduct her own assessment for herself. Whatever she saw, it satisfied her.

"All right," she said. "Let's do this. For Dorothy."

25

As King sat in his booth at the diner, nursing a cup of black coffee, he was lost deep in his thoughts. It was one thing to suspect someone of murder and another to be able to prove it. Did he believe in Lou's compass? Yes. Did he believe that if Lou said Aubree killed Nova, that was what happened? Yes. It had been harder to accept Piper's intuition that Rita had killed her husband—but King's struggle with his doubts weakened the moment Lou put Johnny Golden's jawbone in his hand.

Or at least, what they *thought* was Johnny's jawbone.

There was a way to settle this, of course. Test the bone and confirm that it belonged to Johnny. Once that was done, then there could be no confusion, no reason to wonder. It would also solidify Lou's proclamation of Aubree's guilt. After all, if Lou could find a swamp in the middle of nowhere, walk into it, *dive* into it, and find a jawbone that belonged to a man long since dead, then how in the world could King hold on to an ounce of lingering doubt that maybe she was wrong about Aubree?

Not a chance.

It was important not to undervalue his own work in this either. He had been very thorough at every stage of this investigation. He knew it. Just that morning he'd reinterviewed everyone at the mansion despite Rita's protest, just to make sure he hadn't missed anything.

But the stories remained the same. No one had shifted their positions. There was a bit of embellishment in detail, but that was to be expected the more a person told a story. The farther away they got from the actual death, the more the mind would remake that day in its own image.

Still, the interviews were largely unchanged from what Piper had recorded in her impeccable notes.

So how was he going to do it? How in the world was he going to prove that Aubree Owens and Rita Golden were murderers?

The surrounding diner came into sharp focus when Birdie returned with the coffee pot in one hand.

"Would you like a warm-up, Mr. King?" she asked with a bright smile.

"Yes, please, thank you."

She tipped the coffee pot over his ceramic mug and filled it for the third time.

"Might I ask you how your investigation's going?" Birdie ventured, looking at him over the rim of her tortoiseshell glasses.

"I've hit a snag," he admitted, though he had no intention of being so unprofessional as to reveal the details of a pending investigation with anyone.

"Anything I can help with?"

King looked around the diner to see who all was listening, but there was only one other patron in the place. An elderly man in the far corner slept, his baseball cap pulled down over his eyes. He snored softly.

"Oh, don't worry about Eunice," Birdie told him. "He just likes to have himself a nap after lunch."

"Then if you're not busy, you could join me for a cup of coffee and let me ask you a few questions," King said. He hoped it was perfectly clear that he was interested in her only in a professional capacity. The last thing he needed was the police chief coming after him.

"I'd love a cup of coffee," she said with a broad smile. She went behind the counter and grabbed herself a clean mug before returning to the table.

She poured herself some coffee, added two sugars and a splash of milk, and settled in across from him.

King rubbed his nose. "There are just a few things I'd like clarification on, if you'd be so kind."

"I'd be happy to help," she said. "And *you'll* be happy to know I've got a lot of experience listening to an officer try to work out a problem for himself."

She smiled at him as she stood to return the coffee pot to its warmer.

When she returned, he asked, "Do you know Aubree Owens well?"

Her eyebrows lifted. "Is Aubree a suspect?"

"No," he said, perhaps too quickly. Birdie seemed like an honest woman who could keep her mouth shut, but King didn't want to chance it. He could be talking to the town gossip for all he knew.

"It's just that she was working on the same floor on the day of Nova's death," he said. "That makes her a key witness. It's important to know if key witnesses are reliable before putting a lot of weight on their testimony."

Birdie took a drink of her coffee. "I've known Aubree all her life."

"Then you'd have a decently accurate opinion of her character," King said, turning his cup in his hands. "What do you think?"

He appreciated that she didn't answer automatically. It wasn't that she was hiding anything, she was just considering her words. "I *think* she's grown to be a beautiful woman. She's always been a beauty, actually. A little boy crazy, mind you. In fact, I was so *sure* that she would've run out of this town with a man by now. Just put all of us in the rearview and never look back."

"She isn't happy here?"

"No, I wouldn't say that. She's got a lot of family here. A whole brood of cousins. But maybe that's what's kept her here despite the fact she's a free spirit. She used to talk about moving out of state. Going to college somewhere and getting a good job. I really believed she was going to do it, given how she talked about it. Then she ended up staying. It was strange."

"When was this? When did she talk about leaving town?" King asked.

"Oh, when she was a kid. She's been working at Margo Manor since she was sixteen, and she'd come in here after her shifts and have some pie and talk about how she wanted to see the world. She sat right here at these tables and applied to at least half a dozen schools. And she got into a couple too. But she never went. She ended up staying at that old house. I guess she fell in love with it. She wouldn't be the first. Rita was quite in love with it in the beginning too, if I'm not mistaken."

"Maybe a man kept her here?" King offered. "Any boyfriends you know of? You mentioned she was boy crazy."

"Most recently there was Michael. But I couldn't be sure if that was a rumor or not. I'd only seen them together a couple of times, and if it was love, it was a quiet love. They weren't too affectionate, I mean. And Michael was a good man. He helped Herb pour the concrete in our driveway when we got sick of the gravel. I'm going to miss him."

She had tears in her eyes now, and King let the moment settle before pushing on.

"It's funny because I heard that Nova had a thing with Michael. We're both talking about the gardener, aren't we?" King supposed there was always the possibility that there were more than a few Michaels running around this town.

Birdie scoffed. "Nova didn't have no boyfriend. Even if she was interested in Michael despite the age between them —and both you and I know it happens—Nova's daddy had gone and put the fear of God in that girl. He had her half believing that if you held a boy's hand you were bound to end up pregnant. I'd never seen her look at a boy more than two seconds. It was a shame, really. As she was a pretty girl. I'm not saying a girl's gotta wait until she gets married."

She leaned across the table conspiratorially and lowered her voice.

"Hell, Herb and I fooled around plenty in the back of his Lincoln before we tied the knot, but that's neither here nor there. But no. They weren't connected in any way, except that we've gone and lost them both. Two kids. It's sad when people die young," she said with a sigh, the heartbreak seeping into her features again.

King searched for a way to direct the conversation back to Aubree. Finally he asked, "Before Michael, was there anyone in Aubree's life that you know of?"

Birdie took another sip of her coffee. "Well, you know, I think there *was* once upon a time, but I don't know if he was from here. He might've been a boy from Slaughter or maybe even Coldrup. I never met him myself."

"Then how did you know? Did you hear about him from someone else?" King ventured.

"No. She came in here—Heavens. It must've been a *long*

time ago, because I don't even think my grandson Caleb had been born yet, and he's almost thirteen. Handsome boy." She beamed.

King humored her with a smile.

"Right, so Aubree comes into the diner happier than I'd *ever* seen her. I was asking her what the good news was. Oh, it must've been the summer before she was going to college. Now I remember thinking maybe it was about school. And I was like, 'What's the good news?' And *she* said I'd know soon enough, which I thought was strange. Why couldn't she just tell me? Now it's been so long I can't remember what all she said, but I *do* remember having the distinct impression that she'd met somebody. Maybe they were gonna run off together, or maybe her folks would make an engagement announcement, that sort of thing. Whatever the case, she was on cloud nine."

"But there was no announcement?" King asked.

"No. Johnny disappeared, and it was such a devastating blow to our community, I guess her good news just got swallowed up in all that. Whatever it was, nobody paid attention. All anybody cared about was finding Johnny. By the time I thought to circle back and see how she was, she was different. That spark was gone. I just figured she'd had a fallin' out with her man, or maybe they broke things off. Then fall came and she didn't go to school. She's been here ever since."

King's heart had sped up in his chest. "You're sure it was the summer Johnny disappeared?"

Birdie laughed. "You know how the memory is when we get older, Mr. King. I can't quite recall the exact dates. All I can tell you is that it was about the same time, yes."

The bell above the diner door chimed and three men in construction blazers entered. Birdie excused herself, and Eunice woke in the corner with a start when one of the men called his name. Then he was up, grasping their hands and sharing a good-natured laugh, before the three newcomers joined him in his booth.

King put money on the table for his coffee and excused himself, offering Birdie a little wave on his way out.

"Good luck, Mr. King. I hope you find your man," she called, before giving her full attention to the table.

Your man.

He repressed the urge to laugh.

Instead of climbing behind the steering wheel, King used his key to open the Buick's trunk. He reached into the dark and grabbed a wrapped bundle tucked into the corner. Peeling back one corner, he regarded the jawbone. A part of the metal plate sparked in the sunlight.

He stared down at it with Birdie's words in his ears and a new theory forming in his mind. Could it be *that's* what happened?

He kept vacillating from one theory to another even after he got behind the wheel of the Buick and drove down the road to the post office with the wrapped jawbone resting in his lap.

For several moments, all he could do was sit in his car outside the post office and consider his choices. If he sent the jawbone to the medical examiner, he would find out once and for all if Johnny Golden was dead. And that confirmation would be enough to solidify his confidence in Lou's declaration that Rita and Aubree were, indeed, murderers.

But to do that felt like a small betrayal to the man he was trying to help. Detective Dick White had asked him to work this case as a personal favor. He'd hired King with hopes that he would do what he could to protect Rita. And now King was going to submit evidence that could get her convicted of murder?

He rubbed his forehead and pulled out his cell phone. He found Dick's number in his contacts and pressed send.

It rang four times before Dick picked up. His voice was hopeful, borderline cheerful. Hearing him like that only made King's apprehension grow. He wiped his sweaty palms on his pants.

"Hey, Dick, how's it going?"

"I was just about to ask you that," he countered, the laugh already folding the edge of his words. "What's it look like up there in Vicksburg?"

He'll appreciate honesty, King thought, and wondered if that was a prayer rather than a reality.

"It's not looking good," King admitted. He listened to the thick silence hanging on the line. When Dick didn't answer, King asked, "You still there?"

"I'm here," Dick said. "You really think she hurt this girl, Robbie?"

"No," King said. "Somebody else hurt the girl and I'm working on getting enough evidence to float the case in court, but while working that case, I admit I—"

And here he had no problem telling a *small* lie.

"—I came across some human remains. I'm pretty sure they're Johnny Golden's, and considering how and where I found them, it doesn't look good for Rita."

More silence.

King was partially relieved that Dick hadn't asked for clarification on the *how* and *why* of finding Johnny's jawbone. But the silence still unnerved him.

Into the silence, King said, "I know that Rita is a friend. And I know you asked me to work this case on your behalf, so I wanted to speak to you before I turn the remains over to the medical examiner. I didn't want to start something that you might resent me for."

"If she killed him, Robbie, she needs to go to jail for it. That's the law."

"I still need you to tell me what *you* want me to do," King said, holding his ground. But it occurred to him in that moment that maybe his moral compass had slid a bit off center since working with Lou. Once upon a time he had viewed the world as black and white as Dick did. It seemed as if now those days were in the distant past.

"Turn them in," Dick said finally, his voice weak. The cheerfulness was gone and in its place was only exhaustion. King was sorry to have robbed him of his good spirits. "Just make sure you send it to the Baton Rouge office. It's their jurisdiction, and Pamela—Dr. Mason—is good. She won't make a mistake."

"She working tomorrow? If I overnight the package it would be there tomorrow." King eyed the post office to make sure it was still open. The times painted on its door said King still had two hours.

"She's there until six every day, Monday through Friday. Sometimes later. It's a big department but she'll be there. She's a bit of a workaholic, like the rest of us. But if you're sending it to Baton Rouge, why don't you just drive it in? You'd get there in what? Forty-five minutes? Or maybe something has you tied up."

It wasn't a bad idea. And King could use a long drive. Driving had always helped him clear his head and solve his problems better.

"I'll do that," King said. "And I'll let you know what I find out."

"Please do."

King ended the call, his heart heavy. He'd been honest. That was the best he could do.

Placing the wrapped jawbone on the seat beside him, King pulled away from the post office, the nose of his Buick pointed in the direction of Baton Rouge.

26

———————

Rachel Frisk entered Hellman House with the same sense of disdain that overtook her *every* night she had to return to this godforsaken place. It was the smell. Those bruised and wilted flowers placed in every corner of Hellman brought to mind the stench of rotting flesh.

After all, this place was full of walking corpses.

Only on the nights where she decided to show one of these poor souls mercy did she find any peace in this place. The thrill and excitement of rectifying an egregious wrong was supported by her ironclad knowledge that this was her purpose. This was what she was here for—to relieve this miserable world of its suffering.

She'd found such relief after ending Dorothy Brown's life. She'd done the woman a great favor, that pitiful creature, neglected by her own family, and so riddled with cancer that the pain made it difficult for her to sleep or find a moment of bodily peace. She'd spent nearly every night roaming these antiseptic halls, uneasy.

Rachel *knew* she was right to set Dorothy free.

Yet everyone in Hellman had acted as if a great atrocity had been committed. A scandal. An injustice.

But the only injustice that Rachel could see was letting a woman live so long past her prime as to become a burden to herself and others.

Unfortunately, that brief relief that Rachel had enjoyed in the afterglow of Dorothy's death was fading. Already she felt the lights were too bright. The cloying stench too intrusive. Her own skin itching with unspent energy.

It had been only six weeks between Dorothy and the one before her, Mr. Chavez. Not two weeks had passed since Dorothy's death and already the dissatisfaction had returned. The relief she enjoyed between mercies was shortening.

Why?

What was she going to do about it?

Maybe she should've killed Jesse Elmer after all. She'd almost done it. He was a good candidate, comatose and useless. No family. No one to make a fuss. His care was even paid for by the state, veteran that he was. What a waste.

But something had changed Rachel's mind. An instinct. She'd gone into the room, ready to take care of that problem, only to have a sudden urge to leave. The walls of Elmer's room had closed in on her a little and her desire to be out of there became so intense that she had left. Walked right out without a second thought.

She'd been halfway down the hall before she got ahold of herself.

She'd decided she was being silly. Paranoid. She'd even gone back to Elmer's room, only to find that he wasn't alone anymore.

That woman was with him. The one with the mirrored sunglasses and leather jacket. Rachel was still trying to decide what to do about her because—

"Rachel," someone called.

Rachel's mind spun to a stop as a plump nurse named Nancy waved to her from behind the desk. The nurses' station was a mess, per usual. It was always like that on Nancy's shifts.

"What is it?" Rachel asked, unable to hide her impatience.

Nancy offered her something between two fingers. "Someone left this for you."

Rachel went to the station and took it. It was an envelope with her name printed neatly on the front in that old cursive she'd gotten used to seeing from Hellman's residents.

They don't even teach cursive anymore, she thought as she slid her nail under the corner of the back flap and tore the envelope open.

It wasn't until that moment that she considered perhaps it was better to open the note alone. Too late now. Nancy was already watching her with curious eyes.

Rachel freed the folded paper from its envelope. It was a nice piece of stationery with bluebirds singing in the corners of the page.

I know what you did to Dorothy. I have proof. Leave Hellman tonight and never come back, or I'll turn you in to the police.
—Moira Bradley

Rachel's heart knocked in her chest.

"Is it a tip?" Nancy asked, misreading Rachel's surprise. "Every month when old Mr. Sampson gets his pension, he gives me a fat tip and I love him for it."

"It's not a tip," Rachel said. "Just a thank you note."

Nancy smacked her lips. "That's still nice. Though it does feel nicer when there's fifty bucks in the card."

Face burning, Rachel slipped the note into the front pocket of her scrubs and headed for the elevators.

I know what you did.

I have proof.

Did that old bitch really think Rachel would just take this threat lying down? That she would just pack it up and run because one feeble old woman thought she knew something about anything?

Rachel's anger hardened to a cold stone in her gut.

No.

She wasn't going to be stopped by Moira Bradley or anyone else. She knew what she was doing. More than that, she knew she was *right*.

At the end of the hallway, she pushed the elevator button. The up arrow illuminated green and the steel doors opened. Rachel stepped inside.

There was a better way to handle this temporary problem. And Rachel *would* handle it.

Now.

It was after nine when King made it back to Margo Manor. Before he reached the stairs leading up to the bedroom, he saw the light in Rita's office was on. He considered knocking. He had so many questions, but he couldn't bring himself to ask. If he did, Rita would know the sharp turn the case had taken.

Let her have her peace for a few days more, he thought.

But as he looked at that light seeping out into the dim hallway, he suspected there was no peace for her. Perhaps she hadn't had peace for a very long time.

King tried to sleep. After washing his face and getting ready for bed, he had climbed beneath the covers. He'd found Piper's note telling him that she was helping Lou with something and would be back later.

Scream if the ghosts come for you, she'd written at the end of the note, and King had laughed at that.

If the ghosts come?

It amused him that Piper was more afraid of these supposed ghosts hurting King than the fact that he was sleeping under the same roof as a killer.

A possible killer, he corrected.

It might be threadbare, but King tried to hold on to the fact that Rita remained innocent until proven guilty. The fact was that he didn't want her to be guilty, and he still hadn't figured out why. Was it because Detective White thought so highly of her and King owed him so much? Or was it something about Rita? A feeling that she was trapped under the weight of something terrible and deserved better. And he wanted to be the one to help her free of that weight.

As he tossed and turned in his warm room, the lumpy mattress doing him no favors, King replayed his short visit with the medical examiner.

The lab had smelled of formaldehyde, giving him a headache that had lingered until he was almost back to the manor.

He'd been worried that the jawbone was too damaged, but the medical examiner had assured him that they could pull DNA out of a tooth's pulp, and given that Johnny Golden was a cold case already logged in their system, she might know if it was a match as soon as tomorrow morning.

Tomorrow morning.

That didn't leave King much time to find the exact location where it had been found and come up with a good story as to how he'd come across it.

He would have to ask Lou to take him to this so-called swamp, so he could get the GPS coordinates. He'd also need to figure out what he was going to say to Rita. And why he— the one person who was supposed to be on her side, defending her honor for a crime that she didn't commit—had turned against her like everyone else.

His stomach clenched.

He didn't know how he would face her when the time came.

After an hour of these apprehensive thoughts, King accepted that he wouldn't find sleep lying in this stuffy room, tossing and turning. The best remedy for nights like this was to get up and do something.

King threw back the covers. After some digging, he found the small UV light he'd brought on impulse at the last moment.

The medical examiner had been kind enough to explain that the weapon used on Nova was square but heavy and that it was likely the corner of the object that had cracked the girl's skull.

Instead of lying in bed and tossing through the night, King thought it would be a better use of his time to search the fourth floor and look for the weapon. It was possible that Aubree—*or the killer*, he quickly corrected—had wiped it down and left it where it belonged. After all, if no one ever searched these old rooms and all their many possessions, why would she have to worry about getting caught and go through the trouble of smuggling the item out of sight?

There was a chance that she'd cleaned it well—*too* well— and that the UV light wouldn't show any blood.

You've nothing else to do, he told himself. *You might as well try.*

Dressed, King slipped from his room, down the hall, and up the stairs to the top floor of the house. He kept one ear tuned toward the main floor, should Rita hear him moving about and come to investigate.

But the house remained silent. There wasn't so much as a breeze scratching at the large windows.

Once he reached the top landing, he stood in the darkness for a full minute, listening to the settling house.

He crept to the first room on the left and shut the door

behind him before turning on the UV light. He swept it high and low, searching the walls, the floor, the mantel, and furniture. He combed anything and everything for the smallest stray drop of blood, hoping that even if Aubree—or whoever—had taken or cleaned the weapon, it was possible that they'd left some trace evidence behind.

King struck gold in the third room, the one closest to the balcony.

By the mantel, below the dark-eyed portrait of a domineering figure, King found three drops of blood on the carpet. Where the fireplace ended and the carpet began, those three drops burned bright in the purple glow of the UV lamp.

Carefully, slowly, he combed the mantel, looking for any object that would fit the medical examiner's description of a weapon.

But there was none. There was, however, a small gap, noticeable to the eye, in how the mantel's decorations were arranged. On the left were three objects, but on the right only two, making it look unbalanced.

A wooden horse figurine, a small porcelain girl holding a basket of eggs, and a vase sat to the left of the portrait's frame. To the right, a dog figurine, tail erect, nose pointing to something, and beside that, a silver dish.

Perhaps it was only a coincidence, but King wondered if there had been a sixth object. If there had been, where was it now?

Still, he inspected the fireplace and each object slowly, looking for any signs that they had been scrubbed or washed clean.

When that returned nothing, he combed the room again, looking under the mattress and couch cushions, in corners, any place where someone might stash a weapon in a panic.

He found nothing.

He took two photos of the blood—a normal one, with it invisible to his eye, and a second using the UV light.

Disheartened, he crept from the room and closed the door behind him, wondering if he would be able to sleep now that no other distractions awaited him.

Just before he reached the stairs, a cool breeze slid across his cheek. It felt like a loving caress. A whisper along his skin.

The hair on the back of his neck rose.

Slowly, he turned and looked behind him. But the hallway was dark, still. There was no menacing figure or haunted face rushing toward him.

He was alone.

And yet, there it was again, that kiss of air.

A thought came to him.

Hadn't Mel said there was a secret room up here? Somewhere behind a false wall?

He held his hand out in front of him, centering the cool air on his palm and following it until his hand was pressed against the wallpaper.

He tried to remember Mel's instructions for finding the passageway.

The first two attempts yielded no results. The wall remained firmly shut against him.

On the third try, the wall gave ever so slightly, and he began to sense the shape of the barrier and how it moved under his hands. He adjusted his method accordingly, and sure enough, it opened, revealing a sliver of pitch-black darkness.

He couldn't bring himself to step into that darkness blind, so he extended his hand into the gap between the wall and turned on the UV light. A small hallway, not much wider than himself, glowed purple.

He stuck his head in first, looking one way, then the next.

His heartbeat sped up, knocking uncomfortably in his

chest. He'd listened to Piper too much. There was no reason to believe for even a second that a ghost was going to pop out and grab him.

It was far more likely that he would encounter the killer in here, if this was her secret hideout.

King squeezed into the passageway and shone the light ahead of him. As he moved, his shoulders brushing the walls, he fought against his old claustrophobia. He tried to breathe against the tightening of his throat, the growing panic of his mind.

This isn't a collapsed building, he reminded himself. *You aren't going to suffocate in here.*

Probably.

Just as his fear was about to get the best of him, the passageway broke open and a small room glowed with purple UV light.

"What is all this?" he whispered.

He'd found the shrine.

There were full bottles of unopened booze. Men's clothes, jewelry. There was candy and chocolate and other treats. The most imposing object was the oil painting. A young man featured in its center, posed like a French prince for his portrait. The frame itself was at least five feet tall.

It really did look like Johnny Golden. But given the old style of the painting, it was hard to believe. An ancestor, maybe?

The portrait took up almost the entire wall. King looked up and realized that the ceiling was no more than an inch or two above his head, but he ignored this. No need to give his mind more ammunition to feed his claustrophobia.

He bent down at the man's feet and began to inspect the items one by one, looking for a possible murder weapon. As he searched, he began to understand why Lou and Melandra had called the shrine obsessive. There was no denying it.

Off to one side, wrapped in a towel, King found a horse. A twin to the figurine he'd seen on the mantel in the bedroom. The base of the statue was large and square, just as the medical examiner had described the murder weapon.

It was true that it had been wiped down, but King could see fingerprint whirls in the purple UV light and smears of what could be blood. It had been cleaned but not well.

He carefully wrapped the horse in the towel and stood.

Using his phone's camera, he took a picture of the shrine, though the quality would suffer in the absence of decent light.

His eyes kept being drawn to the man at the shrine's center.

The only question was, why was the shrine hidden in this secret room?

If it was Johnny Golden in the portrait, had Aubree—who'd been reported by her fellow staff members as a bit of a kleptomaniac—stolen these objects over the years and placed them here at her lost lover's feet?

Was it done out of love? Mourning? Madness?

The only way to find out, he knew, was to ask her.

King gave the shrine one more appraising look and turned to go.

Except he couldn't leave.

A dark figure blocked his exit. "What the hell are you doing in here?"

27

———————

Rachel stood in Moira Bradley's doorway for several minutes, her eyes fixed on the lumpy form lying in the elevated bed.

The old woman was turned away from her, facing the far wall beside the unlit bathroom.

She doesn't even know I'm here, she thought. A thrill ran through her.

She doesn't know anything.

Rachel threw one last look over her shoulder, checking both sides of the hallway to make sure she was alone. Satisfied, she pulled the door closed behind her with a resounding click.

A moment before, the room had felt cold, but now a flush of heat pooled in her face. Her cheeks burned.

As she approached the bed, that horrible smell from her nightmares grew stronger. The stench of wilted flowers, of sagging, rotting flesh. Her stomach turned, disgusted. Reflexively, her hand went to the syringe in her pocket, her fingers wrapping around its disposable casing.

She was right on top of the woman now. Rachel saw the

nest of gnarled gray hair sticking out from under the blanket. She couldn't remember if this one was hard of hearing or not. She must be. She hadn't so much as stirred since Rachel had entered the room.

All the better, she thought. A wave of tenderness washed over her. There was no need for her to suffer any longer.

She fingered the hidden syringe again. Unable to contain her excitement, she pulled it from her pocket and admired it lovingly in her hand. The weight of it.

The finality.

Don't get carried away. That's how you get caught.

And she had so much to do first.

Fortunately, Moira Bradley didn't have monitors attached to her body. There was nothing to disconnect so as to not alert the station of the resident's respiratory distress.

There was still the call button. Rachel always moved the call buttons out of reach in case the patients woke before it was done and tried to signal for help. Sometimes the patients believed her when she soothed them, stroked them, told them that everything would be all right. That was, until she pressed a pillow over their faces to muffle the sound.

Only she couldn't find the call button.

Rachel frowned. The small remote was usually fixed in its cradle alongside the bed's rail.

It could be removed, of course, if the patient went to the bathroom and needed to call for help.

But the cradle was empty.

Rachel searched the blanket folds surrounding Moira's body, but it wasn't there. The old woman began to stir.

If she was going to end this tonight, she had to do it now. *Forget about the remote*, she scolded herself. It only mattered that it was out of reach.

With a hammering heart, Rachel pulled the syringe from

her pocket. She uncapped it, held it up to the dim light behind the patient's headboard.

That's when she saw them. Rachel would have sworn that just a moment before that corner had been empty. Dark, but certainly empty.

It was vacant no longer.

She lowered the syringe. "What are you doing here?"

She was unable to hide a flash flood of anger that seized her at this interruption.

"We could ask you that," one said. She stepped forward into the light and Rachel realized she was a girl. She had to be in her early twenties, blonde, silver rings glinting on her fingers.

"Were you looking for this?" asked another.

When this one stepped forward, taking her place beside the first, she saw her dark features and the proud tilt of her chin. She had a confidence that the first girl had lacked.

Rachel realized they had the call button remote.

This was bad. But how bad? What did they want?

The third one didn't come forward. She had a presence that drew Rachel's eye. It was a feminine form, as sleek as a jungle cat who remained in the darkness, just out of sight. The half-hidden creature turned her head and there was a flash of light.

Was she wearing glasses? What had caught the light like that?

Was it *her*?

The woman from Jesse Elmer's room? The one who'd managed to give her the slip before she could make sure she'd exited the building?

Rachel couldn't be sure without seeing her face.

"You need to leave. There are no visitors allowed at night. I don't know how you got in here but you can't—"

Moira began to stir. She was sitting up.

"Don't worry, Mrs. Bradley," Rachel said, plastering on her best smile. "We'll take care of this right away."

"We'll take care of *you*!" the old woman snapped. "This is for Dorothy!"

It wasn't until the woman tried to dig her fingers into Rachel's arm that Rachel finally understood what was happening here.

This was a trap.

A setup.

The old woman grabbed ahold of her and wouldn't let go.

Feet pounded down the hallway. The sound of the calvary told Rachel all she needed to know. They'd pressed the call button and were hoping to trap her here with the damning evidence of her deeds in hand.

If anyone found the syringe on her, that was it. They could test its contents. They'd know what she was doing.

Rachel wrenched herself free from the old woman's grip and darted toward the unlit bathroom, the hint of the toilet's porcelain rim enlarging in her mind's eye.

Flush it! her mind screamed. *Flush it before they find it!*

Without the evidence, she could easily explain away the situation. She could deflect the attention away from her and onto the three intruders. She could say they were lying, feeding the delusion of an already grieving and confused woman. If Rachel really played her cards right, she could get *these* three to take the fall for Dorothy's death.

Rachel had just touched the cool lid of the toilet, syringe in hand, when a boot connected hard with her hip, knocking her back.

She fell, her arms catching her. The syringe clattered to the floor, sliding to a stop a foot away. She began crawling toward it, only to catch another boot to her shoulder.

Rachel cried out, her cry morphing into a growl.

Moira Bradley, from where she sat huddled in her bed, gasped, her gnarled hands covering her mouth.

"Are you going to kill her?" the old woman said with alarm.

But she wasn't talking to Rachel. She was talking to the one who was pressing her boot into Rachel's shoulder, pinning her flat against the floor.

Now Rachel could see it *was* her.

The one with mirrored sunglasses and a leather jacket.

As she leaned over Rachel, smiling maliciously into her face, Rachel spotted the gun in its holster, resting against the woman's ribs.

Rachel wondered if she could reach up and pull the gun before the woman reacted.

As if reading her mind, the boot shoved mercilessly into her aching shoulder, digging in its heel harder and harder, until Rachel cried out.

The boot released her only a second before the door to the old woman's room was pulled open. Billy, Manny, and Amy came into view, with Donna pushing the crash cart behind them.

When they saw her on the floor and Moira sitting up in her bed, they hesitated, looking from one to the other. Their confusion was made plain on their faces.

"Are you okay, Mrs. Bradley?" Manny asked. He was at her bedside first, pulling the stethoscope off his neck, inspecting her with his hands.

"She was going to kill me," Moira said, groping for her oxygen mask. "She was gonna stick me with that and kill me like she killed Dorothy."

They were all looking at her now. At the scratches on her arm. At the syringe at Rachel's feet, the one that Moira pointed to so fervently.

Billy's face was the only one that still held an ounce of

hope in his sharp features. "What were you doing in here, Rachel? Moira's not your patient."

It was a plea. A desperate question. It only served to sharpen the suspicion and horror on the other two nurses' faces.

"Me? What am *I* doing here?" Rachel hissed, pulling herself to her feet. She made to grab the syringe, but Manny was already picking it up, pulling it out of her reach.

They have nothing on me, she thought. *They'd have to prove it was even mine.*

"I'm in here because I *work* here," she said, straightening. "And she attacked me. Look."

She showed them the scratches on her arm.

"I was just doing my job and—"

"Why do you have this syringe?" Amy interrupted, her voice cold. "What's in it?"

How dare she look down on me, Rachel thought. That woman had three kids by three different fathers. How dare she—

"It isn't mine," Rachel said, her teeth gritting. "It was theirs. They brought it in here."

Billy's and Manny's faces pinched in confusion. Amy just looked sad.

"Who?" Billy asked.

These idiots.

"Them—" Rachel went to point out the obvious, the three women in the room who weren't supposed to be there. *That's* who. Only when she turned, they weren't there.

There was no one in the room but Mrs. Bradley and the nurses.

As if sensing what Rachel would say next, Amy turned on the lights, filling the room with harsh fluorescence. She followed Rachel's gaze to the empty corner.

"Who do you think is in here, Rachel?" Amy asked, incredulous.

Rachel pushed open the bathroom door and turned on the light. She looked behind the door, behind the shower curtain.

Nothing.

There was no one.

It was empty.

"I don't—"

Rachel looked to the old woman, half expecting her to tell them the truth. But her eyes gleamed with triumph, her wicked smile hidden behind her oxygen mask.

Rachel lunged at her.

Billy took ahold of Rachel's arm. Furious, she wrenched herself away—or tried to.

"Call Nancy," Amy said to Manny. "Get security up here. We'll need someone to hold her until the director and police arrive."

Rachel pushed and thrashed in Billy's arms, trying to free herself but to no avail.

"I'm sorry," Billy said, his grip firm. And at least it sounded as if he meant it. "But I can't let you go."

"Man, I feel like we should have popcorn for this," Piper said, her gaze fixed on Hellman House.

It stood as proudly illuminated tonight as it had on the first night Lou had seen it weeks ago. Only now Lou was thrumming with satisfaction rather than unease.

"There she is," Dani said, wrapping her arms around herself.

Rachel was being escorted out of the main entrance to the waiting police car with its flashing blue and red lights. She was in handcuffs. Her expression furious. She jerked away as one of the officers tried to push her head down to help her clear the doorjamb.

The car door shut.

"Another day, another life saved," Piper said with a contented sigh. "Good job, team. We should celebrate with Moira. She was awesome."

"You can check on her after you take me home," Dani pleaded. "I'm out of adrenaline and I've got work in the morning."

"Maybe I can come home with you?" Piper said hopefully. "We can snuggle."

Dani squeezed her. "You still have a killer—or two, don't you? Are you really going to leave King hanging?"

"Ugh. No," Piper groaned into Dani's neck while Dani rubbed her back. "I guess you're right."

The police car pulled out of the Hellman parking lot, throwing its lights across the building's façade. As she watched it drive off into the night, Lou's compass began to whirl and click.

"We need to go," Lou said.

Piper let go of Dani. "Why? What's happened? You've got a tone. What's with the tone?"

"King needs us."

"Oh shit, is it the ghosts?" Piper asked. Her hand went to her throat.

"Not a ghost," Lou said, trying to gain a better sense of what awaited them on the other side of the shadows. "Something worse."

28

____

For a moment King could only look at the shadow. Then he noticed the big hair. The woman's voice. Even this late at night, in this dim room, it was hard to mistake Rita's silhouette for someone else's.

"Rita," he said, his breath leaving him.

"Turn on your light again," she said.

King did as she said, in part because he wanted to see her face. He wanted to know for sure that was who he was looking at.

He chose his phone over the UV, which filled the room in a cold blue light.

He was relieved to see it was Rita. Though she had looked ghostly in the ethereal glow of the UV. The shadows tracing the bones of her face gave her a corpse-like appearance, one he could have done without.

She frowned at the shrine taking up the far wall.

"What the hell is all this?" she asked.

"It appears to be a secret room."

"I see that," she said, her irritation thickening. "Why is all of this here?"

She bent down to look at the jewelry, silver dish, and other offerings clustered on the floor.

King let her inspect it all without offering his comments.

When she got closer to the painting, she gasped. "Johnny."

"I wondered if it was really him," King said.

"His grandfather commissioned this portrait for his sixteenth birthday," Rita confirmed. "How the hell did it get in here? It must be sixty pounds. Who carried it?"

It was a good question.

King didn't want to share his theory yet. It wasn't that he was a superstitious man, but information in the wrong hands had a way of running interference in a case. What would Rita do if King told her he suspected that Aubree Owens, the very woman Rita had deemed *harmless*, had built this shrine? That she was obviously stronger than she looked. That Aubree worshipped Rita's dead husband. That she might even have killed Nova because she'd discovered this very room and knew her secret. Or maybe because Nova was going after her new man, Michael.

No, he thought. Now was not the time to show his cards.

"I'm not sure," he said. "But it looks like someone has been taking things from around the house and putting them here for a while. Did you notice these things were missing?"

"Sometimes," she admitted. "I suspected one of the staff must be doing it. They've all got sticky fingers. Every one of them."

King didn't correct her.

"What are you holding?" Rita asked, motioning toward the bundle in his arms.

"I can't tell you," he said calmly.

"The hell you can't!" she cried. "If that's my property—"

"It's evidence, Rita," he said, pulling it out of her reach.

Still she tried to take it. Still he held it at arm's length. Given their height difference, it was easy to do.

When she refused to stop, he groaned.

"Rita, come on! Do you want your fingerprints on the murder weapon that killed Nova Perry?"

This stopped her.

She retracted. "That's what killed Nova?"

"I'll know for sure once I submit it for evidence," he said, straightening his shirt. "But we can agree you shouldn't touch it, am I right?"

"Yes. I'm sorry. I'm just so tired of all this." She collected herself. "Can't I know what it is?"

"I think it's best you don't," he said. "What if they try to interview you about it? If your ignorance is genuine, I think it will work in your favor."

But if that jawbone turns out to be Johnny's, he thought, *there's nothing I can do to protect you. You'll hang the same for one killing as well as two.*

"Someone in this house has been stealing my things, hiding them in this room, and that person is probably a murderer. That's what I'm to understand?" she asked.

"It's a possibility," he said, not wanting to say more.

"Why am I not surprised?"

She sounded so tired. Her voice thin and haggard. And the way she wrapped her arms around herself made King think of a lost little girl.

"This won't be solved tonight," King told her, trying to keep the pity out of his voice. "Why don't you go to bed? It's late."

She looked ready to fight him on principle, but she only shrugged.

"After you," she said.

It took his force of will not to run down the passage away from her. Holding the horse that had most certainly caved in

Nova's skull was a firm reminder not to let murderers walk behind you in unlit passageways.

But King stepped out into the stuffy, warm hallway with his skull intact and a very tired and defeated woman behind him.

"How did you find this?" she asked, gesturing at the hole in the wall.

He couldn't tell her about Melandra or Lou.

"There was a draft," he said. "It was noticeable given how warm it was up here. I followed it and found the seam in the wall."

He let her work out how to close it, watching her pull the door and slide it shut with a click. This suited him fine, considering he didn't want to put the murder horse down for a second.

"So many secrets in this house," she murmured, her eyes still fixed on the wallpaper before her. "I would have never come here if I'd known how it would turn out. Falling for Johnny was the biggest mistake of my life."

"You weren't happy?" King asked.

After a long pause she said, "For a little while. In the beginning. Before I saw him for who he really was."

As if disgusted by this memory, she turned away from King, giving him her back.

"I'd go to bed now if I were you, Mr. King," she said. "I meant what I said about wandering around at night. I can see you listen to me as well as anyone else around here."

But there was no real anger in her voice this time. Only that exhaustion. The disappointment.

"Goodnight," he said.

She made no reply. She only descended the staircase, without so much as a backward glance.

King was about to return to his room when a voice whispered, "Oh man, I didn't know how that was going to go. I thought for sure we were going to have to karate-chop her or something."

Piper and Lou stepped away from the pocket of shadow collecting in the nook above the stairs.

King swore, trying to force his hammering heart back down from his throat. "Let's do this in my room."

Lou placed a hand on his arm and pulled them both through the dark before he could protest. He was still reeling from that nauseating feeling long after she released him.

"You showed her the shrine," Lou said.

"I didn't show her," King protested. He reached out and took hold of the closest post of his bed, still holding the bundle to his chest. "She showed herself by sneaking in after me."

"What are you holding?" Piper asked.

"I think it's the murder weapon."

Piper's eyes doubled in size. "We know that Aubree killed Nova now? We don't have a motive."

"About that," King began. "I have a theory."

"And we have ears," Piper said.

"What if Aubree was the woman that Johnny was going to run off with fifteen years ago, but Rita found out and killed him?"

Piper sank into one of the armchairs by the large window. The moon hung in the black sky outside like a luminous eye watching them.

"Then I would wonder why Aubree is still alive. Why wouldn't Rita kill them both?"

"Maybe Rita didn't know who her husband was leaving her for, only that he was leaving."

"If that's the case, then Aubree would have a reason to hate Rita and Rita would have motive for killing her husband. Doesn't explain how Nova Perry got caught in the crossfire though. What if Aubree had another reason to kill her?"

King considered the boyfriend, Michael. His "It's all my fault" confession. Maybe Aubree did have another reason. Maybe Michael had flirted with the girl, or hell, looked at her for a heartbeat too long.

"We need Aubree's confession," King admitted. "If we can get her to confess, then we will both know why she killed Nova Perry and confirm Rita's motive for killing her husband."

Piper turned to Lou. "What do you think. Another setup? Two for two?"

"You mean three for three," Lou corrected, her hands loose in the pockets of her leather jacket. King had no idea how she could wear that thing so comfortably in this unbearable heat. Her face wasn't even red. She wasn't sweating.

Was she inhuman?

"Even better," Piper said. "Three is my lucky number, and I'm feeling lucky."

King held up his hand. "What do you mean, a setup? Who did you set up? Does this have to do with where you were tonight?"

Piper slapped her leg. "Hoo-*boy*. Do we have a story to tell you."

29

———

Because they spent the better part of the night working out the details for confronting Aubree and capturing her confession, King's eyes were red and raw by the time they were ready to set their plan into motion. And he hadn't even done the heavy lifting. Lou had served as pack mule, retrieving the equipment and supplies they needed—now tucked away in two black duffels beside King's bed.

He was lying in bed trying to decide how to contact Aubree when he received the text.

The medical examiner was short and to the point. King wasn't sure if that was just Dr. Mason's style, or if it was because a human could only give someone so much information before four in the morning.

Confirmed. The remains belong to Johnny Golden.

King's heart sank. That meant that they didn't have a lot of time to get a confession from Aubree. Dr. Mason's report would trigger a response the moment her findings were reported to the proper authorities.

State investigators would descend on Margo Manor in a

matter of hours. Rita might be taken into custody and questioned. Aubree could run—or she could watch out of curiosity to see if her plan would be realized and her revenge complete.

King climbed from the bed, placing his feet on the floor. He composed a quick text to Dick, passing along the news.

By the time he was dressed, Dick had replied, *Do what you need to do.*

What he needed to do.

He needed to get Aubree alone as soon as possible.

He would have to wake the girls. He'd sent them to bed not an hour before with the promise of decent sleep, but it couldn't be helped.

They had no time to lose.

IT WAS STILL DARK OUTSIDE WHEN AUBREE'S HEADLIGHTS swung onto the narrow driveway leading to Margo Manor. King stood in the garden, in the patio at its center, waiting exactly where he'd told her he'd be when he called her forty minutes before, feigning urgency. He watched the lights move toward him, his heart speeding up as they grew closer.

He reviewed his story, practicing it one last time in his mind.

There was a break in the case and I need to speak to you immediately. There was an important discovery regarding Johnny Golden's disappearance. Maybe you can help.

King thought the mention of Johnny Golden would be more likely to bring Aubree out to the house than referencing Nova's case. Mentioning Nova at all might be enough to make her run.

Sure, Lou could find Aubree no matter where she ran to, but what they needed was the confession, the motive that would seal both Rita's and Aubree's fates.

The fact that Aubree had come running at the mention of Johnny's name was damning enough. Who cares enough about their dead employer to get up at four in the morning for a clandestine meeting in the dark?

But Aubree's eagerness wasn't enough to guarantee a conviction in court.

The twin beams of the headlights swung into the parking lot and turned off.

"Are you ready?" King asked the tree awash in shadows.

"My eyes have been dipped in acid, and I have the absolute worst crick in my neck, but yes. I am ready. Somehow." Piper yawned, tears forming in the corners of her eyes. "But you better believe that when this is done, I'm taking a week off to sleep and follow my girlfriend around like a puppy."

King humored her with a nervous laugh. "Duly noted."

He couldn't see Lou at all. She had become one with the darkness beneath the large tree. He thought he glimpsed a pale hand as Piper was pulled into the dark, but he couldn't be sure.

And he couldn't look any harder. A car door had shut. Footsteps were approaching. And one of his two murderesses, Aubree Owens, was stepping into view.

Moonlight cut dramatically across her face, illuminating half of it. The other half remained covered in shadows.

I see your two faces, he thought.

Frogs croaked. Cicadas hissed in the trees. King hoped the microphone he'd left in Piper's capable hands would be sensitive enough to pick up Aubree's voice at this distance despite the interference from nature's orchestra.

"Mr. King," she said, her hair loose and down around her shoulders. Her eyes were wet and shining. The hurried and unkempt look of her made King wonder if she'd ever met Johnny here in this very garden on some night looking just like this.

"What's happened?" she asked.

"I found Johnny's remains," he told her. No point in holding back now. There simply was no time for preamble.

Impossibly, her eyes widened. "Where?"

"In a swamp, here on the property."

She grabbed his hand and squeezed it. He forced himself not to pull away.

"But we looked. We looked everywhere for him."

"You don't seem surprised to find out he's dead." King said it gently, careful to keep any hint of accusation out of his voice. "I thought everyone in this town believed he'd ran off with a woman."

"It—" She considered her words. "It was just something I've always felt was true. Why would he run off and leave behind his beautiful house and all his money? It didn't make sense to me."

Nice save, King thought.

"What I want to tell you now, you might find shocking," he said.

She finally released his hand, and something inside him unclenched.

"You know who killed him," she said softly.

"Everything points to Rita. Rita must have known he was going to leave with another woman, but rather than let that happen, she killed him. Maybe it was planned. Maybe she acted impulsively out of jealousy or rage. Who knows? It doesn't matter. The fact remains that she killed him rather than let him run off with another woman. She drove his body out to the swamp, tossed him in, and has been living off his hard-earned wealth ever since."

It didn't matter that King thought men like Johnny rarely *earned* a thing in their lives. It only mattered that Aubree believed him sympathetic to her lover's misfortune.

"Why are you telling me?" she asked cautiously.

"First and foremost because you've worked here the long-est. I thought if anyone knew who Johnny was seeing back then, it'd be you. Do you remember anything?"

Aubree hesitated, taking a step away from him.

"I know it's been a long time," he said, shifting his weight from one leg to the other. "But maybe you remember seeing a new woman around? Was Johnny giving anyone extra atten-tion? Did he start talking about anyone differently, or maybe Rita even said a name?"

"Why does it matter who he was seeing?" she asked.

"If I could find her and get her to testify, we would have Rita's motive on record. Motive is very important when convicting someone of a crime in court. If we can't uncover Rita's motive for killing him, she might never be convicted. In fact, she probably won't be. The jury will just shake their heads and say, 'What reason did she have to kill him? None,' and let her go."

Aubree clasped her opposite arm as if cold. That was impossible. Even this early in the morning, King could feel the sweat forming on the back of his neck.

He was about to try a different tactic when she finally spoke up.

"It was me," she said.

His heart knocked. "What?"

"It was me. Johnny was going to leave Rita for me."

He gave what he hoped was a convincing portrayal of surprise before saying, "You would've been just eighteen at the time. He was what? Forty?"

"I didn't care about that!"

That was the reaction he'd wanted. "Why didn't you tell anyone?"

She threw up her hands. "I tried! But no one would believe that Johnny—precious, perfect Johnny Golden—would pick me. *Me.*"

It was like now that she'd confessed to this one truth, the rest came easily. Her voice grew louder, her gestures more animated.

"But I *knew* what Rita had done," she growled. "I knew it."

"Would you be willing to testify to that in court? That he was going to run off with you? Would you have any proof that you were having an affair?"

"A few letters," she said. "They're old but I kept them. I kept every single one of them. They're full of the promises he made me about the life we'd have together. Promises that never came true."

Tears formed in the corners of her eyes.

King lowered his voice. "Your testimony could be what puts Rita away for a very long time. If you don't tell the jury everything, then there's no point in pressing charges. Are you willing to commit to this?"

There. King saw, at long last, what he'd been looking for.

The menace. The triumph.

"I'll do it," she said. "I'll tell them everything."

"Why would you do that?" King asked.

She hesitated.

"I'm sorry for pressuring you, but I need to know your reason. Lawyers are very aggressive in court. If they can find a way to cast doubt on your testimony, they'll try to do that. If you're not committed—"

"I'm committed."

He frowned. "Are you? I've heard witnesses say that before. I need a good reason why—"

"A reason!" Aubree threw her hands up. "She took everything from me. Johnny. My future. My dreams. He promised me everything and I loved him, and she took that away from me. I *hate* her."

She struggled to get ahold of herself, wringing her hands violently.

"Okay, I believe you," he said. "You do have a good reason."

Even if you sound a little crazy saying it.

A breeze rolled through the garden and King suppressed the urge to look toward the tree on his left. He kept his eyes focused on Aubree.

Now, he thought, *I need to land the final blow.*

"I need your help to put Rita away. I can't do this without you, so I'm going to be honest. I found something else when I was looking for evidence. I found it right after I found Johnny's remains."

King went to the nearest bush, bent down, and retrieved the wrapped bundle he'd hidden there for exactly this moment.

He waited until her eyes were on it before he began to unwrap it. He watched as her horror grew, the realization of her predicament plain on her face.

"It has your fingerprints on it," he said, showing her the exposed horse figurine.

"Of course it does. I must've cleaned that thing a hundred times." She'd spoken too fast.

"And it has Nova's blood on it," he added. "This says nothing of where I found it. You *know* where I found it."

Aubree swallowed, her eyes still wide with fear. He could see her mind racing, searching for an explanation.

"You struck Nova Perry with this before you pushed her off the balcony. You don't have to lie to me about it. I just don't know *why* you did it. But I need to know if we're going to be a team."

Aubree took another step away from him. She looked ready to run.

"I didn't tell anyone," King said. "I'm telling you this

because I want you to know we're in this together. We can make this go away."

Aubree's face hardened with suspicion.

King was determined not to lose her now. "It happens all the time. Police overlook certain crimes so they can get the *real* bad guy. We both know that Rita is the real monster here, and we need your testimony in order to put her away for the rest of her life. If you'd be willing to testify against Rita, I'm sure the investigation around Nova's death will be closed. It would be so easy to just rule it as an accident."

"An accident," Aubree repeated dumbly, the first sign of hope creeping back into her features.

Close, King thought. *I'm so close.*

"We just have to get your story straight before the police arrive," King said. "Before they come to arrest Rita."

"My story?"

"Yeah." King shrugged as if to say, *No big deal! People kill people, lie to the cops about it, and get away with murder all the time.*

"My story," she repeated.

"Your story. I'm sure you had a good reason for hitting Nova. Maybe she tried to hit you first. Maybe the two of you got into a fight and things got out of hand. It was an accident, but you didn't want to tell anyone because you were scared. And sorry."

Only Aubree didn't look sorry. She looked furious, her jaw tight and gaze burning.

"She wanted Michael," she said, jaw working.

"Michael Reed? The gardener?" he asked. "Were the two of you together?"

"For almost eight years. After I lost Johnny, I was so heartbroken. Every ounce of my will to stay alive was taken from me the night Rita took Johnny."

Interesting choice of words, since it was you who stole her husband, he thought.

"But Michael was good to me. He cheered me up. He made me laugh. He couldn't replace Johnny but he was good company. He promised he'd always be there for me, and he was. Until he wasn't."

King didn't move. Didn't speak. He was afraid of breaking the spell memory held on her.

So close, his mind chanted. *So close, so close, so close. Come on—*

"I saw him helping her into her car, carrying her stuff for her. I saw the way he was smiling at her, laughing with her. That was how it had been for *us* in the beginning, before we began to fight so much. I knew he was going to leave me the second he reached out and rubbed dirt off her cheek with his thumb."

If Michael really was so much older than Nova, King could imagine that he'd thought the gesture innocent. The way one might rub dirt off a kid's face.

Was that why he'd taken her death so hard? Was that why he'd blown his own brains out?

"Were you surprised when he killed himself?" King asked.

She shook her head. "No. I already knew that it wasn't *me* he was in love with anymore."

"It didn't have to do with Johnny?" King asked.

Aubree searched his face. "What?"

"You killed Nova to stop Michael from leaving you. It wasn't to frame Rita and avenge Johnny?"

Don't stop now, Aubree. I beg you. Give me all of it.

"It was both," she said. "I thought if Rita was blamed for Nova's death, Johnny could finally rest in peace. I wanted her to pay for what she'd done. She deserved to be punished."

His heart leapt. He could end this now. He could give the hand signal and end this.

But King thought of Michael's brother, sobbing, heartbroken, desperate for answers.

"That makes a lot of sense," he told her, hoping his real

opinion wasn't reflected on his face. "I just have one more question."

"What?"

"Did you ask Michael if he was flirting with her? Did you ask him if he intended to leave you?"

Aubree drew back from him. "Of course I asked him. I told him what I saw, and he tried to treat me like *I* was the crazy one. 'I was just helping her because it was heavy. I didn't want her to carry all that stuff. She's just a kid.' What bullshit. A kid my ass. I was her age when Johnny first spoke to me like that."

King suspected that said more about the sort of man Johnny Golden was than about the sort of man Michael was.

"Then he asked me if he could give Nova a ride to her brother's ball game and I just—I'm not *stupid*. I knew that he just wanted to get her alone. Take her down the backroads to any of the hundred pull-off spots back there."

"You took care of the problem," King said.

Aubree laughed bitterly. "Yeah. I took care of *the problem*. That very day before her shift was over, I took care of it. If she was dead there could be no ride to *the ball game*, could there? It was done."

King's stomach was sour. His throat tight. The more he listened to her, the sicker he felt. Not just with her but with himself.

How did I not see it? How?

"Why kill Nova?" King asked her. "Why not Michael?"

Aubree's mouth came open in surprise. She looked as if she'd just been slapped.

When she finally recovered, she said, "Because I'm not like *her*. I could never hurt someone I love."

"But you are like her. You're exactly like her."

King didn't think she'd heard him. Her eyes were fixed on the driveway.

Something sparked in the corner of King's vision and he turned to see sunlight filtering through the trees.

The police were almost here.

"Are they coming for Rita?" Aubree's voice was full of excitement.

For you, he thought.

"When will I get to testify?" she asked.

"I'm sure when they take you down to the station, you'll have all the time you want to tell them everything."

Her face pinched with confusion. "When they take *me*?"

King looked to the darkness then, and Piper stepped forward, the moonlight falling on her face.

"Did we get it?" King asked.

Piper held up her thumb. "Loud and clear, boss."

Good. Otherwise, he was going to have a hell of a time explaining why he'd gotten Herb and his folks to come out to the mansion so early in the morning.

Piper pulled her headphones off her head and lowered the recording device. "It was like she was talking right into the microphone."

Aubree looked from King to Piper, back to King. Her face screwed up in rage.

"You!" she screeched, and threw herself at King, fingers hooked like claws aimed at his face.

King managed to raise his arm in a protective gesture, only the blow never landed. A streak of light—no. A streak of *blond hair* crossed King's field of vision as Piper tackled Aubree. With one punch she knocked the woman to the ground.

It wasn't until Aubree was on her hands and knees cursing, spitting blood on the patio, that he realized Piper had hit her in the nose.

"I told you I couldn't leave you alone," Piper said, shaking out her hand.

"Let me see that," King said, taking her hand and inspecting the wrist. "Good punch."

She allowed him to examine it. "Then why does my hand hurt? It never hurts when I box with Bane."

"It's different punching without a glove," he told her.

Something moved in the corner of King's eye again, and for a moment he thought it was Aubree, coming for another attack.

But it was only Lou. She stood there in her leather jacket, eyes hidden behind her shades.

Aubree took one look at her and sank back to the patio. Maybe that was the reason why Lou had chosen to step out of the shadows and reveal herself.

King released Piper's hand. To Lou he asked, "You weren't going to step in?"

"Piper had it under control," she said.

Piper visibly straightened at that. Only her face showed a hint of doubt. "But, like, if I didn't you would've stepped in, right?"

Lou flashed them a smile. Sometimes it was unsettling when she did that.

Herb trotted up the concrete walkway with one of his deputies at his heels. He regarded the four of them, his eyes fixating on Aubree at the end of the sweep.

He frowned. "You're sure about this, Mr. King?"

That was enough to let him know that Herb had gotten his message all right and they were here for the maid and not for Rita. Even so, the criminal investigations unit couldn't be far behind.

"I have her confession on tape," King said. "And it was not obtained under duress."

It felt necessary to say that considering that Aubree was now cradling a bloody nose.

"She attacked me after she realized we were recording her."

"She do Michael too?" Herb asked, his face stricken.

"No," King said. "I think it was only Nova."

"As if that weren't terrible enough," Herb said. "Aubree, how you're going to look into the eyes of God, I don't know."

His disappointment was thick as he and the deputy lifted Aubree from the patio.

The officers carried her between them back up the walkway to the parking lot. King, Lou, and Piper kept a polite distance behind.

When the walkway ended and the door to Margo Manor loomed, King saw that Rita had come out to investigate the commotion. She stood on the porch of the great house with her bathrobe pulled tight around her.

She watched as Herb and the deputy shoved Aubree into the back of the police car.

When she saw King, she asked, "What's going on?"

"Aubree's being charged with the murder of Nova Perry," King said. He handed the wrapped murder weapon over to Herb, who took a peek at it and shook his head again.

"A damn shame. She was just a kid. This is gonna break her parents' hearts. I think they were dead set on believing it was an accident. The will of God and all that."

He slid the wrapped horse into a plastic evidence bag and tossed it into the front seat. King didn't think that was how one handled evidence, but this wasn't his town. Hell, in a couple of hours, none of this would be his problem anymore.

Rita descended the stairs and went to the police car. She stared into the backseat and regarded Aubree with disbelief.

"Aubree, why?" she asked.

"Because Johnny loved *me*."

King's breath caught in his throat. He watched the

emotions play across Rita's face in real time. The confusion, the shock, the disbelief.

Then, at long last, the anger.

"You," Rita said. "It was *you?*"

"You didn't know Aubree was the woman he was leaving you for?" King asked. He hoped the honesty as well as the unexpected nature of the question would be enough to startle the truth from her. More importantly, he hoped she would answer here within earshot of five witnesses.

And it worked.

"No," she said. "I had no idea."

30

Lou found Konstantine in the church. He was sitting in the pew, staring lovingly at the statue of Mother Mary, who beamed down at him. He did that sometimes, gazed at the Virgin, his mind lost in thought. But her compass was never wrong. He'd called her here for a reason.

He turned and looked at her suddenly as if sensing her. *"Amore mio."*

"You rang?" she asked. She had wanted to hunt after the excitement of watching the murderous maid get arrested. It was anti-climactic sometimes when capture didn't end in a kill.

He lifted the file folder off the pew beside him and held it out to her. "I completed the search on King's woman. Rita Golden."

Lou suppressed a snort. She wasn't sure King would appreciate Rita Golden being referred to as "his woman."

"It's interesting," he said as she took the folder. "He must have been a powerful man."

"What do you mean?" She took a seat beside him, the wood creaking under her weight.

"I had to dig for those," he said, nodding toward the folder in her hand. "He must've had the power to *make it go away*, as they say. Only someone with a lot of money or power can do that."

Lou opened the folder and began to thumb through its contents.

The photographs were horrifying snapshots of broken limbs and bruised flesh. A face so disfigured from a beating as to be unrecognizable.

A cold rage filled Lou. "How many?"

"At least seven women," he said. "He nearly killed one. She was in the hospital for six weeks."

Lou wondered if he'd really broken his jaw in a car crash or if some pitiful woman had had the gall to swing back.

"It was never about the cheating," Lou said. "The women left to save their lives."

"The first wife had a great deal of evidence," Konstantine said. "But she signed a non-disclosure in the course of their divorce in exchange for a large settlement. Her mother as well."

Lou snapped the folder shut.

"You look angry, *amore mio*. I am sorry I couldn't give you good news."

"I'm only angry that I can't kill a dead man twice," she said. She tapped his leg with the folder and stood. "Thanks for this."

"Where will you go?" he asked.

"To save Rita," she said. "King's going to blame himself for this."

"Good luck, *amore mio*. Come home to me soon."

Lou was halfway across the cathedral before she turned back. The beauty of him, with one arm draped over the back of a pew, his legs slightly spread. Everything about him made her want to stay.

"What is it?" he asked.

"If I can't stop this, how soon could you make a new life for Rita somewhere? She'll need a place to live, money. Maybe a whole new identity."

He gave her a devil's smile. "No time at all."

KING WAS PACKING HIS FINAL BAG. IT WAS THIRTY MINUTES before the manor opened for the day and he planned to be gone before it did.

He'd been looking for one of his belts when Lou stepped into the bedroom. He swore at the sight of her. "You scared me."

She handed him the folder without comment.

"What is it?" he asked. The very sight of it made his heart sink.

"Proof of Johnny Golden's crimes."

Despite his twisting guts, King opened the folder. The photographs made him feel sick. After a dozen of them, he pinched his eyes closed.

"He was a sick bastard," he said.

"He liked having a punching bag," Lou said. "He specialized in young women without much family."

"Women like Rita."

"Makes you wonder if Rita really killed him because of infidelity. I'd think his promise to leave her would be cause to celebrate."

Rita.

"Shit."

King abandoned his bag and fled the room. Still clutching the folder, he ran to the front office, skidding to a stop at its door.

"Rita? Rita!"

She wasn't there. The office was dark, the papers on the desk tidy and undisturbed.

At the far end of the hall, he spotted her on the porch looking out over the parking lot.

"Rita!"

He heard the cars screech to a stop. Someone in the driveway was asking for her name.

"What is this about now?" she called, stepping out of view.

"Rita, wait!"

He couldn't reach the entrance fast enough. When he stepped out into the morning, the dampness clinging to him, he saw Herb's patrol car and two unmarked vehicles beside it.

"Hey! Hey!" An officer was trying to cuff Rita.

Upon seeing him, one of the investigators in plain clothes approached him.

"Are you Robert King, the private investigator?" He was kind enough to extend his rough hand toward King.

"I am." King shook it with agitation. "Are you arresting her?"

"We've got enough to hold her and question her, thanks to you finding Johnny Golden's remains on this very property. That was good work."

King's stomach twisted. "I—"

"But it'll probably be the other one's testimony that sends her away to prison. Aubree Owens. If she's really got letters with Johnny promising to run off with her and marry her, then we'll get a trial at least. It'll be up to the jury to make the charges stick."

Rita saw King at last, her eyes locking on his.

"Don't let them do this, Robert! Don't let them do this to me!" Rita screamed over her shoulder as she was forced to the car.

All he could do was stand where he was and watch as her

emotions shifted from desperation, to surprise, to finally what he'd feared most—betrayal.

It was as if a horse had kicked him in the guts.

He went to her. He placed a hand on the officer trying to push her into the backseat.

"One minute," King said. "Just a minute, okay?"

The investigator scowled at him. "Talk to her through the window."

He shoved Rita into the unmarked car and shut the door. At least the back window was down.

King spoke quickly in a hushed voice. "Rita—"

"I trusted you!" she spat.

"I'm sorry. I want to help you. I really do."

"You have a sick way of showing it."

King opened the folder he'd been clutching this whole time and shoved it into Rita's face. Her anger disappeared. Horror rose up to replace it as she realized what she was looking at. The photographs full of her dead husband's handiwork.

"I know what he really was," King said, closing the folder. "Okay? I *know*."

The pain didn't leave her eyes as she searched his face. "Then how could you? How could you do this to me?"

"I'm sorry. I'm so sorry, I wasn't fast enough," he said. "But I will fix this. I promise."

"I'm going to need you to step away from the car now," the plain-clothes inspector said.

"I promise," he said again. "Just hold on, Rita. Please."

"Mr. King," the investigator said, his voice turning cold. "Step away from the car now."

King had no choice but to pull away from the window.

The manor's employees had begun to line up at the edge of the parking lot, watching the spectacle. Their expressions were a mix of curiosity and displeasure. King supposed he could understand. If Rita was going to prison, then the manor would be shut down and the "best job in town," as Birdie had called it, would be lost.

"Now, now, everybody," Herb said, speaking up over the commotion. "There's no need to worry. We'll sort all this out one way or the other and y'all can get back to livin' your lives in no time. Why don't y'all take the rest of the day off and check back with me tomorrow."

The footman didn't have to be told twice. He pulled his wig off his head and walked toward a beat-up red truck at the edge of the parking lot.

The others were just behind him.

"Are they going to be all right?" King asked the police chief.

"Oh, they'll be all right. We all will be. If Rita loses this place, I suspect the ol' lord of Basswood will buy 'er. I can't imagine he'd like anything more."

King barely acknowledged this. His eyes kept going back to Rita.

All he could do was stand in the parking lot, twisting the folder in his hands. He itched to show it to Herb or the investigators—anyone—and make a desperate plea on Rita's behalf.

But it was too late for that now. The damage was done.

King waited until the parking lot was vacated before retracing his steps back to his room, defeat heavy on his shoulders.

Lou was sitting beside his bag, one leg crossed casually over the other.

"I fucked up," King said. "I *really* fucked this up."

"Don't worry about it."

"Don't worry about it!" King threw the crumpled folder onto the floor. Several of the photographs slid out. "In case you forgot, Louisiana has the death penalty, and everyone in this town is ready to hang her as it is."

"It doesn't matter," Lou said. "She won't spend more than a night in jail."

"What?" His heart leapt. The relief coursing through him was enough to bring him to his knees. "You're going to save her?"

"When you fuck up"—Louie Thorne stood and flashed him a wicked smile—"it's time to do things my way."

31

Rita hadn't moved in twenty hours. She was starving. She needed to pee. She had managed to sleep at least, slipping in and out of consciousness on her stiff jailhouse cot for a few hours here and there, since her arrest and imprisonment.

King had told her to hold on. But she wasn't sure if she could do that. She'd been holding on for twenty years—ever since she'd married a monster and lost her life before it had even started.

Two black boots scuffed to a stop by her cot. She expected a guard.

What she had not expected was a woman in a leather jacket, packing two Berettas. Her eyes were hidden behind a pair of mirrored shades.

"Get up," the woman said.

Rita sat up, pressing her back against the cinder block walls in terror. "Are you here to kill me?"

Even in death, Johnny had friends in high places. Maybe they'd sent this woman to deliver retribution.

"No," the woman said. "I'm getting you out of here."

Before Rita could comprehend the situation or mount a defense, the woman took hold of her arm and pulled her through—what?

Rita didn't understand it. A moment before she was on the unforgiving jailhouse cot. Now they were standing in a room with city lights and pulsing traffic rushing by outside.

The woman released her.

"What?" Rita stumbled to the window. She stared out, uncomprehending.

It looked like a city. Rita didn't know the buildings or the street name. Were those Canadian license plates? "How—"

"I'm a little disappointed that you killed Johnny. I would've liked to do that myself," the woman said.

Rita turned to her. "What are you?"

"I think you'll be more interested in opening that duffel bag than hearing my life story," the woman said. She pointed at the bag sitting in the middle of the living room floor.

Rita felt like she was in a dream. Her legs were shaking from the lack of water or food since her arrest, but she barely noticed. Her mind was struggling to understand what was happening here.

She bent and unzipped the bag. A disturbing amount of Canadian cash was stacked neatly inside. On top was a wallet, complete with a license, credit cards. Beneath the wallet was a folder of documentation, even a Canadian passport. All of it had her photo but was in the name of Maxine Marsh.

She looked up. "Maxine?"

"I didn't pick it." The woman shrugged. "But he could change it if you hate it."

"Who? King?" she asked hopefully.

The woman said nothing.

Rita looked at the bag's contents again, her shock dilating.

"There are bank cards and everything," Rita said. *Is this real? Am I losing my mind?* "How is this possible?"

"This apartment is in your name too. It's leased for six months. You have everything you need to start a new life here in Toronto, or you could go somewhere else."

Rita looked at her photo—at *Maxine's* photo—in disbelief. Maxine was even smiling.

She began to cry and couldn't stop herself.

"Maybe Canada is too cold for you," the woman said at last.

"No, no, I'm sorry. I'm just—this can't be happening. He has friends. There's an investigation. What if someone finds me?"

She wiped her eyes with the hem of her shirt.

"He'll take care of that too. It might take us a minute to make sure we destroy *all* of Johnny's connections, but it'll get done. Can't have any vigilantes looking for you now, can we?"

Rita looked up at her through her tears. "You can do that? You can really make sure no one finds me?"

The woman smiled, and it sent a chill through Rita's bones. *Who the hell is she?*

"Finding people is my specialty," she said. "It won't take me long."

Rita didn't know what to say.

"Take a hot shower. Get yourself some dinner, some clothes. Hang out and rest for a few weeks, and then after that, you can do whatever you want. I'd avoid Louisiana for obvious reasons, but anywhere else should be fine."

Rita looked around the modest but clean apartment. The sack of cash at her feet. The promise of a new life.

"This has got to be a dream. It can't be happening. I've been trying to escape that house for twenty years."

"And now you have. Congratulations," the woman said.

She was leaning one hip against the island counter. "I've got to ask. My curiosity is killing me."

"What?" Rita sniffed.

"Why didn't you leave him when he said he wanted Aubree? You must have wanted to."

Rita held the duffel bag against her chest as if it were a shield. She was scared it—along with her freedom—was going to disappear.

"You're right. I did see it as an opportunity. At first. When he said he was seeing someone else, I asked for a divorce. Things had already been bad for a long time. I'd tried to leave before but he found me every time and dragged me home. And when we would get home, he'd hurt me so bad that I believed him when he said he would kill me if I ever tried again. When I asked for the divorce, that was the meanest I'd ever seen him. He lost it. *Completely* lost it."

"But you were ready," the woman said with a knowing smile.

"I'd bought a gun off of Michael Reed, my *gardener* of all people. It was under the table. I thought if I'd actually gotten a permit and all that, Johnny would have found out about it. I'd begged Michael not to tell anyone and he didn't. He didn't even ask what I needed it for, and when Johnny went missing, he didn't say a word. I was really surprised about that. Turns out he'd been friends with Johnny's first wife, Tricia, since they were kids. Maybe she'd told him what he was really like. I don't know. And now I'll never know."

"You asked for a divorce and that set Johnny off," the woman said. "Is that when you shot him?"

"Not right away. He started in on me. Punching me. Kicking me. Pulling my hair. He really liked to pull hair. There was a moment when he started choking me—I could actually feel my heartbeat slowing down in my head. I couldn't breathe. My vision was going black. I'd shot him twice in the chest before I even realized what I'd done. I was as surprised as he was. But there was no taking it back. He was dead. So I rolled him up in the carpet, threw him in the back of his huge truck, and drove six miles out to one of the hollows at the edge of the property. I about broke my back throwing him in there, but I did it. The very next day—like an act of God—a hurricane blew through and washed the truck clean. Flooded the land a bit. Erased all my tracks. I thought for sure Herb and them would find his body, but somehow they never did. It was a miracle. And this feels like a miracle, too. Is this really happening? Am I really free?"

"You are," the woman said. "Have a nice life, *Maxine*."

She turned to leave. Rita sprang to her feet. "Wait. What's your name? What about Robert?"

The woman stopped. "Louie Thorne. And I'll tell him you said thanks."

Louie Thorne.

Rita vowed to never forget the name.

"Please tell him—tell him I'm so grateful for everything. Tell him that—that asking him to come to the manor was the best decision of my life."

Louie Thorne smiled. "He knows."

KING KNOCKED ON MELANDRA'S APARTMENT DOOR AND Lady barked in response. He could hear her pressing her snout against the frame and sniffing deeply, trying to catch the scent of whoever was on the other side.

"Come on now," Mel told her. "Move aside, *ma grande*."

The door opened.

"Hi," King said.

Melandra returned the smile. "Welcome back, Mr. King. You're all in one piece, I see."

"I saw a ghost."

She arched a brow. "Did you now?"

Mel stood to one side so he could come in, and he did. Without asking, she poured him a glass of sweet tea and gestured toward her couch.

"Sit down and tell me about it," she said.

So King did.

In as much detail as he could recall, he recounted the moment he'd been about to drive away from Margo Manor for the last time.

He had just thrown the Buick in reverse when he saw a figure in his side mirror.

King pushed the door open and looked back at the house. On the balcony above the garden was a girl.

Young. Pretty.

She gave King a bright smile and a friendly wave. She looked familiar. He was certain he'd seen her face before. He lifted his hand to return the wave, but in that instant, she disappeared.

That's when he'd realized who she looked like.

Nova Perry.

When he finished his story, Mel said, "She was probably thanking you for solving the case and capturing the person who killed her."

As difficult as it was for King to accept what he'd seen with his own eyes, he did hope that was true. That maybe, just maybe, he'd actually helped *someone* this time.

It was still painful to think about Rita and that look of betrayal on her face as she was shoved into the police car. Even though Lou had reassured him that she was settled and doing well in Toronto, it still hurt.

Part of him was desperate to go to the prison during visiting hours and throw the—admittedly crumpled—photos of Johnny Golden's crimes down in front of Aubree. More than once he'd imagined himself telling her the truth. Making it clear that Rita had done her a favor.

She hadn't stolen Aubree's future. Aubree had done that herself.

But each of these mental rehearsals only ended in amplifying King's own shame, as he was forced to confront again and again his own failings in Rita's case.

If King had done a better job, if he'd been more careful and had asked the right questions, if he hadn't made so many assumptions...If he hadn't turned in that stupid jawbone, Rita would've never been arrested in the first place.

Mel seemed to sense his turbulent thoughts. The struggle he was trying to keep to himself.

"Have you eaten?" she asked him.

"No. But I don't want to go out either. Maybe I'll just make myself a sandwich before bed."

After searching his face, Mel said, "If you wouldn't mind a bit of company, I say we order takeout and watch a movie."

Lady put her head on King's knee, her tail wagging encouragingly.

King touched her on the soft spot between her large brown eyes and smiled. "How can I say no to that?"

32

————

Lou stood beneath the large fir tree and read the news article on her phone. Rachel Frisk's mugshot was centered in her screen, her gaze haunted and hollow.

Nurse Facing Four Lifetime Sentences, the headline read.

The mud sucked at Lou's boots as she walked farther out into the center of the lake. In the distance, a hawk cut across the sky without so much as a glance in her direction.

Once the water was waist high, Lou bent her knees and sank beneath the surface. She rested in the gray water, enjoying the feel of it against her face. When the cool waters began to warm, she opened her eyes to find red all around her.

She climbed onto the shores of La Loon and squeezed the excess water out of her hair.

Jabbers wasn't waiting for her. That was just as well. Lou hadn't brought an offering, and she'd only come for one thing.

She retraced her path to the mountain, and then down the unlit corridor to the water's edge, only to find what she'd feared.

The eggs were gone.

Every last one of them. The cavern was empty.

She was standing there in the glow of the water, her disappointment sharp, when something sparkled in the water.

She waded out a foot and bent down to pick it up.

Once it was in her hands, she recognized the cool surface. It was a fragment of one of the shells.

She stood there admiring it as the water shimmered along the walls around her.

A black shadow formed beneath the surface. Growing, stretching, rising.

Lou stepped back, ready to run, only to realize it was Jabbers coming out of the pool.

Coming out of the pool?

That meant the water didn't stop at the low rock ceiling as Lou thought it had. In fact, it must be deep enough to accommodate a beast of that size.

And if it was only a watery passageway and not an underwater pool, it begged the question, where did it go?

Jabbers pressed her enormous head into Lou's stomach and purred in greeting.

"Where did you come from?" Lou asked.

Jabbers dove beneath the water again, and when Lou didn't follow her, she circled back, raising her head in question.

Lou arched a brow. "You want me to come with you?"

There was the possibility that the passageway was too long for Lou to swim on a single breath. Then what would she do? She would slip through, she supposed. Either back to Blood Lake or home.

What do you have to lose? she asked herself.

Lou waded out into the water. She made it as deep as her hips before she could reach out and touch the low-slung rock wall. She would have to dive underwater to go any farther.

Jabbers dove with ease, circling back again when Lou showed hesitation.

Only this time, she seemed unwilling to wait on Lou any longer. Her long tail coiled around Lou's waist.

There goes my choice, she thought. All she could do was hold tight to the beast.

She'd had only a moment to take a deep breath before Jabbers dove.

Her black serpentine body moved with incredible speed. Even without her tail, which Lou was sure she could use to propel herself underwater, she was fast and full of grace.

The water grew a brighter and brighter turquoise but did not turn red.

Lou's chest began to burn only a second before Jabbers thrust them both upward into the light.

They broke the surface and Lou took a deep breath.

Before her was a rocky shore. Lou stretched her hands out and grabbed ahold of it. With a generous shove of Jabber's tail, she was able to haul herself out of the waters onto a rock ledge.

Then she was standing alone, looking out over an incredible sight.

It was a large cavern.

Rock walls encircled a sizable pool at its center. The walls ran straight up, forming a circle to frame the open sky. The forever-twilight shone down on the shimmering pool, giving it a soft purple glow that mingled beautifully with the turquoise blue of the water itself.

Lou would have never guessed that there was a secret world hidden here inside the mountain.

A splash in the water drew her attention, and Lou looked down in time to see the contraction of a black body at her feet.

It wasn't nearly as large as Jabbers. Perhaps no more than

four feet long. It was more serpentine than Jabbers as well. Its head more diamond-shaped. No legs.

That's when Louie knew what she was looking at.

Her baby.

More dark shapes darted in the pool, coming closer, drawn either by Lou's scent or by the appearance of their mother. Lou couldn't say.

But just like that, they were there.

Their heads stuck a few inches out of the water. They watched Lou with large toad-like eyes, silver in color.

Lou thought of Jabbers's webbed feet.

"You start in the water," she said, kneeling down. "You're like tadpoles."

One of the babies began to blow bubbles with its nose slits, and Lou had no idea if that was intentional or simply how it breathed.

She counted the heads once. Twice. Three times to be sure.

But there was no mistake.

All six babies were there.

One even dared to come close to her, its eyes impossibly large as Lou placed a cautious hand on its head.

It didn't bite or snap. It only blinked at her, as if waiting for her to do something.

Six babies.

Jabbers hadn't eaten a single one.

The beast pulled herself to the stone ledge beside Lou and shoved her head into Lou's abdomen once more.

Lou smiled and placed a hand on the creature's massive head. "I owe you an apology."

. . .

KONSTANTINE WAS ALREADY IN BED, NAKED FROM THE waist up with a paperback open in one hand and a glass of red wine in the other, when Lou finally came home.

"You couldn't look more inviting if you tried," she told him, stepping from the closet in her wet clothes.

"You are always invited." He looked her over. "But please shower before you get into bed, *amore mio*. Are you hungry?"

"A little," she admitted.

And by the time she'd showered and dressed, he'd set out a plate of leftovers for her on the counter.

"Is it done?" he asked as she took a seat at the table. "I saw the news."

"It's done."

Of course he would have seen the news, both about the cold case in Louisiana being reopened and about the arrest of the murderess nurse.

"All of it?" he pressed.

"All of it."

"I am asking if you plan to leave me alone in our bed again anytime soon," he said with a little pout, pouring her a glass of wine. "I don't know if I can stand it again."

"No," she told him as he placed kisses on the side of her throat.

"I found the babies," she said between bites.

He hesitated.

"The babies?"

Lou told him all about the underwater passageway and the secret cavern where Jabbers's six babies could grow safely in their very own pool until it was time for them to—to do whatever it was they did once they outgrew the water. Find territories of their own? Share Jabbers's?

Lou had trouble imagining that far ahead.

"You touched it?" he asked incredulously. "You actually touched it?"

"Just one of them," she said. "I think the others were too shy."

"Shy." He laughed. "I would be scared I'd lose a hand. Or an arm."

"You wouldn't have pet it?"

"No," he said, too quickly. "They sound terrifying. Even if they are babies."

"I thought they were cute."

"You would," he said. "Given your affinity for their mother."

"Six of them," she said, cleaning the last of her supper off her plate. "Can you even imagine having *six* babies?"

He was looking into her eyes, his smile contented.

"Yes, *amore mio*," he said. "I can imagine."

Did you enjoy Hell House? Louie's story continues in *One Foot in the Grave: Shadows in the Water #10*

GET YOUR THREE FREE STORIES TODAY

Thank you so much for reading *Hell House*. I hope you're enjoying Louie's story. If you'd like more, I have a free, exclusive Lou Thorne story for you. Meet Louie early in her hunting days, when she pursues Benito Martinelli, the son of her enemy. This was the man her father arrested—and the reason her parents were killed months later.

You can only read this story by signing up for my free newsletter. If you would like this story, you can get your copy by visiting ➜ www.korymshrum.com/lounewsletteroffer

I will also send you free stories from the other series that I write. If you've signed up for my newsletter already, no need to sign up again. You should have already received this story from me. Check your email and make sure it wasn't marked as spam! Can't find it? Email me at ➜ kory@korymshrum.com and I'll take care of it.

As to the newsletter itself, I send out 2-3 a month and host a monthly giveaway exclusive to my subscribers. The prizes are usually signed books or other freebies that I think you'll enjoy. I also share information about my current projects, and personal anecdotes (like pictures of my dog). If you want these free stories and access to the exclusive give-aways, you can sign up for the newsletter at ➜ www.korymshrum.com/lounewsletteroffer

If this is not your cup of tea (I love tea), you can follow me on Facebook at ➜ www.facebook.com/korymshrum in order to be notified of my new releases.

ACKNOWLEDGMENTS

Here we are with our *ninth* Shadows in the Water book finished at last. For those of you who keep asking, yes, the series will go on for at least three more installments. Thank you in advance for your patience, you ravenous fiends!

The usual thanks are in order to my amazing team: editor extraordinaire Toby Selwyn, cover designer superb Christian Bentulan, and the very best assistant a woman could ask for—Alexandra Amor.

Thanks also to my critique group, The Four Horsemen of the Bookocalypse: Katie Pendleton, Angela Roquet, and Monica La Porta.

And as always, many thanks to my lovely street team. Thank you for reading the books in advance, reporting those lingering typos and posting your honest reviews.

Without my team and the best fans in the world, I don't know if I could have kept doing what I'm doing for this long. So thank you from the bottom of my heart for all the love and support you've shown me over the years as I continue to chase my impossible dreams.

ALSO BY KORY M. SHRUM

Dying for a Living series

Dying for a Living

Dying by the Hour

Dying for Her: A Companion Novel

Dying Light

Worth Dying For

Dying Breath

Dying Day

Shadows in the Water: Lou Thorne Thrillers

Shadows in the Water

Under the Bones

Danse Macabre

Carnival

Devil's Luck

What Comes Around

Overkill

Silver Bullet

Hell House

One Foot in the Grave

Castle Cove series

Welcome to Castle Cove

Night Tide

2603 novels

The City Below

The City Within

The City Outside

Standalone Novels

Jack and the Fire Eater

Learn more about Kory's work at: www.korymshrum.com

ABOUT THE AUTHOR

Kory M. Shrum is author of more than twenty novels, including the bestselling *Shadows in the Water* and *Dying for a Living* series. She has loved books and words all her life. She reads almost every genre you can think of, but when she writes, she writes science fiction, fantasy, and thrillers, or often something that's all of the above.

In 2020, she launched a true crime podcast "Who Killed My Mother?", sharing the true story of her mother's tragic death. You can listen for free on YouTube or your favorite podcast app.

When she's not eating, reading, writing, or indulging in her true calling as a stay-at-home dog mom, she loves to plan her next adventure. She can usually be found under thick blankets with snacks. The kettle is almost always on.

She lives in Michigan with her equally bookish wife, Kim, and their rescue pug, Charley.

Learn more about Kory and her work at
www.korymshrum.com

www.ingramcontent.com/pod-product-compliance
Lightning Source LLC
Chambersburg PA
CBHW071213210726
48293CB00002B/413